Ever

That's Yellow

Penny J Bond

For those who've experienced a broken heart, may your heart heal and you find the love you deserve.

For those dreamy celebrities, keep doing what you do, and we'll keep dreaming.

And for those friends of ours who are always there, when you need them the most, you make the world a better place.

Prologue

Bunny Boiler = a woman who acts vengefully (acting in a way that expresses a strong wish to punish someone who has hurt her) after being spurned (to reject) by her lover. She's considered unstable and prone to sudden changes of mood.

I was never a person where revenge ever came into my thoughts; but you know what they say, never say never.

The thing about revenge is it never works if it's instant.

It works best when the person on the receiving end never suspects a single thing. It's the timing that delivers the fatal blow to revenge.

That perfectly timed moment when the unsuspecting victim of the revenge plan thinks their world is all calm and wonderful. That period when they believe their life couldn't possibly get any better because everything is on the up. They're walking on clouds, and then suddenly, out of nowhere, revenge storms uninvited into their life, like a destructive twister, ready to turn their entire world upside down.

Now, the person delivering the revenge must be patient; they have to keep it together long enough to not rush in and risk spoiling the maximum impact of damage they could cause from biding their time.

It's crucial that by waiting for the perfect moment to unleash their dose of revenge, the result will be worth it, when it knocks their victim entirely and utterly off their feet, because that's what they want to see, the person who has wronged them on the floor at their lowest, the very opposite to the cloud nine feelings they've just had stolen from them.

And there it was, my plan...

A plan formed with pain being the heart and soul of it.

I want maximum impact so desperately, along with the maximum destruction I can cause, because it was this that would help to make me feel better for all the tears and heartache I've had shed over him.

The result I desire is for his perfect life to be destroyed inch by inch.

I want him to feel unwanted, for him to feel jealous, I want to humiliate him, and most importantly, I want to watch him fall at my feet, begging not only for forgiveness from me but also for acceptance back into my life once again, for my affection.

I want him to realise the huge mistake he's made by breaking my heart into a thousand pieces and then turning his back on me. The lowest point for me was when he didn't even raise an eyebrow while I slowly picked up the broken pieces of my heart one by one. He was utterly blind to the amount of love I gave him, blind or just completely oblivious, but either way, he did nothing to make the end of our relationship any easier for me.

In fact, he made it as painful as possible for me.

It hit me like a storm breaking through a perfect summer's day.

The sky suddenly turned as dark as the night, while lightning bolts hit my heart repeatedly.

The storm blasted through my entire world, destroying everything I'd loved about it, and what was once my perfect life was left tattered and shadowed by the greyness of the dark night sky. The storm tore my body open from the inside out, and it left me eternally exposed to the entire world.

I became vulnerable, and all those peering eyes around me could see my vulnerability from a thousand miles away. I lost my footing and was forced to watch my happiness dragged away as quick as a Monday morning hits after the most perfect weekend.

My entire body was broken, and my mind would spend all of eternity spinning out of control, with thoughts and questions that came with no answers. Questions that would haunt me forever and throughout all of it, all I could do was watch, watch as pieces of my heart became lost in the earth. I was trapped inside a storm created by him, Reed, my destroyer, and no one could pull me out of this chaos, no matter how hard they tried, and all I could do was sit in the audience and watch as my life slipped further and further into more chaos. I somewhat accepted defeat by handing my spirit over to the storm I was caught up in.

Hitting the lowest point of my life, as everything spun out of control, I knew I would never be the same person again.

The echoes of *It'll all work out in the end,* and *you'll be ok,* faded into the background of my mind.

I wouldn't be ok, and it wouldn't work out in the end, or so I believed whilst in my darkest hour tangled up inside this ever-spinning nightmare.

I never thought I had it in me to seek revenge towards another person; I'm too quiet, slightly naïve, and completely compliant in society to think of ways to hurt others. But a broken heart and a large dose of humiliation can bring out sides to a woman that even they didn't know was quietly living inside of them.

And being inexperienced at revenge, my plan was flawed, for the twister I had carefully called on the weather gods to awaken and implement in full force, was about to hit my world just as much as my unsuspecting victim, which was something I didn't see when I carefully hatched this well timed and very detailed thought out revenge plan.

The most important detail I didn't consider is that twisters don't just affect one sole person; they affect anyone or anything that's in their path, and I was standing blind and unaware it was heading directly for me. I was about to be suddenly and, without warning, knocked off my feet by the twister I myself had summoned...

"I do solemnly, sincerely, and truly declare and affirm that the evidence I shall give shall be the truth, the whole truth and nothing but the truth."

I take a seat on the heavy wooden chair in the witness box.

My instant thought is how uncomfortable the chair is. I guess court room chairs aren't meant to be relaxing; I assume they designed them to be specifically uncomfortable, to make people part with information quickly preventing wasting anyone's time.

But this is just my theory. I wish they could've at least put a cushion on it, because I know I'm going to be here a while, this prosecutor is going to tear me apart.

I've watched and listened to them this morning and I predict they're going to take their time with me and they're going to enjoy every second of the interrogation they will put me through.

It doesn't help me that there is such a large audience for them to play up to, which consists of a large amount of reporters that are gathered in the courtroom with us.

Most people collect stamps or coins. Not me. I've recently taken up collecting criminal charges. It's not as difficult as one would think, and it certainly helps if you're slightly unhinged.

I look around the courtroom and wonder who most of these people are, and how my court case has peaked their interest so much.

But, I guess that happens when you go from being a no-one to everyone knows you, even if it's for all the wrong reasons.

The prosecutor looks at me as though she's looking through me and I find her to have an intimidating demeanour. She comes across as someone who thoroughly researches every last detail of a case and isn't someone who could have the wool pulled over their eyes. She has an assertive tone and I'm not sure if the wig she's wearing is too tight for her, or she usually has the chewing a wasp facial expression.

"Miss Fletcher, you are here today to answer to six alleged offences, and despite you admitting to all but one, how does a person go from never having committed crime to wilfully endeavouring to partake in several criminal activities?"

I look around at the faces in the courtroom and take a deep breath as I prepare to share the most difficult time with a room full of strangers.

"Well, it all started several months ago. My life was great, and also crime free. I had a job, a home, money, friends, and the love of my life, Reed. But then on our anniversary of nine years, everything took an unexpected turn, so in order to explain to you on how I've ended up here with these charges, I have to take you back to that day, the day I thought Reed was going to ask me to be his forever."

Chapter One
Anniversary

As I open my eyes, the first thing I see is the golden ray of sunlight that has sneaked through my curtains and into my room.

I rub my eyes, wiping away the mist accumulated from a long night's sleep, and I'm now far away from the perfect dream world I've just left and back in the perfect real world I live in.

I look over at the sunlight and welcome it in, and my lips curl upwards with happiness, knowing today is a glorious summer day once again.

My eyes suddenly avert to a bright red rose lying on the side of the bed.

It's blood red, with a streak of Merlot, that perfect colour of love if you're a total romantic like me.

It's the same colour as my heart, my big over-beating blood red totally in love heart.

I reach gently for the flower, and as I pick it up, it feels like the first time I've ever touched a rose before; I experience it like a whole new sensation, touching it gently and allowing my fingers to run over its velvet, feeling petals and around its thorn. I know it's rough and ready to bite me.

There's something dangerous and yet exciting about your fingers being so close to the bite of a thorn.

As I look lovingly at this beautiful and somewhat dangerous flower in front of me, I appreciate this beautiful sight more than I ever have because it has such a special meaning today.

I twist it around so the flower is in full view and pull it close enough to inhale the sweet aroma hiding from me like a shy child.

Today, to me, this is the most beautiful rose I've ever held, and the muscles in my face awaken as my lips form a cheeky smile.

My eyes are alert to the red danger I'm holding in the palm of my hand.

I know how this rose got on to my bed; it won't take a private investigator to solve this mystery.

My eyes trace the line of petals that flow from the flower, and as I sit up, I see the entire bed is covered in roses; someone has been busy destroying my beautiful flower family, but I can't help thinking it looks so mesmerising, the way the blood-red lays against the snow-white sheets. It feels naughty that I'm happy with this crime scene. But I can't help it and now my smile is in full bloom, much like the rose I hold so carefully in my hand. It's almost like we've opened up together.

I wrap my tousled bed hair around my ear and let out a huge yawn that wakes all of my senses up.

The sun is still beaming through the bedroom window as though trying hard to be noticed. It wants the same attention as the rose, but I'm too sluggish to stretch out and feel its heat. I feel a happy sense covering me; how many people can say the sun tries their hardest to wake them up in such a fantastic, gentle way?

This is one of those perfect moments.

Today is mine and Reed's anniversary; it's been nine years since we got together, and what a way to rise with love scattered all over my bed from my man, who is a serial killer of flowers.

Could today be the day that Reed gets down on one knee and asks me the question I long to hear?

Recently, he has been quite mysterious, and my crime-solving skills have been exhausted.

But after piecing the evidence together, the verdict is that he will probably ask me to be his wife tonight, and I long for this so much.

He's my soulmate, and I couldn't imagine feeling this way about anyone other than him.

I know in my heart that he's the one for me.

After nine years, the butterflies are still there, and when his name flashes up on my phone, my knees still turn to jelly.

I know we're going to a fancy restaurant in the city tonight.

He told me it would be a very special night that would change our lives from that moment; I mean, could he be any more obvious that by the end of the night, I will be wearing a part of him on my finger for the rest of eternity.

I have the sexiest little black dress currently screaming out from my wardrobe to be worn, and let's not mention the underwear I've purchased.

I'm not confident when it comes to sexy underwear, but I've gone all out on what I will have on underneath my dress, because I want Reed to always remember what I was wearing the night I said yes to him.

Even though I'm not confident, I want to be sexy for Reed tonight, so that when he reminisces about the night he proposed to me, he will remember how I looked standing over him on our bed, with my stockings running tight up to the red lace thong I will have on, and the tight red bra that shows him more than he expected, and while we're making love on the night that he asked me to be his forever, I will keep my high heels on the entire time and this memory will be the only one he will ever need to go back to in times of need.

Everything will be perfect, and although I'm happy laying here on my bed of roses, I'm excited for the day to hurry by so we can skip to our evening meal of wine, romance and a marriage proposal. I don't think I can contain my excitement today, and at any point, I could pop like a cork on a champagne bottle, exploding with happiness. Reed is so romantic; I trust him to get everything right, and he will deliver the perfect marriage proposal.

There'll be love in the air, music in my ears, wine pulsing through my veins, the scent of flowers surrounding me and, most likely, the sparkle of some very expensive diamonds.

My heart has switched into race mode.

I need to calm my beating heart and try to stay contained, or at least somewhat calm, at least on the exterior.

But it's so difficult when this is all I've ever wanted, a man that I love, that loves me back the same, there's just something so wonderful about it.

Right now, my guess is that Reed is in the kitchen making me breakfast.

I can just see him now, my very own breakfast God slaving away to ensure his Queen is fed with nothing but the best.

This will undoubtedly consist of cereal because I need fibre, and there will be orange juice, because I need vitamin C and some egg dish because I need protein.

My health is very important to him because he wants me around forever.

I can see him now, stroking back his hair when the heat from the pan gets too much. The sweat is messing up his perfect hairstyle, so he sweeps it back.

Reed has no knowledge that his swept-back look gets my insides fluttering. It's like love at first sight all over again and then there's his eyes, those dreamy pale baby blues, that always make me lose my breath.

I imagine how busy he is in the kitchen with his arms going from one job to the next. Oh, those perfect arms;

and I imagine he's squeezing an orange when what I really want is him in this bed squeezing something else.

The thought of all of this is getting me hot under the collar, and I brush my hair off my forehead, catching that one trickle of sweat that's running down my eyebrow caused by my naughty thoughts of the man I love.

Reed doesn't need to be reminded about anniversaries or dates; he has them all stored on his phone, and what woman doesn't have a good nosey on their partner's phone every now and again?

The fact he sets alarms to ensure he never forgets knocks me off my feet every time, and it just makes me love him even more.

Arrrr, my man, I float backwards, and my quilt and pillows form the perfect clouds to fall into.

I reminisce on the beautiful man I have, this beautiful specimen that belongs to me. I have rose petals moving into the creases of my toes, and excitement builds up inside of me that my man makes me so happy.

I'm so excited about today! I think about how much of a clown Reed is; he always makes me laugh, which is why I love being with him.

I don't seem to have many down days; because he won't allow it, and he pulls out all the stops to cheer me up if he feels I'm not myself. He's kind and sincere and he always tells me how he feels, which is unusual, as most men I know hide their feelings, fearing letting women know their feelings somehow makes them weak or vulnerable, but it's not true; it's endearing.

Reed tells me anything and everything, and I love how honest he is with me. He would do anything for me; he would never lie to me about anything; I can trust him with my life, and I think this makes our love so strong; because we understand each other, and we always put each other first every time.

He makes me feel like I'm the only woman in the world, as though he is unaware there are billions of other beautiful people out there.

He passes them in the street, but his eyes never gaze; I even notice how stunning other women are, but he appears to only have eyes for me.

I know this is the man I want to spend forever with.

I feel this in my heart, and I feel I'm his world; it's just Reed and me.

Well, me, Reed and Dalton Rivers.

Most men have hobbies such as going to the gym, men's clubs, sports, and sneaking off to play poker and drink beer, but not Reed; his passion and secret guilty pleasure is Dalton Rivers. An actor who Reed looks up to. He will be the first person to know when one of his films is being released, and he will be the first person in line to buy the tickets; he will be sat on the front row, and he won't leave the cinema until he has seen all the credits. Dalton is also in a TV series that originates from a comic book. Reed keeps trying to get tickets to the comic conventions Dalton does meet and greet's at, but the tickets always sell out too fast, so he can only ever see him from afar. He has sent him thoughtfully penned fan mail, and he constantly follows him on all the social media sites.

It's safe to say Reed is slightly obsessed with this man, and his dream is to meet him in person.

But it's a harmless obsession.

He looks up to the man. He isn't going through the unstable stalker phase yet; I see it as his hobby. Reed enjoys it; and it doesn't take over his life too much.

However, the screen saver of Dalton on his phone is odd, and I now know more about Dalton Rivers than Dalton probably knows himself.

Our daily conversations will always have some sort of update on him, and I listen to Reed because it's something he enjoys talking about; and I love Reed, so even if I can't bear to hear another word about Dalton Rivers, I do it because I care about Reed, and whatever he is slightly obsessed with, I will make time to take part in his conversations regarding it.

Considering how happy Reed makes me, it's the least I can do.

I accept his slightly over-the-top obsession with his favourite celebrity because if this is the only annoying trait he has, then I'm happy to accept this.

I mean, it could be worse; he could have ended up a serial killer of people and not just flowers, but this won't happen because Reed is too loving and too gentle to have any anger issues.

He doesn't enjoy upsetting people or hurting their feelings; he doesn't have a temper, and he's mellow all the time. The most excited I see Reed get is when it's something to do with Dalton flaming Rivers. However; I accept maybe he didn't have this when he was a child, a celebrity idol that's plastered all over the bedroom walls, so perhaps he is reliving this time now.

As I look to the side, the ray of sunshine beams across the wooden floor, forming a beautiful glow of smoke that rises from the planks, and at this perfectly timed moment, Reed sweeps around the door and into our room, and as I predicted, he has made breakfast.

He looks at me with that cheeky grin of his; his hair is all tousled but swept slightly off his forehead, the primary evidence he has worked extremely hard in the kitchen this morning, and I sense his main priority today was waking me up with a smile, which he had already achieved with the beautiful array of roses. Reed is carrying a tray of food.

"Good morning, beautiful," he says, with a gentle whispery tone, and he leans over and kisses my head.

And I want this kiss to last forever.

I love the sensation of his gentle lips pressed against my forehead; I catch his delicious scent, and I have a split second to decide whether to lick his perfect neck; it's fair to say that whenever my mouth is anywhere near his neck, it automatically opens up like a slow-moving garage door, obviously without the creaks and noise.

It isn't just his neck that gets my tongue going; it's every part of him.

But in this perfect moment, Reed didn't think about the tray of food he was holding when he bent down to plant that smacker on my head.

And the tray tips up with breakfast quickly sliding to the floor.

It's all mashed up together, from the slither of milk and cereals down the side of our drawers to a concoction of mess on the floor, now ready to be cooked by the wood and sunlight working together. Reed's legs are covered in different fluids, from sticky vitamin C to milky calcium.

I glance at the slow-cooking cereals and then back over to his simply divine face; he looks embarrassed, his cheeks flush a cerise pink glow. He's so gorgeous when he's blushing, and I love seeing it.

Reed jumps up and starts clearing up the disaster of a mess he's just created, and I know this is mainly to hide his embarrassed face. I laugh; it's part nervousness and part embarrassment, but I can't control it.

Soon enough, Reed laughs with me; he has caught my contagious laugh. He throws the plates down and jumps on the bed laughing, and like magnets, we're drawn together. Only Reed could turn something so funny into something romantic.

As we lay together, I feel so comfortable and warm from Reed's protective cuddle, with the smell of him freshly showered, and that aftershave of his that sucks me in.

His wet hair makes me tingle as the cold tips of his hair stroke me.

I look over at the sunlight that has now moved across the room to the bed, and it hits my arm as if it knows I'm missing Vitamin D.

]I'm so happy and the aroma of roses sneaks up to my nose, giving me such a pleasant, invisible surprise.

There is nowhere in the world I'd rather be; I feel as close to heaven as possible.

"I promise I will love you forever, R," I whisper.

"I will always be devoted to you and you alone, C."

Reed gently kisses my cheek.

I feel like a child who's just heard they're going to Disneyland; because my inner self is jumping up and down, whereas my outer self lays calm in the arms of my Reed. I ignore the fact my leg is now sticking to Reed's leg, thanks to the vitamin C he spilt all down it. Still, it's satisfying to know we're stuck together through our choice.

I feel so safe in my man's arms, gently nuzzled on our perfect fluffy cloud together, where we are both totally and utterly in love.

Before long, I begin to start drifting back to sleep again, ignoring the smell of what will soon become stale milk, cooking on our bedroom floor from the indoor BBQ, courtesy of the sunlight.

Who knew that the next time I'd wake up would be three months from now...

Chapter Two
Charity Fletcher

There's being a plain Jane, and then there's Charity.

She became so comfortable with her life that she forgot about all of her dreams and ambitions.

As a child, she had a wild imagination and big plans for her future, but somewhere in between the transition of being a child and becoming an adult, she misplaced that imagination.

Her plans were put in the *I'll get to it later* boxes in the back of her mind, where she eventually forgot about them.

Adventurous, she isn't, but loyal, she is.

One of her most significant flaws is her naivety, which makes her an easy target for those looking for a doormat in life to wipe their muddy shoes on.

Her kind heart makes her even more of an easy target for those who seek givers, who they can emotionally and physically drain, and because Charity has such a good heart, she forgives and forgets almost instantly. Charity is driven in life regarding her relationship, but not what's good and healthy for her.

She consistently puts everyone else's feelings above hers, and when she's in, she's entirely in. Reed was her first proper love, and she believes she can't survive in the world without him; he is her oxygen.

She's disillusioned and can't seem to understand real true love, which isn't her fault. She has nothing to compare it with and she believes that this is the real deal.

She's a watcher on social media. She never posts interesting updates or shares motivational quotes; she simply spectates in other people's lives by living through their posts and interactions. She blends in and could easily be missed unless you're seeking her out. She isn't into fashion or beauty and has no hobbies.

She has built her life around Reed; he is her social activity, hobby, and the centre of her universe.

When she's not working at her mundane job as a receptionist at a local solicitor's, she devotes all of her time to Reed and their home.

Charity considered going to university and learning law so she could at least progress in her company. But, she never even got a brochure to show she's that serious about it and that idea quickly disappeared.

She considered fostering 300 dogs but quickly realised she would need money and land for this, which she didn't have.

She's considered changing jobs frequently, to become an Uber Eats delivery person to a librarian, and each time, that's all it's been a consideration.

She's in her early thirties, so she believes there's still time to decide as and when she gets to it. Charity isn't overly fussed about her appearance either; she's comfortable being her, she's not worried about ageing, and she doesn't bother with heavy make-up, anti-wrinkle creams or nail polish.

She's pretty, with lovely, thick brown hair, which she was blessed with and luckily it doesn't need any expensive or timely upkeep.

She also has beautiful clear skin; again, she's blessed not to have to use fifty-two different creams daily to maintain such a glowing complexion; she just wakes up with it.

When she was a young girl, she loved dressing up and pretending to work the job she always dreamed of doing, an author of children's books.

She loved witches, wizards, fairies, trolls and all the fairytales she was read as a young child. She wanted to be like the authors of those books and create magical fantasy stories for children, to inspire them to believe in all the magical things we can't see.

She would spend hours writing stories, which she read to her parents and younger sister, and she thought she had it all ahead of her.

She never doubted she would become the writer she always dreamed of being.

She studied English Literature and Creative Writing at university and had her plans, dreams, and ambitions ahead of her. But as life goes, or divine intervention, she met Reed at university, and everything soon became about him; there was no money in writing for her, and she was encouraged to get a paying job so they could move in together and slowly over the years, the dream spark that used to be inside of Charity, burned out.

The magical imagination soon became about adult life, bills, work, and a relationship, which in itself is a full-time job.

Charity doesn't have time for a large friend circle, so she keeps Della close by; she's been her longest friend since the days of school.

To Charity, it's not about quantity; it's about quality. Della is everything you would ever need in a friend and more.

From an outsider's perspective, people would describe Charity as bland, uneventful, and perhaps lost. She's too good for her own benefit, and putting other people's feelings above hers has moulded her life into what it has become.

She's relied upon, the person who is always there to pick up the pieces, she's a nurturer, responsible, but what she doesn't realise is the girl she once was is still inside of her, deep down inside of her, waiting patiently until it's time for her to make a guest appearance in life once again.

Chapter Three
Awakening

When I said, *who knew it would be three months until I woke up*? I didn't mean it literally. I meant woke up to my realisations.

I have spent the past three months spinning inside a destructive twister of emotions, to be literal.

That lovely romantic moment was the last one I had with Reed, so to get you up to speed on what's happened in the past three months, here goes.

I was let down on our anniversary night.

Reed left me sitting at a table for two hours, the table he booked, where he would propose to me, or so I had thought.

A hundred missed calls to his phone with me going entirely out of my wits' end, thinking he was hurt and was lying somewhere with no one to help him, led me to using a shared location tracker we both have on our phones.

Reed was the one who encouraged me to get the location tracker app, in case he ever lost his phone, or for emergencies, which until now I'd never needed to use. But now I had an emergency and a reason.

I saw Reed's location on the app, and it led me to a restaurant that was a lot more exclusive than the one we had booked. The glorious sunshine that I started my morning with had long disappeared and the rain had come to pay us a visit.

I should've seen this as a sign of how the rest of my night would go, and as I stood in the pouring rain looking as pathetic as possible, I saw through the restaurant window my Reed had affections for what looked like some bleached blonde knockoff version of a Barbie doll.

Whilst trying to piece together what was happening, I saw his lips hit hers.

In complete shock, my arm did an involuntary act of banging on the glass; however, what I didn't expect was the window to crack; I'm not sure if I was completely taken over with anger and I didn't realise my strength or whether the fact I was holding my phone in the same hand impacted the damage I caused.

I can't remember the walk away from the window; all I remember is that I vomited like a newborn baby with projectile vomiting; it just wouldn't stop; it was like it had been stored inside me for years, just waiting to erupt like a volcano, a volcano of sick. I put it down to the excruciating pain of the stab wound I was feeling in my loved-up heart, that and the many red wines I had drank whilst awaiting my prince charming to arrive for our dinner; I had powered through the wine, which, as I'm not a big drinker, probably wasn't the best idea.

But I drank mainly through nerves of what I thought was about to be a proposal to me. As I stood emptying my stomach of the grapes and heartache, it was at this moment my whole life was ripped out from under my soggy, soaked feet.

I felt a hand on my back, and a voice said, "Excuse me, Miss."

I told them in between retching to leave me alone. I did not want anyone to help me or give me any form of sympathy, especially while I was at my lowest point. Still, they persisted, and wouldn't leave me alone. It was at this point that the last thing I wanted was to be touched by anyone; while my heart was bleeding from the inside out, I didn't even have time to feel embarrassed about the fact I was throwing up in public.

As they continued, "Miss, we need to talk to you." My patience snapped. I turned around and lashed out to push them away from me.

They fell backwards onto the floor, hitting their head. Through what I can only say was shock and upset, I vomited again, this time all over the gentleman who was now lying on the floor with a head injury.

When I stopped being sick, my eyes inspected him.

The first thing I noticed was the dazzling bright yellow visor that gave it away to me that the person I had just emptied my stomach of heartache and red wine on was a police officer.

I watched as another officer helped him up. His partner, I assumed. While I stood in bewilderment at what was happening, there was lots of chatter from the officer across her radio and a lot of groans from the officer holding his head. I realised I had never had anyone look at me with such disappointment before. The people walking by looked at me with a look that people only gave to criminals.

I was now officially a criminal.

What followed next was I was arrested for Drunk and Disorderly, Assaulting a Police Officer and Criminal Damage from the restaurant window (you've got to love CCTV).

Which explained why the officer was so persistent in talking to me. He had an ulterior motive.

So now I'm being summoned to appear in court later on these charges.

When I told you I lost everything, this also included my spotless, non-existent criminal record, and I now face a considerable fine, community service or, the worst scenario, a prison stretch, where I know I will never survive.

I have seen prison shows, and I know I would become everyone's prison bitch, because I can't fight to save my life, and I detest confrontation.

On my anniversary night I spent twelve hours in a police cell thinking about the possibility that in the coming months, I could end up with a prison girlfriend that I don't want, and how could Reed do this to me, how could he be so cruel, this wasn't the Reed I knew and loved, and nothing made any sense to me, all I kept thinking was there had to be an explanation to all of this.

Was this all just a bad dream?

Wake up, girl, wake up!

But you can't wake up if you're not asleep, and I certainly didn't sleep in that cell because the prison-style blanket I was given felt like too sure a way of getting scabies, so I sat shivering in self-pity because this felt like a safer option.

I mean, the last thing I needed to contract as a newly single woman was scabies to add to the dating profile, the dating profile I never want to create.

I spent the night beating myself up, thinking that maybe if I hadn't had that last large red wine, I wouldn't be sitting, deciding whether the risk of getting scabies was worth being warm for or not.

If Reed had just turned up, my life would be how it was less than twenty-four hours ago.

This morning, the sun didn't invite itself into my cell.

It knows I'm a criminal, so it shone through the window of a good person instead.

I didn't have a lovely experience at the police station, but I guess I shouldn't have expected it after word got around that I had assaulted one of their own; Derek was the officer's name; I heard from several officers what a good man he is, which made me feel a thousand times worse than I already did.

And depending on my mood when I talk of her, this is the nicest thing she will be called the man stealing w***e. So, in my denial and just because I'm a naïve idiot at the best of times, I discovered this had been going on right under my nose for months before that night.

In the three months that have passed, I have gone through many phases, the first one being heartbroken, not a nice place to be; I cried a lot and a lot more. In fact, it felt like I did nothing for weeks but just cry. That sadness soon turned to anger; how dare some BOOB just come along and steal my Reed! the anger phase is still present.

I've gone through the *I feel sorry for myself* stage and I've spoilt many nights out with friends, (I say friends, what I mean is Della and a few of her friends from yoga) they tried to cheer me up by trying to make me forget about my disastrous relationship, and in return, I get drunk, cry and then turn the whole night into a counselling session with whoever will listen to my sorrow and sadness over Reed.

One night, I found myself huddled in the corner of a club, pouring my heart out to the best listener I've ever had; they didn't judge me; they just listened and let me rant out my anger over everything.

It turned out my therapist was not to be completely human but to be an image of myself; I spent the entire evening talking to myself in the club mirror.

Alcohol has not helped me through this episode; alcohol is not my friend, it is that kid at school that dares you to do something, so they can sit back and watch you fail.

Me and alcohol are no longer getting on. I have reached a point where I no longer recognise myself, and it's only because Della captured the whole embarrassment on her phone that after sitting and watching it back it's made me realise, I need to wake up, well there's that and the threat that if I continue this way, she'll post this on every single social networking site we both use.

I now loathe social networking sites where everyone can show off their amazingly impressive lives. Come on, admit it; that's all it is.

Everyone goes on to see how bad someone else's life is or be nosey over how good someone else's life is. I never posted anything online, but now I'm finding solace in sharing updates with everyone about how depressed I am. I wanted to delete Reed's profile through anger.

But, the inner curiosity I have wouldn't allow me, and no matter how many times my finger hung above that remove button, my inner strength wouldn't let me do it, so I kept him, and this was the worst thing I could have done because I now see someone else filling my space in Reed's life.

Photos, love messages, kisses, kisses everywhere, f*** off with the kisses already!!! BOOB has to put a million kisses every time she writes anything on Reed's profiles, and it angers me, her secret messages that are so easy to decrypt; I sit shouting at my laptop; I was with him; we did that probably much better than you ever could you pathetic cow. I'm surprised I haven't smashed my laptop; the amount of times I have slammed it shut and thrown it on the floor through anger.

The moment you're no longer together on a social networking site is the worst; that moment I was removed from being Reed's girlfriend and someone else's name was there. It felt like I'd had my heart ripped out and chewed up in front of me. It was then spat out, and then I'd been told it tasted like desperation.

I cried a lot that day.

I have also gone through the *I'm not good enough* stage. The unwashed emergency ponytail is now my best friend. I don't care about how I look.

I got the impression it must've been bad when I sat waiting for a bus and a woman next to me gave me some spare change. It's fair to say I've let myself go.

I've been an absolute mess for the past twelve weeks, and I've now lost my sense of who I am.

What made me wake up was an incident that happened last night when I was in the local shop, whilst getting my supplies of Ben & Jerry's and tissues, ready for the subsequent viewing of *The Notebook*, when I heard a voice I recognised.

As I peered around the corner of the aisle looking like some sort of stalker/security guard, my heart sank into my feet.

From behind, I realised the delicious backside looked familiar. I was right; it was Reed.

He and BOOB were strolling down the aisle without a care in the world, laughing and all loved up together, that sickly honeymoon phase type of love.

I felt the sick crawling up into my throat; I felt the skin on my neck shuffle up and nearly swallow my entire head, and I felt the volcano erupt inside my face. At this moment, I felt like the Hulk, about ready to tear down this whole shop and rip BOOB apart like a savage dog.

I hid around the corner of the aisle for what felt like a million years, and I saw my entire life with Reed play out before my eyes. I stared at the reflection across from me in the glass fridge door, and it looked like the image of someone who hadn't bathed or changed their clothes in at least two months.

I saw how destructive I had become toward myself, and a part of me cried inside at how low I had sunken. To make matters worse, if Reed saw me this way, he would be glad he had left me. My anger once again turned to sadness, and in sheer panic mode, I needed to exit the store. I couldn't bear to even breathe the same air as them both.

Last night, I was arrested for stealing a tub of ice cream, a four-pack of toilet rolls—which wasn't even Andrex; it was the cheap shop brand—and a copy of *The Notebook* on DVD.

I don't think Reed recognised me being dragged back through the store as the mop of unwashed hair hid my face. Della told me there are people who have lived on the streets for years who look after themselves better than I have the past few months, and the feelings of shame swallowed me up.

This time, I only spent eight hours in the cell, where I sat thinking about how nice that ice cream would have been and how I could have been snuggled up on the sofa with my teddy bear feeling blanket, swooning over Ryan Gosling while wishing I looked like Rachel McAdams.

Still, instead, I have that flea-ridden, itchy blanket to comfort me and a copy of a woman's magazine that was published four years ago and it's sticky; I do not want to think about what made this magazine sticky.

Rupinder and Derek, who were once again at the scene of my crime, said it would be a shame to waste a good tub of ice cream, and I heard them tucking into the Ben & Jerry's, and I heard them mention that cookie dough was a plain choice and that I should've stolen Karamel Sutra. I tried to tell them my favourite flavour is actually the Vermonster.

But, once again, Rupinder's face didn't make a single movement when I spoke and she showed minimal regard for breathing the same air as me.

When ice cream wasn't the topic of conversation, I had hours alone to reflect on how well Reed looked.

I'm broken into thousands of pieces, and he looks like he's just walked off the front cover of a magazine.

It doesn't feel right; there's no justice from this breakup, no closure for me; he destroyed me and then moved on quicker than a hungry dog taking a treat. It all seems one-sided, like I'm the idiot here, and all this time, I have kept my decorum (well, if we don't count the crimes I've accidentally committed); I haven't messaged him or even posted anything about our breakup.

I know I will spend my whole life loving him no matter what happens. This is how much I gave to our relationship: I gave him my body, mind, and soul. I didn't think I had anything to worry about. We were always solid together and best friends, not just partners. This hurts because I lost two in one when I lost him.

Then I think about the night he left me alone at that table for hours. Alone. And then I think about her, that knockoff, the man stealer who saw my name in a relationship with him and didn't care; she is not a true woman; she broke girl code, oh how I long to get revenge on her, how I would love to win Reed back and for us to sit laughing over a romantic dinner, while she's standing outside in the pouring down April showers, all broken inside and never to be fixed. I want this moment to happen; I want Reed back, despite everything. But I've decided I want revenge on him first. Then he will come crawling with his tail between his legs when he realises I'm in control. So, it's time to focus on the revenge part first.

Then everything will fall back into place like it used to be when the sun woke me up in the morning and beautiful merlot rose petals were scattered across my bedsheets.The only way to move on from this heinous crime he has committed against me, is to deal with the tragedy itself, get myself back to me or a better version of myself, commit the most terrible act of revenge and leave Reed wholly exposed for the fraudster of a man he is, where he will beg for me to take him back.

I also need to deal with the anger issues I'm feeling, and what better way to channel these feelings than to put my energy into getting back at him when he least expects it. I have thought about starting a relationship with BOOB, where she and I cheat on Reed, but I then recall the feelings I had when I thought I would end up with a prison girlfriend, and this isn't for me. I've thought about posting some uncensored photos of him I know he doesn't like, but that's not very tasteful, is it?

Della reminds me I will fall in love again.

However, I can't fall in love with anyone when I'm still in love with Reed, and I don't think I could ever imagine not being in love with him, so if I can't love anyone else, then I need him back. So, with no self-respect, no confidence, a lot of split ends, terrible nails, a bad complexion, puffy eyes, pending charges from the police and an embarrassing video of me talking to myself and It's now time to do something about all of this.

And what better way to make yourself feel better than with a bit of revenge, and a *I don't care about you anymore* attitude that only a broken-hearted woman could pull off.

Oh yes, I'm at that point now; after a lot of self-wallowing, I'm bitter, and not just a bit bitter, I'm very bitter. Squeeze a thousand lemons into a glass and drink

it in one, and you're still nowhere near to my bitterness
levels yet…

Chapter Four
Reed Walker

Reed is attractive on the outside, but he's wholly self-centred and hollow inside.

He thinks being arrogant is a great asset.

Being in his early thirties doesn't worry him because he still feels like he's in his early twenties and he's emotionally immature.

When he's not dishing out attractiveness for dinner, he's accused of superficiality.

He thinks chatting up women is a valuable skill to possess.

Still, he doesn't stay around long enough to hear smart women's thoughts and comments about him after he's left their presence, because certain women can read him like a book.

He's an only child, and it shows.

He's spoilt, and he only wants toys for him to play with.

He was the child at school who refused to share the crayons with any other child during art time.

His oxygen in life is feeling important, and he likes to believe he's popular.

His goal is to become as successful as possible; this is his drive.

He works in I.T., and he has ambitions to climb his way to the top, even if it means stamping on a few people who are also working their way up the same corporate ladder as him. To him, the only casualty he's concerned about is himself.

He surrounds himself with people who make him feel important and needed. So he usually buddies up with those at work who appear to have few friends, and over the years, he has collected an army of work colleagues who would usually be in the losers club.

Other than being obvious when meeting him for the first time that he's smarmy, he's actually brilliant when he puts his mind to it and knows his job in his sleep.

With his dreamy eyes, he knows how to be charming and how to treat women, a skill for which he wears a top badge.

He can make a woman feel like she's the only woman in the world, something he often uses to his advantage.

He's caring, but caring in a way that has something in it for him.

He's not altruistic.

He disregards people's feelings without even realising he's doing it, because he's so wrapped up in himself. He's entirely unaware of how cold he can be towards people sometimes.

If he offends someone, he doesn't lose sleep over it. He needs his beauty sleep to keep his handsome good looks. He's the only child monster whose parents still run around after him, despite him being the age he's at, and he's happy for them to do it.

Even in his thirties, he expects his mother to put a plaster on his knee and kiss his boo-boos better. A smiling assassin, where sadly, his looks and charm are enough to draw women in, and like a Venus flytrap, there's no escape once you get close.

But, the part people don't see early on is that unless you're pleasing his every whim, he won't have any purpose for you.

Chapter Five
Unemployed

Having a criminal record was never on the list of reasons I could think of ever losing a job.

I received a not-so-friendly email from my boss, Janet, demanding that I come in on a day that I wasn't due to work, and I sensed immediately that something was wrong.

Janet isn't the nicest person, but even this email was ruder than usual.

When arriving at my place of work, you could cut the atmosphere with a knife, as voices appear lower and all eyes are on me.

I take a seat in the reception area that I manage, but it feels like I'm a stranger in the building today.

There were no friendly hellos or how are you.

There was just hushed silence, and everyone pretending to be busy.

As I await my fate, I put two and two together and feel I'm about to get into some form of trouble.

Janet, a stern-looking woman with glasses on that make her look even sterner than without the specs, opens the ribbed glass door with force as though she is making a statement that she's arrived.

"Charity, this way, please."

And with this, I'm summoned to meet my sealed fate.

Janet has always made me feel a little on edge because she doesn't have the warmest personality. She's a forward-thinking woman in her late fifties who doesn't believe in not saying what you're thinking, because she believes there's no time for it. She often said, "Just get it out and cut to the chase."

When we were once making coffee, Janet once told me how she'd had no friends at her workplaces.

"Oh dear, no, you can't be friends with these people; they aren't my friends. I get paid to talk to them, and that's all. Could you imagine me inviting Jeff round to my home or going out for the day with Jessica? Certainly not. Out of work, I have no time for these people. If I saw one of them getting mugged, I wouldn't get involved, and I'm sure the feelings are mutual; I'm sure they've no time for me; it's always been this way and will always be this way."

I knew this meant Janet was very detached.

She separates work and home, and work and friendships, and according to Janet, it's served her well over the years. She said *there's no emotion involved then*.

Now I stand opposite her, and as I pull the chair out from the desk to take a seat, Janet quickly remarks, "Oh, I wouldn't bother sitting; it won't take that long."

I immediately stop pulling the chair out and stand utterly still, sure to win this game of frozen statues.

At that moment my phone quacks.

How did I not switch it on to silent.

Janets raised eyebrow tells me that she's not a fan of the sound of a quacking duck.

I however, love it as my message tone.

"Sorry," I try to sound as sincere as possible.

"You're sacked," Janet says, as frosty as a winter's morning.

And before I can say anything in my defence, Janet adds, "I'm sure you know you did not have a criminal record when we hired you, and I'm sure you know it wouldn't look good for a law firm to be hiring the criminals that pay their wages, so on these grounds, we are formally letting you go. No notice is required; your employment has been terminated immediately. You will receive the hours you've worked, and any annual leave you have left will be paid to you." Before I can say anything, she continues. "We're surprised at you Charity. We thought you'd be more forthcoming with your recent

activity, but it took a source to tell us instead of you being honest."

I know I can't fight this because—one, I'm terrified of this woman, and two, because Janet is correct, it makes sense from a business point of view. Right now, losing this job is the least of my worries.

"Thank you, Janet." I turn around to walk out, hoping there's a shred of decency in this woman, where she will at least thank me for the work I've done, or just say something nice so we don't leave it on a sour note, but no, from behind all I hear is "close the door on your way out, it's chilly today."

On my way out of the building, I pick up a plant that's sitting on top of the reception desk.

"This is coming with me," I say to a young male at reception.

He's obviously a new hire to replace me, and he's far too junior to pick a fight with a sacked woman over a plant.

I pick up a business card from one of the dark oak tables just before I get to the door. It's the solicitor's contact details. "I might need this," I laugh.

And just like that, I'm officially unemployed after working for the firm for eight years.

Chapter Six
Social Media Stalking

I'm emotionally tiring myself out looking at Reed's social media profiles.

I jump from Facebook to Instagram, to see if he has any new updates. I constantly refresh the pages to ensure I miss nothing; frankly, it's embarrassing. But I miss him so much, and this is the only way I can see him. Even if it's a virtual way, it's a way. I know it's been a few months, but it still feels like a fresh cut.

I go through our photos religiously on my profiles, because one of the first things Reed did was to remove our photos from his profiles.

It's sad how Reed wasted no time in cleaning up. However, as I have time, I've noticed he's missed a few photos of us.

I had to go back years to find them, which is probably why he's not deleted them. But why would he have the time to look through years of his photos online, when he's clearly busy with his new relationship.

I know the day will come when these last few photos will be gone and he will have deleted every trace of me and no one will ever know that Reed and I were once in love.

I don't know why I'm doing this social media stalking, because it just upsets me. It makes me angry. Several times, I've slammed my laptop shut in anger at seeing photos of them two together, and I've even contemplated throwing the laptop out of the window. If I don't have a laptop, I can't put myself through this.

But then I remember I still have a phone, and I'm not throwing that anywhere, so what would be the point

There will always be a way I will see him; I can't avoid it.

The worst part about his profiles is how quickly I've been replaced, and he's just carrying on with his new life. It's almost like nothing happened, like we weren't even together, which makes me sad. I wish we could switch places, and the shoe was on the other foot because it's exhausting being me. I feel so low, pining for him and still trying to figure out what I did wrong.

The worst part is how happy he looks, like he seems pleased with himself and his actions.

Was I that bad as a girlfriend?

Is he now relieved he's free of me? Is she a better woman? Does she make him happier than I ever could?

I look at his updates of where he's recently been and what he's doing, and he seems to be having fun, going out to the theatre, nights out drinking, and lots of dinner dates with BOOB, and I feel jealous. Why didn't he take me out more? He always said he loved staying in and being at home, which was his favourite place.

But looking at his updates, he's never at home. Home, our home that I've been evicted from. There wasn't even any discussion about who would stay in our house; he just turfed me out like I was a squatter.

I bought all the things over the years to make the house we lived in a home, and now I won't ever see the items again.

It feels childish, but all those things are mine, like my fridge magnets from where I've travelled, my fluffy pillows, my favourite throw I'd curl up on the sofa with, and the one that infuriates me the most is my favourite mug that no one else was ever allowed to drink out of.

Visitors like workmen were only allowed the tramp mugs we called them, that lived at the back of the cupboard and we never used them.

Then there's the coffee table I up-cycled; I spent days sanding it down, staining it and painting it; I even learnt how to use stencils and paint on little leaf designs and flowers, all with the help of a YouTube tutorial. Knowing Reed and BOOB could be having coffee in my favourite mug is killing me inside. I bet she's not using the tramp mugs.

They will put whatever mugs they're using on my table, the table I worked hard on, and they probably won't even use coasters.

They are that low class, and before long, the paint will chip away from all the coffee mug ring stains.
It makes me feel physically sick to think about BOOB snuggled up on my sofa, with my favourite pillow,

where she falls asleep, and Reed covers her with MY FAVOURITE THROW.

It's like all the things I spent my life buying, collecting and creating. She's just been given them all. She's walked into my home, and everything is now hers.

If I'd known the future would look this way, I wouldn't have purchased such nice things. I feel robbed.

I'm finding it increasingly difficult to resist the urge to look at his profiles. It's like an addiction I can't shake.

But each time I give in and scroll through them, I'm left feeling ten times worse than before.

It's a battle I can't seem to win, and I'm left wondering why I'm subjecting myself to this self-inflicted pain.

I could delete him from all the channels I use.

I hover over the unfriend button on Facebook.

I can't do it!

My finger is shaking.

My heart rate has increased.

Do I?

Don't I?

What if I delete him and he never accepts my friend request again?

How will I keep up with the updates that are tearing me apart? The fear of losing this last thread of a connection is paralysing. As I hover over the unfriend button, fear rushes through me.

What if my finger slips and I can't take it back?

I place my finger as far away from the unfriend button as possible, with the weight of this decision heavy on my heart.

Chapter Seven
Revenge Plan

Revenge is a way of making one's self feel better.

Anyone who says they don't enjoy revenge is not being completely honest with you.

There's no better feeling than karma dropping by and smacking someone in the face with a reality check because they've somehow caused you upset or harm.

The preparation of revenge takes the most thought and planning.

You can't go too far, but you can't be too gentle either.

After all, that person clearly didn't think about your feelings; they didn't sit and feel bad that you may have watched re-runs of romantic comedies and cried that much that you nearly drowned.

They don't feel guilty that you may end up with shoplifting being placed neatly on your newly born criminal record. Do they sit and feel bad that you had your whole life with them mapped out, that you couldn't wait for the day when they got down on one knee and asked you to spend forever with them?

You sat staring at them while they slept, thinking about how beautiful your future children would be, being fathered by such a delicious specimen. They don't care about any of it, and so I must seek some satisfaction myself and regain my self-respect by getting revenge.

As I sit plotting, the first thing that comes to my mind is the scene from *Fatal Attraction* when Glenn Close goes too far with the rabbit; no, I wouldn't ever do that. I wonder if BOOB has any pets? No! I shake that feeling away. I could NEVER harm any animal, never!

So I think about how amusing it would be if she lost her job, not so attractive unemployed and I'm sure that hair would soon go to waste with no money to maintain it.

I wonder how I could slip laxatives into her food?

Now we're on the sinister level of revenge, but I laugh at how funny it would be for Reed to watch his new girlfriend constantly running for the bathroom.

I soon realise I'm thinking of doing things that could get me into trouble. As I'm heading for a court date because of the recent crimes I've committed, I need to think of something that wouldn't get me into trouble if I got caught.

Every girl who's had her heart broken thinks about dolling herself up and showing her ex what they're missing. I intend to do this, but it's not enough.

I need to conclude this chapter of my life, but I'm not walking away without gaining some sort of payback for being such a good and quiet ex; that's not how it's meant to be.

Could you imagine letting them get on with living their lives happily together, without so much as one word from me or about how I've been feeling?

What kind of person could manage that?

49

Not me, that's for sure. I need to at least try to win him back, or how will I ever know if I could have got Reed back if I don't at least try.

As I lay on the sofa listening to *The Beautiful South's 'A Little Time'*, this song seems fitting; for the thoughts I have today, all I need is a little time, and before long I will have concocted the perfect plan.

I think about the makeover I will undertake to get myself noticed, where Reed's head turns and his mouth drops open; and his thoughts are, s*he looks hot. I never realised how beautiful she could become with all that new makeup and fake eyelashes. How does she look so good? Does she miss me? Urgh what am I doing with BOOB? How can I win Charity back? I'm such an idiot. What have I done?*

The annoying sound of an incoming call rudely interrupts my happy daydream; it's Della; she's at one of her temporary jobs and she doesn't care if the boss finds out she's calling her best friend on work time.

"Hello," I try to sound awake.

"Hey, do you have plans this weekend? I was thinking we could go to a singles night?"

She's trying to sound enthusiastic and I know she's doing this for my benefit.

"Yay, sounds, err, great," I say in a sarcastic tone; I wish I was still daydreaming; I will not bump into Reed on a singles night.

"Come on, it'll be fun, I promise," Della tries to sound more excited; I know what she's doing, but it's not working.

As I think about the weekend ahead and whether I can use any excuse not to go along to this singles mix, something suddenly dawns on me.

"I need to call you back," and with that, I rudely hang up on Della, realising the date for this coming weekend.

As I tear through the mound of post and letters that Reed keeps forwarding to Della's for me, which I have been promising myself to finally get around to organising.

As letters fly about, and paper is sprawled out all over the living room floor, my eyes scan each piece with great detail, as though I'm carefully trying to find a needle in a haystack, and suddenly my pupils enlarge.

A feeling of utter evilness creeps over me and an evil grin forms on my lips as I slide out the gold envelope.

All my plans have come together at once.

My inner devil claps her hands and jumps up and down excitedly, and then she pats me on the back for coming to my senses with the most fantastic revenge plan of all. I carefully walk back to the sofa and gently sit down while holding the envelope like it's some sort of rare archaeological find.

As I sit staring at the envelope, I feel a sense of sadness creep over me again; my little broken heart gives me a nudge to remember why I'm about to do what I'm about to do.

I open the envelope as though I'm not supposed to be looking inside it.

As the inner contents slide out, my sadness quickly turns to excitement.

I feel like the world's greatest genius right now; and without averting my eyes from the paper I hold in my hand, I somehow speed-dial Della back without even looking or blinking.

As I slowly raise the phone to my ear, I try to contain my excitement. Della answers, "Finally, what's going on?"

"Della, we can't go to the singles mix this weekend; we have other plans."

I'm staring at the paper as though it's a newfound wonder of the world.

"Other plans? Like what exactly?"

I pause, and there's an awkward silence.

"We're going to a comic con."

"Why on earth would we go to a comic con? You're not making any sense; I don't want to find a Star Trek fan as a boyfriend, and I'm not dressing up either They're all geeks that go there." I hear her huff down the phone, and I imagine she's rolling her eyes right about now.

"So the gift I bought Reed for our anniversary, well, I didn't get to give it to him." I'm so ecstatic about this

"O..kkkkk?" Della's confused; one of her little habits is when she doesn't have an absolute clue what's going on;

she always drags out the last letter of the word she's responding with to enhance the fact she's confused.

"This weekend, Della, we're going to a comic con to meet and have our photo taken with…"I'm now dragging it out because I want to wind Della up.

"TELL ME WHY WE ARE GOING TO A COMIC CON NOW!"

I suppose I should put her out of her misery, and I can't keep it in any longer.

"Because Della…..we're going to meet……. DALTON RIVERS!"

"Dalton Rivers?!??!?!" She screams down the phone.

"You got that idiot tickets to meet Dalton, and you kept them and you didn't tell him and he doesn't have the tickets and we do?"

Della is highly excited; it's fair to say I haven't come across anyone that isn't obsessed with Dalton Rivers, well except me, and I've realised over the past few months that I'm not missing the daily update on this man's life and I've also realised that I only tolerated this conversation because Reed loves him so much. Della hangs up; and I guarantee that within seconds she will update her status on her social profiles for all the world to see, bragging that she will be meeting the iconic DR.

I won't put anything on.

I know Reed doesn't have these tickets, and I know the chances of him actually getting to meet Dalton are near on impossible, because of how difficult it was for me to get them.

But what I do know is that Reed wouldn't miss this convention for anything.

This will be the first time we'll be in the same room together since the morning of our anniversary (we can't count the shop as he didn't know I was there).

If I know Reed, he will watch everyone else meet his hero, like a creepier version of Michael Myers from *Halloween* and this'll be the perfect moment for me to walk in, looking better than I ever have in my life.

I visualise laughing with Dalton because I'll say something funny when I meet him. He'll laugh, and I'll laugh, and we'll laugh together. Then he will put his arm around me and I will do the cheesiest smile I've ever done in my life for our photo, which I will then plaster all over my social channels, and Reed will vomit like I did the night he broke my heart. Only his vomit will go all over BOOB, because that's what she deserves after all. I imagine it ruining her fake hair extensions and she will have to go to the salon, where all the hairdressers will pull straws out the back away from her because none of them want to touch her sick, stained fake extensions.

Right now, I have a reason to smile, even if I'm smiling from the inside only.

But for the first time in a long time, I feel happy and almost excited about this weekend.

Now, what to wear?

I imagine there'll be a lot of Catwoman and Wonder Woman's attending this convention and they'll look stunning in their all-in-one leather suits and short hot pants, so I need a showstopper outfit that makes jaws drop. I scour the internet for comic heroes and villains; after all, I'm feeling bad lately. I decide on the perfect character to go as Supergirl. I have, after all, overcome a lot recently. But I'm going to have to sexy up this costume, and make it more alluring.

I could cut the top from the skirt and show off my stomach. I look down and notice that my stomach's a little bigger than it usually is; this is all that goddamn comfort eating; I kick myself and decide I won't eat anything but grilled romaine lettuce for the next three days, and that will for sure help.

No, this is too excessive.

I will go for a walk every day, a very long walk and I will cut out anything that has sugar in it until after the weekend, and that's final.

My phone is going off like a duck being strangled, and it's Della texting me constantly; she's acting more excited than Reed would have been if I'd given the tickets to him, and he is, after all, Daltons number one fan.

I have a split-second thought about giving the tickets to Reed; thinking indeed, this would win over points for me against BOOB.

But then I see him happy, smiling with BOOB and the jokes on me because I gave them the tickets, the golden tickets to meet Dalton, and I shake off any altruism inside of me.

I put the tickets safely on the side table; and as I pass the hallway mirror; I stand and stare at the tired and broken person I look.

I'm a shadow of my former self, consumed with self-pity.

I really invested in Reed, and it really never occurred to me that one day we wouldn't be together; I was so sure it was for life; if I had known, maybe I could have prepared and managed all of this better, but it didn't ever once occur to me that this is how my life would become overnight.

I'm homesick; I'm like *Stitch* all alone in the woods lost and I don't know my place in the world; I want to be fixed; I don't want to feel like this anymore; I think I'm not good enough; and not only Reed, but the world has rejected me.

I feel embarrassed, believing he was going to propose to me. I feel like I'm being laughed at; he must hate me because we haven't spoken once.

All I want are answers to how he could treat me this way.

What did I do so wrong except love him and do everything to make him happy? All of this feels like it all happened to me in another life.

I slide down the wall, but the mirror still haunts me with my reflection staring back at me and I think back to the first time I saw Reed; we were both in the library, and he was following my eyes through the book shelf gap.

At first, I thought he was a strange boy, but then I got a full view of his pale baby blue eyes, and I was locked into that look forever.

The moment he introduced himself to me, I fell head over heels in love with him, and that smile of his made all of my insides flutter, something I'd never experienced before.

Every week, I went to see him at the library and before long; we took our encounters out to coffee shops and restaurants and strolls through the park in the late evening. Picnics in the afternoon and one evening we sat watching a film at the cinema, sharing our popcorn and laughing at all the same jokes, with his safe protective arm wrapped around me, and I remember looking at him and knowing he was the one I always wanted to be with for the rest of my life.

He smiled back at me; there were no words, and as we gazed at each other, I hoped inside; I longed inside that he was thinking the same thoughts as me.

We talked about marriage and what our wedding would be like, almost as though we were playing out how the day would exactly be, and we talked about having children.

Reed wanted children; I recall him saying he wanted children with me and even if I didn't want kids, I would have to have them with him, and I felt so secure knowing this was what he wanted, and in my mind I had it all to look forward to in the coming future.

But why would someone put these thoughts out there if they never intended to take part in this?

I feel as though he went fishing with me; he reeled me in by tempting me with a future I wanted, to then throw me back in the river when I had run out of air, moving quickly on to his next fish, which is now BOOB and she's a smelly fish at that! I would immediately throw that trout back into the river and return to your rainbow carp.

But those days seem so long ago, and they almost feel as though they happened to someone else, because all the love I once felt has been overshadowed by dark feelings of resentment and anger.

These feelings are heightened right now. I know this, and I know deep down underneath all of this, that no matter how he has treated me, I still long for him and I still love him dearly.

Right now, I need to focus on this coming weekend, because once he sees me, things will change. I know this for sure; I'm going to hurt him. He'll want to know how it felt to be close to the person he idolises the most in the world (after himself).

I will lavish in all the details of how Dalton felt and smelt, and how much of a gentleman he was, and how I feel like we're closer now that I've met him, touched him, and made him laugh.

Outfit ordered, hallelujah to next day delivery.

I book an emergency hair appointment for tomorrow. So, Reed likes blondes, does he? Well, I have always been a brunette and I suddenly fancy a change. Emergency eyebrow, nail, and waxing appointments booked.

Suddenly, my calendar has just filled up over the next few days; now, if this running around doesn't flatten this kangaroo pouch of a stomach, nothing will.

It's all coming together nicely.

Thank heavens for Dalton Rivers; he's finally come in useful for once in my life.

Chapter Eight
Location Stalking

When someone breaks up with you and quickly moves on to the next person, they have little time to focus on wrapping up minor details of their past.

Not only am I still on all of Reed's social media channels, but he's still sharing his location with me, so it seems he hasn't had time to think about turning it off, and that's probably because he's far too preoccupied with his new love.

It's weird that I'm sitting here, seeing all the places he's going.

I know it's wrong to look, but it's there for me to see, and I can't help it.

It's strange that when we were together, and it was normal for me to have the opportunity to see where he was, I never checked his location. I had no reason to; I trusted he said where he was, and I often forgot we were even sharing our locations.

If I'd checked on it sometimes, maybe I'd have seen that he was not working as late as he claimed to be, or he was not having an extra long session at the gym, despite telling me this.

Maybe I could have cottoned on to his cheating sooner, and ironically, now we've broken up, and I don't have the right to check where he is; I am.

It's funny how things take a full circle.

Della says he must have a burner phone.

I haven't even heard that name for a phone before, so I guess I've learnt something new. But how on earth could he have had two phones without me noticing?

I find this really hard to believe. Is he really that calculated? I guess if he had two phones, then he must be.

He appears to have a new coffee haunt, as he visits that place more than he goes to work. I can also see where he's eating out with his new trophy girlfriend.

I can see when he's at the gym, and it's almost as though I've become a peeping tom, sitting here spying on his life from the outside—well, at least through the location app. I've thought about signing up for his gym.

Would that be a bit too far?

Would it?

I've thought about ringing the restaurants he's in and subtly dropping them a tip that a male who's currently having dinner in their establishment is on a certain list. Maybe it's because of certain photographs or certain search histories found on his computer, or maybe he's on a certain list that I'm not allowed to disclose, just planting the seed for it to grow in their own mind, and he would be sat there all happy, enjoying his dinner and the tough-looking manager would come over and quietly ask him to leave.

He'd have no idea what's happening, and I would sit outside, somewhere in the shadows, and I'd get to see the utter confusion on his face as he's frog-marched out of the building and kindly told by the manager to never return there again.

But then I realise it's illegal and immoral.

Why shouldn't I spoil his life a little? After all, he's spoilt my entire life.

I don't know what I get from checking where he is. I have thought about casually turning up at the coffeehouse or accidentally being in the same restaurant as them both.

Then I could finally approach them both, and cause a huge scene, with onlookers stopping what they were doing to watch the dispute play out, and I would be in tears because both of these people had ruined me.

Reed and BOOB would get tuts and gasps from strangers who will take my side because I'm crying, and because I must be telling the whole truth and nothing but the truth because the tears say so.

I'm not brave enough to go through with it, and it's certainly not in my nature to cause such a scene, even if I enjoy daydreaming about it happening.

One afternoon, I started heading towards a supermarket I knew he was in.

It wasn't too far from Dellas, and it would be so easy for it to be a coincidence that we're both shopping there.

But then I recalled the last time I accidentally ended up in the same shop as both of them, and it was so unexpected that I freaked out, (It was my fault, as I still wanted to shop in my local shop, but what were the chances of bumping into them) and I ended up with another charge.

I know what I'm doing is wrong, because if I told Della that I'm watching where he's going or admit that I'm having the occasional spy on his location, she would call me crazy and make me switch it off. Once it's switched off, he would never reshare it with me again, so I guess that would solve the problem.

Can I even justify it by saying it's just a habit that I'm finding hard to break now?

I'm just trying to adjust to a new life, one without him in it, but there are just a few things that I'm really struggling with.

I've sort of accepted that he's with another woman, but I can't help not knowing what he's doing or where he's going and I just want to know that he's okay.

I guess my behaviour is the opposite reason for having a location-sharing tool.

It's meant to be for one another to check in on each other when you're together and in love, but when you're no longer together, it becomes sinister that one of you is still using it and monitoring every move of your ex-partner.

I'm ashamed I've become this way, and I know it's borderline stalking without his knowledge, and what do I get out of it, except detailed information of where he's going and what he's doing, and am I causing anyone any harm? I am, though, because what right do I currently have to access this information on him? I don't, and I know I'm taking advantage of this situation, and my behaviour is wrong. However, some of this has to fall on him. It's not like he's even thought to check his own security settings on his phone, so that's his fault.

The truth is, I'm really struggling to let go.

Isn't that why there's a saying that old habits are hard to break?

Chapter Nine
Della Davis

You'll always hear Della before you see her; she's that type of woman.

Loud and proud is what she coins it.

Charity and Della met in school and have been inseparable ever since.

Even as a child, Della never had a filter on her thoughts or her mouth, and she continues to be this way to this very day.

But that's what drew Charity to want to hang around with her. She saw Della as the bundle of fun she is.

Even as a youngster, Della always spoke before thinking. Charity always remembers in school when a teacher said to Della, "Do you know the alphabet, Della?" and Della responded, "Yes, why?" And the teacher reminded her that "B comes before M in the alphabet, so remember brain before mouth; it may help you in the future." Della didn't listen, and she's still the same to this day.

Wiser than her age and somewhat of a mother hen, Della has a strong intuition, and she can read people within minutes of meeting them.

She's into horoscopes, tarot cards and reading tea leaves, and she loves anything colourful. Whether that's tie-dying your favourite t-shirt without your permission or painting.

She loves painting in her spare time, and the messier the better.

Della loves how she can express herself on a canvas and she has a stack piled on top of her wardrobe, because she has limited wall space left in the flat, because of the amount of her previous work she's currently displaying.

Della got along really well with Charity's mother, Alice, as they both shared a love of painting.

Alice taught Della about the common mistakes of watercolour painting, such as too much water on the brush or too little water on the brush.

Alice loved to paint ladybirds.

That was her signature object, and she enjoyed teaching Della.

Della quickly followed Charity to the capital city of London to live, ensuring she is always close to her best friend, something Charity was very grateful for.

She's full of energy and often compared to the Duracell bunny because she never sits still and barely stops.

Adventurous, caring, and wild are three ways of describing her.

Della is currently single, but she chooses this and loves not being tied down to anyone.

She sees herself as a free spirit and loves dating, but no one has captured her enough yet for her to take the plunge into serious relationship territory. She's the friend you need in your circle; she brings fun, laughter, honesty, and madness. Della cares a lot about Charity and only wants to see her happy. She sometimes finds this challenging because she often has to remind Charity that she needs to get out there and be more adventurous. She's been telling Charity for years that she needs to put herself first and stop centering her whole universe around a man, that man being Reed.

Della hasn't ever really been a fan of Reed; her intuition tells her the type of character he is, and despite her warning Charity over the years and telling her she could do so much better, but her advice is always ignored.

Della's polite (if you can call it that) towards Reed for the sake of Charity, but if it came down to pick him to be on her sports team, it would never happen.

If the boat was sinking and there was a stranger and Reed left on it, and they only had one space left in the lifeboat, she would most certainly give it to the stranger.

She floats from job to job because this aligns with her free spirit attitude, and she doesn't want to settle with anything in her life, relationship or career.

She works temporarily as a florist, and she loves bringing home colourful bunches of flowers, mainly because they're free and she can use them in her painting.

Next week, she will no doubt have another career; she's done everything and more you would expect a human to do, and this all adds to her life experience and seems to make her wiser than her years. Charity's nickname for Della is 34 DD (Della Davis, with her current age), and it's a pet name she adjusts as they age.

Their friendship is built on a solid foundation of humour and truth.

Della is someone you would look at and think is 100% on an illegal substance, but the truth is, she isn't.

Her high is life, and Charity admires this about her. She trusts Della with her life. She might not always agree with Della, but she knows she's always got her back, and without her, Charity would be very lost.

Chapter Ten
Transformation

Over the past four days, I've been transformed from a miserable prickly caterpillar into what Della now describes as a beautiful, intense, needs-to-chill-out butterfly who needs several tequilas and a few one-night stands.

It's incredible looking at the outcome of myself in the mirror. I'm unsure whether I looked dog rough before the breakup, and nobody informed me, or whether the breakup just added a few additional slices of roughness.

Della and I spent a day at the spa, which was interesting.

I've never experienced being waxed before. This was an experience I'm not sure I'm in a hurry to endure again so soon.

I could feel the entire hairs on my legs being ripped from the seams.

It's an experience I would put close to torture, and granted, I had let myself go somewhat and that didn't help the situation.

I could've given an average chimpanzee a run for its money with the amount of hair that got tore away from my poor legs. I'm feeling sensitive, metaphorically and physically, from the experience.

Smooth and silky legs, check.

That's not the worst part about my little trip to the spa, though.

I'm embarrassed to say this, but I did something I never thought I would.

Della had the most ridiculous idea of me having my lady part shaped; I argued this, telling her how silly this idea was and how no one would see it anyway, so what would be the point? Della delivered a speech similar to the tense court scene at the end of a drama film, where the defence is giving their closing statement. She declared I need to do something crazy to get all this out of my system. That it would be a secret only she and I would know about, but how it would make me feel somewhat mischievous because no one would know.

She wanted me to take myself completely out of my comfort zone, and eventually, she wore me down; I mean, my prison girlfriends going to love it, so I did it. I can't believe I did, but my pubic hair is now the shape of a love heart, and that's all we need to say about this.

Lady part styled, check.

Now moving upwards, my eyebrows now have a shape; they look like brown slugs sitting above my eyes, and I've spent a significant amount of time pulling faces and frowning in the mirror just to see them move. I call it the slug exercise workout. I will need Botox at this rate, Because I keep utilising my facial muscles with this new workout frown. Della says, *It's all the rage*, so I took her advice and had them. I can't say I like them, but they're definitely different. I never realised eyebrows were this important for beauty.

Eyebrows, check.

I've been spray-tanned; I agree I needed it; the breakup has drained me somewhat, and I was looking like I could be a part of the *Cullen* family.

My only other alternative was to get an emergency IV from out of nowhere to put back into my body all the life that's been sucked away.

Glowing body, check.

I've had my hair cut and coloured, so no more root job for me and not a grey hair in sight; it's fair to say I have accumulated a few more of those over the past few months. It may be down to the breakup or the looming prison girlfriend that awaits me.

I now have a gorgeous colour of honey blonde highlights to complement my brunette hair. The cut alone has given my face a rude awakening. It's taken Della's power of persuasion and the use of my savings to make me see how better I now look.

Hair check.

My nails have been done, and I no longer have stumpy nails and hands; I have acrylic, perfectly french manicured nails, and oh, how I love them; they've made my hands come alive. Now, I use every excuse to flash my hands off so everyone can see how nice my nails look. I've noticed my hands now stay on the counter longer when I'm paying; I hand over my cash in shops slowly so the cashier can see this girl's got nails, and I find every excuse to rest them in the eye-line of everyone, including tapping them gently on the counter to get them the attention they deserve. I have found a newfound love for nails.

Why didn't I ever have my nails done before? I simply love them. They've made me feel so good about my hands. All I need now is Reed, so I can run my new long fingernails down his back, and he, too, will question why I never had my nails done in all the nine years we were together.

Nails check.

I've been shopping for clothes, and it feels marvellous to wear feminine clothes again. It's been so long, and I forgot how nice they are. I got so used to being with Reed that I realised I had got so comfortable with casual clothes; so long gone are the slouch trousers, and the comfy hoodies.

Now I have slim-fitted jeans and feminine tops that reveal some, but not too much, of my breasts, which I forgot I had. I have a new, gorgeous, fitted black trench coat that makes me feel like a stylish woman.

New fashion sense, check.

Right now, I know I shouldn't be spending my savings on flashy clothes, but it feels incredible, and that overshadows my guilt; losing my job should've been a brutal hit, but as I'm dealing with losing the love of my life and my home, I don't have time to feel guilty about making myself feel better by spending money that I shouldn't. I still have some savings left, and I'll worry about finding a job when the savings run out and the credit card's maxed out; I know this is irresponsible, but to be honest, all I've been is responsible, and where has that got me lately in life, plus what company is going to hire me with a criminal record and the possibility that I'm heading for prison?

So, I will deal with my finances later because for the first time in a long time, I feel good about myself.

It's a temporary fix; I know this.

I miss Reed so much, and I know I shouldn't because of what he's done, but my heart can't help loving him; I wish I could stop loving him; it's killing me slowly by holding on to feelings for him, but how can you just erase everything? There's no magic button for all of this. If there was, it would be so much easier and somewhat kinder to press it.

As I stand looking in the mirror, I can't help but frown.

The slug thing gets me every time. I look at myself and wonder where I've been hiding all this time.

A sense of sadness creeps over me, and I wonder how long I will feel like this. I always seem to wait for that small moment that will send me back into that bottomless pit of despair that I've been in for months now. It's like being in a dark tunnel, and you can see the light at the end, and then out of nowhere, it goes dark again, and I have no control over it. I can't get to the end of the tunnel because I can't find a way out. I should think positively about everything.

But I have this little voice whispering to me that no matter how many spa days I have or how many shopping trips I go on with Della, Reed won't want me back.

He made his choice on our anniversary night. It was so easy for him to choose between BOOB and me, and he did his decision-making like he was picking a dessert from the menu.

Then there's me and I feel I can't ever forgive him for what he's done, for his lying, or for the cheating he was doing behind my back; it feels like our relationship just seems like one big fat lie, and he wasn't mine, because I was sharing him with her.

Who does that?

Pretends to be with you and hides this other life behind your back.

The deceit and levels of lies this takes I just can't imagine ever being able to do this to another person; I just don't think I have it in me to be this cruel and cold.

Oh, how quickly the flames of anger alight inside of me. A fire lit without the use of matches.

I tire myself out thinking of all the bad things about our relationship and how much hate I seem to hold for Reed.

And I know it's not healthy, and I know it's a process that I need to take myself through, but I need one night with him, just one night to hear him say sorry, to make him sit there and for him to have to listen to what he did to me. I need my chance to tell him how he's made me feel and how hard it's been for me because sitting and looking through his social profiles like the crazy stalker I've been; it appears I never existed.

There's nothing left of me.

All our memories are gone, and our relationship status has vanished as though we were never together, and it hurts.

It hurts to be deleted in life this way, with nothing as much as a simple *I'm sorry* message. I'm grieving for a loved one who hasn't gone away, and it feels harder than if they had actually gone.

As I look down at the tickets for tomorrow, I hold them as securely as Charlie in the Chocolate Factory gripped his; he knew this ticket would change his life; he knew this ticket was a once-in-a-lifetime experience he would never get to do again. So I remind myself of the plan.

I know this ticket will deliver the revenge Reed so deserves, and boy, I'm looking forward to it.

I remind myself I have to stay focused on the plan; because I won't get this chance again; I can't mess this up.

Once I meet Dalton Rivers while all dolled up and the best I have in years, that perfect photo will be uploaded to all my profiles.

I can only imagine the sick feeling of jealousy that will creep across dear Reed.

They say revenge is a dish best-served cold, but it's safe to say that revenge has been coming for a long time.

We're now at cryogenics level.

As I place the tickets on the dresser, ready for tomorrow's performance, I feel excitement rushing through me. I realise that, finally, there is a wicked side to me, one I haven't met until now, and it took heartache to bring her out.

I sit with a cup of tea, staring at my outfit for tomorrow that's hanging on the wardrobe door.

I realise how brave I've become this week, with my spray tan, my slugs, my nails, and now this one-of-a-kind Supergirl outfit, which, Della and restyled, we cut the top off the dress and turned it into a crop top so it reveals a little bit more and we stitched Velcro around the top of the skirt because it wasn't holding up, that must've been the sauna me and Della sat in for three hours the other day, its miraculously sweat away that Ben & Jerry's I was carrying around.

As I sit fixated on the outfit, which, until this moment in my life, I don't think I would ever have been brave enough to wear, my eyes avert to the knee boots I will wear, and with my new look.

I don't think Reed will even recognise me, I'm sure he'll walk straight past me, while the other men stare at the beauty I've transformed myself into and they'd never guess that it only took me four days to come out of my chrysalis.

Reed will be speechless when he discovers why I'm there, and despite there being thousands of people there, I could spot him in a crowd of a million people because when you truly love someone, you can just find them.

The question is, now he doesn't love me anymore, will he see me?

Della comes into the room, stops, and stares at my outfit.

"You're going to be the hottest girl tomorrow, Supergirl."

She sits down next to me and puts her arm around me, and we both marvel at how much progress I've made this week, going from the pits of despair to now looking like a completely new member of humanity.

"You deserve so much more, Charity," She puts her finger up to my lips to shhh me and to stop me from arguing back.

I know this conversation has been a long time coming.

"Get your revenge, sweetheart; you don't want someone like him in your life; you're smart, beautiful and funny. I know you've forgotten who you are, but you're finding her again. If not, you're finding an even better version of yourself who's now shining through."

As tears form in my eyes, it makes the image of my Supergirl outfit all blurry; I know she's right.

But I don't want to fall in love with anyone else; I just want my life back, and Reed is the missing part to that jigsaw; he's the missing piece that once you put it in the centre of the puzzle, all the other pieces just fall right into place.

Della pulls my face around to look at hers and you can see she's serious.

"And anyway, have you ever noticed his forehead? He looks like a cartoon character. I mean, come on."

This makes me laugh; then it sets Della off and we both sit laughing, and I realise its been a long time since I laughed.

I look at Della's green eyes and curly red hair; she's always been outrageous and has never cared about fitting into the mould of society.

She's true to herself, and I love this about her, including the bright rainbow-coloured wardrobe she wears every day.

She's always there for me, always. I don't know what I ever did to deserve her, but I don't know what I would do without her; it would break my heart even more not having Della in my life than it has not having Reed. I wish I could tell her this, but even the thought of saying this to her gets me choked up, so I need to find a time I'm not this emotional, to thank her for everything she's done for me, more so over the past few months.

Della gets up to leave but wants to leave it on a good note tonight.

"And one last thing, with him being Mr Perfect and all, there's no chance of you two being together again."

"How come?" I'm confused by this statement.

"Well, you're a jailbird now. Are you going to tell him about your criminal damage, vomiting on a police officer, assaulting the same police officer and your shoplifting offence?" She cackles and I throw my pillow at her. She leaves the room, and I sit smiling to myself, thinking about the situations I've got myself into.

I don't think I'll be able to sleep tonight; I'm full of nervous anxiety for tomorrow. I'm worried my alarm clock won't go off, so I set it and then re-set it no less than five times; I also set three alarms on my phone just in case the clock fails. I have everything ready; all there is to do now is come up with the funniest thing I can think of to say to Dalton Rivers when I get my thirty seconds with him for our photo opportunity.

As I turn in, all I can see in the darkness of my room is my life being replayed repeatedly on the ceiling, like a comedy doomed to flop on the first weekend of release. But no matter what I think about it, my mind always goes back to our anniversary; why did he make such an effort in the morning to slam me down like a ton of bricks in the evening?

Why did he book a restaurant to take me to, if he never intended to meet me? Why the roses, the breakfast in bed, the significant build-up to the evening meal, leading me with breadcrumbs to believing he would propose to me that night, just to leave me alone and embarrassed, let down, insecure and sad?

To not explain why, to not say to me we are no longer together, that it's okay, but then he moves on the same night with another person. I pick my phone up and go online; I look at all the photos of him and his creature recently, and sure enough, he's taking her everywhere.

Wow, busy little bees, aren't they.

I can't help but despise her when I see photos of her; as a woman, I would never hurt another woman the way she hurt me; I would love to wipe that smirk off her face and tell her who she really is, a home wrecker, a man stealer, a complete and utter hoe.

I move away from the photos as my laughter quickly turns to anger again.

I know replaying all of this just gets my back up repeatedly; in fact, there is a pattern that I've noticed whereas soon as I see him and her online, it brings it all back again.

I don't know why I keep looking at it all; I just need to see if I'm missing out on anything they're doing, or maybe I'm hoping they've broken up suddenly because he's realised what he's done to me.

I check his status; it's all about tomorrow; you can tell by the way he writes that he's feeling like a child on Christmas morning right now.

Gutted I can't meet my hero, but I'll be there tomorrow DR and I'll be close by to see if I can catch a photo of you.

This is a good sign. I knew he'd be there. He wouldn't miss an opportunity to be in the same room as his hero. He just doesn't realise his jilted ex-partner will be there, too.

So, if he really is close by then I can do the walk I've been practising with Della, the head held high, pretend not to notice him, and walk straight past him, and then I slowly turn around and say *Reed is that you? You look older somehow, I didn't realise it was you, sorry I can't stop at the moment I'm having my photo taken with DR, but if you're free after, we should really catch up, toodles,* and then I walk away, brimming with confidence, while trying to keep my shattered heart together inside my body, and making sure my heart doesn't spill over the floor for everyone to witness.

Oh, if only he knew I would be there to ruin his day tomorrow.

He will though eight hours and counting…

Chapter Eleven
Beatrix aka BOOB

Beatrix Ola Orson is a princess.

She's never heard the word 'no' in her entire life.

If Beatrix wants a pony, then Beatrix will have a field of them.

She's the apple of her parents' eye and a complete daddy's girl.

She works at her father's company, barely doing any real work. She does, however, do a good job of floating around the building, chatting to the male colleagues there.

She's self-centred, and she knows it, and she doesn't care.

She loves attention and needs it constantly.

She has to be the centre of everyone's attention; if she isn't, she will divert attention to herself.

She plays the dumb blonde, but she's more clued up than she lets on to those around her. She's quite calculating and always one step ahead of the games she plays with people.

Her evenings are filled with dates, and her weekends are filled with appointments, from hair extensions to nails to spray tans. She has regular Botox injections, which she started far too young in life. It's showing because she no longer looks her age, which is mid-twenties. She appears older, resulting in overusing Botox for many years. Her face doesn't move, so she's hard to read; you never know if she's angry or happy; and you'd get more emotions from a potato.

Lip fillers, crystal wand massages, waxing, microdermabrasion, she's never short of somewhere she needs to be for a treatment.

Her passions are beauty and fashion, and her parents' salary is splashed on these passions, ensuring their princess never wants for anything. She lives with her parents rent-free, and she tags along on their holidays with them, not because she wants to spend time with them, but because it's free and she needs something new to post on Instagram.

She doesn't see consequences of anything because her parents constantly clean up any mess she creates, and she's also not out looking for love; she's far too wrapped up in herself to make room for anyone else in her life.

She sees men as toys, and as soon as she's bored with one toy, she throws it away and grabs another out of the toy box; some toys she keeps in the box and goes back to as and when it suits her, she likes the fact they hang around waiting for a call from her, this feeds her ego and makes her feel important to them, they, however, are not crucial to her.

Beatrix is a woman who is in complete control of her own life.

Chapter Twelve
Today's the day

I'm awoken by every alarm clock in the house after having very little sleep, because from dusk to dawn I tossed and turned, thinking about today.

I awake with the notion that today's the day.

It feels like waking up on your birthday with that celebratory feeling that it will be a good day no matter what happens, because the day is all about you.

But there is also a sense of nervousness around today, so I have mixed emotions.

As I roll over, I see the sun shining through my curtains.

Finally, it's come back to me.

This is a metaphorical sign that my relationship with Reed will follow.

I ignore all the negative thoughts and focus on the positives of what I'm trying to achieve today. One positive feeling is that today will be a memorable one, one that I sit and tell our (in the not so distant future) perfect little children about. I can see it now, over a family dinner, sitting around our dark oak table, which is covered in a delicious meal that I've worked hard preparing.

Reed will be at the head of the table and I will tell everyone the story of the lengths I went to, to win my little darlings father back, and how my efforts are the reason we're all sitting here together as a family, and how different life would be, had I have not been crazy in not wanting to accept that Reed and I weren't destined for each other.

My eyes scroll around my room, and they stop at the attention seeking outfit hanging on the back of my door.

This outfit will surely make Reed wonder where this woman was hiding all this time. Because it's not the usual clothing he would've seen me in.

The very short red skirt that will show the legs that Reed used to kiss. The tight-fitted crop top that says I'm a woman, and people won't be able to help but look while wondering if my breasts are ok, as they look as though they're struggling to breathe.

Their eyes will avert to the ruby red bra strap that is peeping out of my tight top that bears the letter S, which says I'm super and that also says that when I chose this outfit, I felt empowered inside, and went for sexiness, and it will be finished off with the red lace thong that will sit underneath that oh so very short skirt.

I can't bend over in this outfit under any circumstances.

Forget the S on my chest; my underwear's my superpower, empowering me to know I'm a different version of myself today.

I'm out of my comfort zone and intend to enjoy every second. I need it so much today.

To finish this daring outfit off, I'll be wearing red-heeled knee boots that show I'm a woman who can not only hold my balance but can also hold her own in life.

It's funny that the new me seems defined by how I look and my outfit. Perhaps it is my fault that Reed lost interest; maybe he needed someone who took more care of themselves and presented themselves to the world in a more feminine way. I imagine BOOB has nice nails and wears feminine outfits, and maybe this is where I went wrong. He probably didn't feel he could tell me I had given up looking nice. So instead, he found someone who maybe wasn't so lazy and was more focused on themselves and their appearance; and perhaps this is on me and not him.

I glance at my phone, and see Della text me over an hour ago asking if I'm awake.

It's crazy that we live in a time where we send each other a message despite being less than ten feet away from each other, separated only by a wall.

Yes Della, I reply. **I'm awake and feeling ready for today.**

Della seems more excited than me for what lies ahead for us today. She's over the moon with my new transformation and has said several hundred times this week, how it's about time I took time for myself; I've also had several lectures from her about how Reed doesn't deserve me, how I'm better off without him, how I could do so much better than him, how I need to realise how much of a favour he's done me by ending our relationship, because I was far too comfortable, not only in my dress sense but apparently in my choices in life. She's also shared with me how she wasn't a fan of him because she thinks he overshadows me; he's never let me be myself. She also described how she viewed our relationship as me being a caged bird that needed freeing.

The thing with Della is that even when she doesn't say it bluntly, she still says it. I already knew how she felt about Reed because she made plenty of subtle comments to him, and to me, and she isn't one for not sharing her thoughts and feelings. Sometimes she can just about keep her opinions to herself, but only sometimes.

The one thing I know about Della, which I learned from the first day I met her, is that she only has my best interests at heart. She's never competed with me; she's the one consistent part of my life that never changes. She's always there for me through the good, the bad and, more recently, the ugly.

I'm so lucky to have her as my best friend because she's always there on the sideline of my life, cheering for me louder than anyone else ever does or could.

I take a moment before getting out of bed to recall the dream I had a few nights ago; it was an erotic dream of my former man begging for me to take him back and how much fun I had teasing him.

In this dream, I had all control; I was a strong, independent version of myself, and I liked her and her attitude.

Although it was only a dream, it felt so real, and this brings back memories of nights Reed and I spent together;

there was so much love and passion between us; where did it all go so wrong?

I shake these feelings off, reminding myself that today will be filled with revenge.

The girl in my dream is about to enter the real world and show everyone who has control in this situation and she's bringing the attitude along.

I get out of bed and head for a shower, where I know my thoughts will follow me along with that dream.

After showering, I stand looking in the mirror at this new creation of me and for once; I look fresh and alert; I'm almost rosy, although this could be from the adrenaline that's speeding through my veins; I'm probably headed for a further charge of speeding at this rate.

My stomach is in knots, knowing I will see Reed today, that I'm probably going to face my enemy BOOB and also that I will leave the house in my very revealing outfit.

I look down at my nails and marvel at the beauty that the nail technicians created; they are artists in their own right, and I again wonder why I left it so long to look after myself in this way.

As my eyes fix back to the mirror, I notice the slugs. Urgh they're still there, and although this is fashionable, I'm still in disagreement.

If I have a fringe today, it will somewhat hide them. But then I decide no, today is about not being me, and the old me didn't have slugs. But this new woman does, and I will embrace them, along with my latest nails, perfect eye-catching outfit, and everything else I will do this morning to make myself look as stunning as possible.

I take just under an hour to dry off, moisturise, and style my hair; I've gone with curls, not all curly, but fun, more like a wave, a style I never have.

My makeup is perfectly applied (thanks to the makeup influencer I found online, who talked me through it), and I'm now standing in my look-at-me outfit.

I leave the bedroom and head to the living room.

I catch myself in the full-length mirror hanging in the hallway, and I'm shocked this is actually me.

Who is this woman?

What am I doing?

Is this normal behaviour?

My mind is suddenly overwhelmed with doubts, doubts about what I think I'm going to achieve, doubts about making myself look like a fool, doubts that Reed will look at me and see straight through my soul and know what I'm playing at, doubts that coming face to face with BOOB will make me realise that the better woman won this battle and doubts that I'm going slightly insane because I look unrecognisable to myself.

But then I wonder what if this is the real me?

Maybe I was stifled in my relationship, and this version of myself was boxed away; and maybe Della is right. I was a caged bird, and this is the real version of me, as a free bird. Besides the broken heart, the hardest thing for me right now is understanding who I am. I don't know who I am anymore.

I argue with myself over why it takes a break-up and a broken heart to find yourself. Did I get too comfortable and forget there was a woman hidden under that smitten love slave to Reed?

A part of me feels ashamed now, looking at myself, that I let myself get so lazy, and then it occurs to me that maybe Reed really wanted more, and perhaps I made it too difficult for him.

It's not as though you can approach your partner and say, *You're looking rough, sweetheart; how about a makeover?* Without them feeling somewhat hurt inside.

Did I cause this?

Was I not attractive enough for him?

No wonder his eyes wandered if I wasn't.

Why am I getting revenge on him if I'm the one to blame here?

Lost in my own thoughts, I don't hear Della come into the hallway. She stands behind me, mouth agape.

"F*** me, you look insane, like insaneeeee, like if I wasn't into men, I would offer myself to you on a plate right now, jeez."

She bounces my wavy hair up, straightens the invisible crown she's given me and wraps her arms around the top of me. "One day Charity, you're going to realise how beautiful you are, inside and out, and I can't wait for this day to come. Now let's get this all out of your system, so you can focus on the great life you've got ahead of you, and the great love life you don't know is heading your way, especially looking like that."

My eyes start to sting.

"Hey, there's no time for tears today; today is about revenge, and revenge is fun, right? There's no time for a broken heart today; we have to switch it off for 24 hours, so pick that bottom lip up and straighten your crown because you're a Queen," Della says in a motivational tone.

"It's not that, it's…." I can't seem to get the words out.

"Whatever it is, I'm here for you, so share with me, so I can help you," Della has gone from motivational speaker into concerned friend mode instantly. "Well, I feel foolish saying this," Despite being pressured by Della's full-on stare at my face, I still can't say the words.

"Nothing is stupid, Charity; please tell me so I can help you."

"It's…… it's the thong."

"The thong?" Della was not expecting that response to come out of my mouth.

"It's severing me…down there; it's far too small." And with that, we both burst out laughing.

Della falls against the wall, and I can't help laughing at her contagious laugh; I love these moments in life, unexpected mini doses of laughter, right when you least expect it.

"Rip it off then."

"WHAT! I can't leave this house in this tiny skirt with nothing on down there. Are you crazy?"

I can't quite believe she's suggested that as an option.

"You have to now, one, to prove that you're not that stupid that you would let a lace thong ruin your day and two, so you can prove your fearless, because it's not in your nature to go knickerless, so just do it."

She stands staring at me, tapping her foot, after giving me an ultimatum that involves me having no option but to remove the dental floss underwear.

I mean, she has a point; I'm transformed into a new version of myself, standing here wearing clothes that I never would have worn, going to seek revenge on my ex, which is something I've never done before, so I may as well just continue this pattern of doing everything that isn't me right?

"Fine!" I declare.

"Come on then, get it off. There's a strong coffee here with your name on it." And with that, Della walks into the kitchen.

She sits at the breakfast bar, coffee in hand, eagerly awaiting me to remove my underwear to prove I'm now this fearless woman, and I take the bait of her words and slip it off.

Walking into the kitchen, noticeably it's drafty down there, and the doubts I had earlier now have another one added to the list. This skirt is incredibly short, and it's a very revealing, it really doesn't leave much to the imagination and to top it off, it's held together by a velcro strap and wearing this without underwear, has just given me the most significant amount of anxiety I've ever experienced with clothing.

I sit on the kitchen stool and instantly feel the impact of not wearing underwear.

I sip my coffee and notice the lipstick mark I've left on the rim of the solid white cup. And it's a sense I have left my mark, which is what today is all about, leaving my mark on Reed, and by the end of today, that boy will wonder what he did, and he will have regrets of this, I am sure. He will glance at BOOB and think, what did I do? Either that or he will have a belly full of fire when he sees my photo; it will rise and burn all of his insides, then seep into his head and finally, he will feel some of the rage I've been experiencing all this time.

Meanwhile, I will sit back with a sense of satisfaction that I was that heat that crept under his skin and did this. I feel as though my wicked inner self is having far too much fun and there's a chance it could get out of control at this rate.

I look up from the coffee cup and see how beautiful Della looks.

I was so consumed by myself that I didn't realise how great she looks.

She's dressed as Catwoman, and what a Catwoman she is, with her tight black catsuit, her drawn-on whiskers and those big friendly and loving green eyes of hers.

I know as I look at her that the only reason I'm brave enough to see today through is because I have her on my side. She's always rooting for team Charity.

Without her, I would not be leaving this house, and if I were, I would most certainly be wearing underwear.

"The lifts here…you ready?" Della says as she frantically grabs her bag, she's super excited about today, and then she turns around and stares at me. She gives me a look that says, *don't you dare put that thong back on*, and then she heads out the door.

As I walk back through the hallway, I take a final look at myself and say to myself; "I'm ready; you can do this, Charity, you can…let the games begin."

I grab the tickets and slam the door, and all that's left behind is a lipstick-stained coffee cup and a red lace thong on the kitchen counter, as we're on our way to a more memorable day than either of us realised.

Chapter Thirteen
Comic Con

We arrive at our very first comic convention.

Both standing at the entrance of the building, marvelling at all the colourful characters standing in front of us.

My eyes don't know where to look.

There's people dressed up from *Harry Potter* to the marshmallow man from *Ghostbusters*, there's Jareth the goblin king and Sarah from *Labyrinth* to *Walking Dead* characters, and then there is me and Della, who are currently sticking out like a sore thumb, mouths open, just staring at everyone, making it completely obvious we are comic con virgins. Della flicks her hair and gives someone dressed as Superman a flirty smile. "I thought you said this was too geeky for you and not somewhere you could meet anyone, Della."

"Well, look how handsome he looks. How can I not?"

Her eyes fixated on Superman.

"You realise he's in costume, right? I doubt he actually has muscles or a penis that big." I wave my hand in front of her face to break the hypnosis she's currently under.

"Right, we need to find where the signings are for Dalton," and I drag her away unwillingly. The convention is not how I imagined it to be, although I'm not sure, having never been to one before, what I expected. The event has a pleasant atmosphere; everyone seems laid back, chilled, and happy to be here. There is so much to see as we stroll by stalls of things we could buy if we were the world's number one fan of *Game of Thrones* or an avid fan of *Marvel*; I realise there really isn't anything you can't buy here.

Della seems to be enjoying herself, taking endless selfies with people dressed up. As I stroll behind her, I wonder how Reed and I would be acting if we were here together today. I think about how Reed would be walking on cloud nine, knowing that shortly he would get to meet his idol.

I notice the stalls have endless things to do with Dalton Rivers, and we would indeed be carrying hundreds of bags from all the merchandise Reed would have purchased by now. A part of me feels low inside.

My mood changes from a good-time girl having fun with her best friend to a desperate ex-girlfriend missing her loved one, who cannot possibly enjoy today, as this is all wrong and not how it was meant to be.

While wallowing in self-pity, Della quickly awakens me with the loud, enthusiastic voice only she can have this early in the day.

"I love this place; why did we never think to come here before today? It must be the easiest place to pick up geeks and guys...hello, is anybody in there?" she snaps her fingers in front of my face.

Through her eyes, I see a reflection of misery. "Oh no, you're not doing this today, missy; today is all about you;

stop wallowing and remember the mission and why we're here." With that, she pulls my arm, and within seconds, we are sitting in what looks like a pop-up bar.

"Two white wine spritzers as fast as you can make them," she says to the barman, who looks far too young to be working in a bar.

She leans on the counter like a young schoolgirl getting served underage, twizzling a strand of her hair around her finger, while sticking her Catwoman behind out.

"We don't have any soda, so I can't make you that; I can do two white wines if that's OK?" the young man says, smiling at Della.

"Perfect, although you may have to find a way of making up the missing soda for me."

I wonder if there isn't anyone she doesn't accidentally flirt with, and with that, alcohol has now become my liquid breakfast for today.

Della pays for the wines and we go and take a seat.

"You need a good stiff drink before your photo, Charity; it will make you look more relaxed and less, erm, uptight." She gives me a long, slow wink while looking over at the young barman to see if he's still checking her out. He gets the end of her wink, so she's just done a double whammy with us both; and yes, he's still looking at her.

"Should I slip him my number, the hot barman?" Della awaits my permission and advice. I'm confused as I'm the last person qualified to give this advice.

But I respond, "You should. He's clearly interested; he hasn't stopped looking over at you since we got here."

"I'm going to do it; more wine is coming up," Della says excitedly, as she heads to the bar.

I look at all the happy characters and attendees walking past the bar. Everyone's in high spirits. There's so much noise with voices chattering, and it's at this moment I catch sight of the man who has broken my heart.

In slow motion, I see him walking towards the bar, and he looks like an angel. I freeze in my seat, and suddenly, feelings of excitement, rage, sadness, and fear take over me. I watch him; he has happiness spread across his face and he looks so beautiful.

It's like he hasn't aged a day in our three months apart.

In all honesty, he looks better than ever, like he's glowing, his hair looks perfect, and he has a pale blue shirt on, with a bright white collar, it's new,

I know this because I've never seen that shirt before in my life; I wonder if she purchased it for him, or whether he's gone on a new shopping spree like I've recently done to create this new and better version of myself.

He looks stunning.

This was not a part of the plan.

He's not meant to look this good.

I know I should be so mad right now about everything that's happened with us, but I look at him and miss him more than ever. Della shoves a fresh glass of wine in my face, and as I stare at Reed, without blinking or moving an inch from the vision of him heading towards the bar, I down the glass of wine that's just been given to me.

He looks over at the bar, smiling and laughing; he seems so full of life, and I catch sight of the blonde hair draping next to his shoulder. But I can't see BOOB's face because she's overshadowed by those walking in front of her, but I can tell he has his arm around her.

"Charity, what's the rush!" Della exclaims.

Della wants to stay in the bar so she's close to the man she's got her eye on, and I want to leave the bar to follow the man I've got my eye on.

"I'm ready; let's go." And with that, I jump from my seat, and receive a sharp reminder I'm not wearing underwear, as I nearly tear my arse off on the suction from the seat its been stuck to.

"Wait, Charity!" I hear Della call; but her voice fades in with all the background noise, and I'm not slowing down. I need to catch up to him, and I need him to see me.

In all the chaos of the convention, and with the amount of people there, he's becoming more and more out of sight, and as I rush past people like the crazy follower I've become, I'm frantically trying to reach him, it's like I will never have another opportunity again for the rest of my life, I'm that frantic I don't even apologise to the people I am pushing out of the way and suddenly my arm is grabbed

"Charity, what's the matter." Della pulls me back to earth as she swings me around to face her. She breaks me away from the red mist that's in front of me, and I can see the annoyance on her face that I just upped and left her in the bar.

As I turn back around, Reed is nowhere to be seen.

I scour the crowds, searching for the pale blue shirt with the white collar, but it's nowhere.

I feel disappointed and sad that in a venue this big, with the number of people in it, I've missed my one opportunity to confront him face to face and for him to see me dressed up this way.

Della sighs, "Did you just see him?"

She pulls me in and hugs me, and I want to break apart right here in the middle of a comic con. I don't though, because right now, getting emotional is not an option; for it will ruin the make-up I taught myself (well thanks to the influencer online).

I need to hold myself together, but I'm now feeling the full effects of the glass of wine I just downed and even hugging Della is hard work, and things are feeling somewhat heavier than before that additional glass, and I'm going to need some water very soon. "Right, get it together. The photo meet and greet with Dalton is over there."

She points to an overcrowded area that looks like a health and safety risk.

"You see how everyone is on the balcony. They're watching Dalton have photos taken, and we're heading for there. There's going to be a very high chance Reed will be one of those people watching his idol because he couldn't get tickets. That photo op is your stage, and Reed is in the audience, OK?"

She's right. I need to pull myself together, or I'm going to waste this opportunity.

Della fixes my hair, straightens my invisible crown once again, and holds my face in her hands. "He's going to be sick with envy, sickkkkk, I tell you, and you're going to feel much better shortly about everything."

She grabs my hand and starts leading me over to my stage.

How can I have the worst case of stage fright at this precise moment?

Chapter Fourteen
Meeting a Celebrity

As I stand in what seems to be a never-ending snake queue of obsessed fans, I realise I'm probably the only person in this queue who's a fraudster and isn't actually a fan of the man everyone is so desperately waiting to meet.

Della has taken the time to touch up her makeup, which gives me time for my eyes to scan the queue for the love of my life.

There's no sign of him, and I feel very disappointed that I didn't get to see him face to face, especially after practising how unimpressed and not bothered I would act at seeing him. It all seems silly and a waste of my time now, making me see how childish I've become from this breakup.

The queue is moving down quicker than I thought it would. There's so much chattering around me, Dalton this and Dalton that, and my outer shell portrays a fan who can't wait to meet her dream actor.

While my insides are screaming out, *As if I need another minute in my life dedicated to spending any of my time on Dalton Rivers.*

I've realised I have awoken to the fact that I loathe this man, like real-life loathing, to the point I don't even want to hear his name anymore. It all stems from jealousy that the person who has broken my heart cares more about a man who pretends to be someone else in films than he does for me, and over the past few months, I have relived all of those cringe-worthy moments where I have had to appease Reed, listening to every boring fact about Dalton Rivers.

From hearing about his upcoming films (yawn) and what news stories have just dropped about him (yawn) to what size shoe he is (yawn) to what he eats for breakfast (yawn). I've remembered how when my partner should've been interested in talking about us, instead he spent his time obsessing over this man, who frankly is not that interesting, and he also isn't the best actor on the planet like everyone seems to think he is. He's also not god's gift to women and men from what it appears.

"No joke, but I think I'm going to faint." As I turn around, I see a woman clutching onto her friend's arm, and I quickly notice that the woman has a lot of sweat coming from her armpits, her head, the front of her chest and, more strangely, her top lip.

She's sporting an 'I love Dalton't-shirt; I mean, it actually says 'I love Alto' as she has large breasts, but I got the message loud and clear of what it's meant to say, and I'm slowly feeling really desperate being in this queue.

"Take deep breaths." Her friend tells her, and I turn back around, trying to mind my own business. How is it possible my life has come to this? I look for the nearest exit because I'm now in flee mode and I don't think I can go through with this.

"How do I look?" Della interrupts. "I need a nervous wee; it's that or the wine we just tanked."

The exit plan is aborted, as the realisation that Della fits in with everyone in this line perfectly and she's ecstatic that she got to take Reed's ticket for this meet and greet.

"You look beautiful, D." I try to pretend to at least be a little happy to be where I am right now. Then Della drops a bomb on me. "What are you going to say to him?"

"Oh, you know, just how much of a mess I've become, how I can't seem to repair my broken heart, how desperate I've become of late, and how kind it was of him to cheat on me and then not apologise, and how I've stayed up late on many nights thinking of committing the worst crime possible to his new partner because I now have a criminal record so what does it matter, something like that." I sigh.

"I meant Dalton, but it's good to know where you currently are, Charity," Della gives me one of those half smiles, and before I can react by trying to cover it up by saying it was a joke, the loudest crash happens behind us.

As we both turn around, the 'I love alto' woman has dropped.

She wasn't lying when she said she felt faint.

Suddenly, out of nowhere, what looks like the secret service, but dressed in bright yellow, all crowd around her to move her out of the line. Obviously to prevent delays, because the last thing the venue needs is a riot from everyone having to wait.

We live in a time where everything blows up quickly.

Della and I look at each other, and we're both hiding the fact that we're about to burst into hysterics despite us both knowing it's the most inappropriate time to do it. It's very insensitive, so we both turn our backs on each other because all it will take is that one look to set us both off.

As the 'I love alto' woman is carried away, It suddenly dawns on me, I hadn't planned what to say to Dalton Rivers, I had a plan of saying the funniest thing to him, but I didn't get around to figuring out what it would actually be and now I feel under too much pressure to muster up a comedy line, damn it!

We're both still nowhere near being able to turn around to face each other, so Della and I hutch down the queue back to back, and I realise how we must look, but considering the surrounding audience, I don't think we stand out too much.

Looking to my right, I see a new woman replacing the 'I love alto' woman with her friend.

And the new woman is heavily pregnant; she's holding a piece of paper in her hands.

Della notices."What's on the paper?"

The woman turns the paper around to show us, and what's written across it in bold black marker pen is -

THIS IS YOUR REAL DAD

She explains to Della; she intends to hold the paper up next to Dalton in the photo, to give to her unborn child as a joke for them in however many years and with that, Della looks at me and hysteria sets in as we both burst out laughing. However funny the sign is, and you have to admit it's a genius photo to show your child in the future, the laughter coming out of me is a combination of the 'I love alto' woman, the wine I've had for breakfast and the broken version of myself I'm trying so desperately to hide from the world.

"Oh Charity, you've got to laugh; if you don't laugh, well...." Della links arms with me, and that's the silent reassurance she always gives me. No words, just that arm linked in mine. That arm that says, me and you girl, we've got the world at our feet and a never-ending line of appletinis waiting at the bar for us and there's nothing we can't achieve.

The queue is going down quickly, and I see the booth we're heading for.

I can now also see the people on the balcony, and all of them are watching the booth, which is weird because they're watching the booth, we're watching the booth, they're looking at us, and we're looking at them, it's all one big watch fest going on.

I look down at my boots and wonder what people think of me; I've never really been one of those people that this affects, as I usually blend into the environment; I'm sort of magnolia, I never stand out, and no one ever notices me, and yet here I am, knickerless, dressed in the most provocative version of a Supergirl outfit I could pull together and I smell of desperation and wine.

My self-pity moment is quickly spoiled

"Charityyyyyyyy," Della says suspiciously.

"Yeah?" I respond, wondering what could go wrong now

"Look up on the balcony, right in the corner to the right-hand side of the booth."

My eyes scan the balcony, and it doesn't take long for me to realise what she wanted me to see. Reed.

There he is, taking the front-row seat to spy on Dalton Rivers; of course, he's up there, I say to myself. I can't see BOOB, though; he obviously ditched her for this spot, as Dalton is, of course, more important than anyone else to him.

He looks so happy; I mean, he would look happier if he was stood where I am, holding a fast-track ticket to meet his idol.

Still, he's not, and this fuels my wicked side, and suddenly, I'm brimming with confidence. I feel entirely in control; I have something he wants, and he will have no choice but to see me in mere minutes. I plan to look up at him, dead in the eye, in a real smarmy way, just in case he has any confusion whether it's me, and my eyes will say, *Oh yes, it's me, Reed, hello stranger.*

"You ok?" Della breaks my thought pattern.

"Oh, I'm great; I mean, obviously, he's in that spot; we knew he would be," I say, trying to convince her I have everything together; despite being confident, my insides are torn, and sadness is now throwing unwarranted punches at my confidence.

107

"Do you want me to go first? So you can make your grand entrance?"

"Sure, that works for me," I agree, because one, I'm feeling very nervous suddenly, like the worst anxiety has just sneaked out of nowhere, and two, I still don't know what I'm planning to say to Dalton Rivers, and I'm running out of time.

Loud chanting begins in the queue of *Dalton, Dalton, Dalton,* and this is the last thing I need right now, this man's name being forced into my ears, but as I look to Della for support, it quickly becomes apparent she too is one of the chanters.

My eyes scan up to Reed. I'm curious to know if he's spotted me yet. He's not looking my way; maybe he's pretending not to have seen me. He seems fixated on Dalton, and he, too, is one of the chanters.

I look at him and feel annoyed that all of today's performance is for him. The clothes, the meet and greet, the makeover. Della thinks it's to make me feel better, but it isn't; it's to make him notice me, to see me again, because if he sees me, maybe he will miss me and realise what he's done and then perhaps I can get my life back.

My arm is tugged, and as I come back from my stalker stare at Reed, Della is dragging me into the booth that contains the world-famous Dalton Rivers.

I didn't realise how loud all the noise in the venue is; it's full of constant chanting from so many people; there are people excited, people cheering, people laughing, people shouting, and here's me, drowning in the noise of it all, along with my wallowing and still despite all the noise, my thoughts still function, never giving me any respite. We enter the small booth area, which has a tiny line of people inside, and we're seconds away from meeting the man everyone is here to see.

I glance over and see a person taking a photo with Dalton Rivers.

So there he is, the man everyone loves. He looks normal, nothing extraordinary, just a man who seems happy to meet people. Despite all the noise in the venue, this area has fallen deathly quiet, and everyone is now holding their excitement in from being feet away from their idol.

I look at Dalton's clothes; he seems casual but smart. But what is it about this man that everyone loves?

It still baffles me; he looks normal, like someone I would pass on the street, not giving them a second glance. They don't have thousands of people following them and throwing themselves at their feet, or fainting, for that matter.

What am I missing, I wonder?

Della has fallen silent; she is also wholly mesmerised by the man we're here to meet, and it's not very often that Della loses her voice.

As she approaches Dalton, she whispers something to him, and he laughs, and I realise I still have nothing to say. She smiles for the photo, gives Dalton a hug and then turns around, looks up and shouts, "REED, YOU'RE A DICK!"

And somehow, the silence just got even more silent.

I look up and see Reed staring down at her, mouth agape. He's recognised her, and he then looks directly at me, and it's one of those moments where time seems to stand still.

Me and Reed just stare at each other, no words, nothing.

The only emotion I can work out he's experiencing right now is shock.

I don't know if it's from Della's insult, or that he's just seen me standing here, about to meet his dream man, or whether it's how I'm dressed or all of the above.

The moment is rudely interrupted by the sound of "Miss, it's your turn, move along please," and a worker ushers me towards Dalton Rivers, and now's the time to switch into actress mode myself.

Walking the few steps towards Dalton Rivers somehow, feels how it would if you were walking on the moon; it's slower than it should be, and taking way longer than expected.

Dalton holds his hand out to greet me.

As I take it, he says, "It's lovely to meet you."

My response is wholly unplanned and not rehearsed; in fact, it couldn't have been more off-script than expected. "I wish I could say the same it's my ex up there that loves you, not me," and that's when I realise what an unnecessary bitch I'd just been.

I look at the confused expression on his face and realise I'd just been cruel and unkind, and he has no details about the backstory leading up to this moment.

"I'm sorry to hear that. Shall we have a photo?"

He seems a little off-kilt, like he isn't sure what to do, and I'm embarrassed as I caused this awkwardness, which was certainly not what I had planned.

As we stand awkwardly together for our photo, I say,

"I'm sorry, that was rude of me, I didn't mean it," and that's it, I've shown Reed what he's missing, I've met Dalton Rivers, I've been rude to Dalton Rivers and had a photo with the most sought after celebrity on the planet.

Well, I wish that's how I could tell you it ended, but it didn't end there.

I didn't realise how close I was standing next to Dalton.

As I go to quickly walk off, embarrassed about my petty behaviour, my skirt got caught on his belt, and what followed was my skirt being pulled off, leaving me very exposed in front of the most sought-after celebrity on the planet and all the watchers on the balcony, along with my ex, and the 'I love alto' fans waiting in the booth.

The watchers all just started watching something else, and the cameras are now turned away from snapping photos of Dalton, to snapping photos of a random woman they'd never met.

Among the gasps and eerie silence of the bigger awkwardness I'd just created on what quickly became one of the worst days of my life, all I hear in the chaos that I created is, *Is that a....love heart?* At this moment, I realise I will never agree or think it's a good idea to not wear underwear; I will never get my lady area shaped again, and I plan to never leave the house again for the rest of my life...

Chapter Fifteen
Dalton Rivers

Despite being one of, if not the most famous man on the planet, Dalton is also one of, if not the most insecure person on the planet.

He loves acting and knows it's a privilege to do what he does, but when the day is over, he goes home alone.

He has no real deep friendships, as everyone he knows in the industry and it's work. He feels like people only want to be friends with him because he's famous, and he's been hurt him over the years because of this.

He has celebrity friends, but misses the connections he had as a youngster with his friends when it wasn't a friendship built on work.

He's thoughtful, kind, and trusting.

He knows good manners cost nothing, and he certainly doesn't have the ego one would expect with his status.

He's polite to all of his fans and has the time of day for everyone, but he also keeps his guard up and can be closed off to people until he's really got to know them.

Born in the United States of America, he loves his country, but he has a special place in his heart for England.

He's filmed many films over the years in England and he finds it a slower pace, he loves exploring alone in the countryside. He usually signs on to do a role based on where the location of filming is, and if it's England, then there's a higher chance he will say yes to it.

Dalton is humble; he's come from a hard upbringing.

His parents split up when he was very young, and his mother turned to drink. She sent him to live with his father years after her and her drinking habit had already done irreversible damage to him. This damage happens when you make a young child grow up too quickly, and the role reverses into making them the adult in the relationship. It's fair to say he's from a broken home, one that was turbulent and troubling, one where he eventually ended up in foster homes and has grown up with his own loneliness and abandonment issues.

He has more money than he could ever have imagined and he does good with it.

He regularly donates to charities and helps as many causes as close to his heart as possible. They're all to help animals and children, and because the adults around him let him down, he feels donating to causes that support them feels wrong. He wants to help those with voices that are not loud enough to speak.

He carries a lot of trauma from his childhood, but he manages it well. He's had extensive therapy, and it doesn't impact his life like it once did. The one thing he's missing in his now privileged life is love. This area of his life is a problem.

Every time he falls for a woman or is interested in pursuing someone, it doesn't take long for him to realise that they aren't interested in who he is away from his profession.

It seems fame and fortune attract people to him and they're not the type of people he wants in his life.

As a child, his future aspirations were to live in a house where there wasn't violence and fighting.

He just wanted a job.

It didn't matter whether it was cleaning toilets or delivering mail; all he wanted was a job that could give him enough money, where he could build his own safe fortress, somewhere he would feel secure, that would be his and no one could move him out of it whenever they had drunk too much.

He dreamed of having somewhere that he could call home.

He went into acting as therapy because playing someone who wasn't him gave him a break from the everyday struggles he carries around with him.

It turned out that he was very good at it. With his dashing good looks, it didn't take long for an agent to snap him up, and the rest is history.

Dalton has everything he could ever want: money, fame, possessions, and an apartment overlooking Central Park in New York, where he feels safe.

But despite having what most people are on the chase in life for, he feels empty. He works a lot to mask this loneliness, barely allowing any time for his inner demons to come out and play with his mind.

He's in his mid-thirties and is anxious he won't ever find true love.

He needs genuine relationships, and he longs for the day when he can fall in love and for them to see who he is beneath the image of him that's portrayed to the world in every film he's in.

He would give up his acting and wealth to settle down and have a typical family and home, as this is his real dream.

Chapter Sixteen
Who is Charity Fletcher?

Not leaving the house hasn't helped me. In the twenty-first century, everything is online, and online is inside of everywhere.

I can't escape the fact that I've become somewhat famous—famous for all the wrong reasons, of course—and for the rest of my life, there will be photos out there in the world of me, in the worst way possible.

That's the thing about the twenty-first century, we've advanced so far with technology that, thanks to our camera phones and social media apps, you can't do anything wrong and not expect it to be shown to the world.

If I thought my confidence was shattered before the comic con, then it's really taken a battering.

I'm now being commented about on every site you can imagine and most are sharing a similar headline - **Who is Charity Fletcher?**

I'm all over the news for being the girl who flashed the most famous man on the planet, and no one even mentions how this was accidental.

My face is plastered everywhere, and people are seeking to find out everything and anything about me, including my recent breakup and my fresh criminal record.

Is everyone in the 21st century a private detective?

The worst part about all the coverage is that Dalton Rivers is once again inviting himself into my life uninvitedly, and my loathing has reached a new level towards this man. I feel everything to do with him causes me pain; when I hear his name, it takes me back to all the times Reed would share stories and news about him or when we'd go to the cinema to watch his new film, and now we've come full circle. I've become a part of Dalton's news. Me?. No doubt Reed will now sit and tell BOOB all about it. It will be the breakfast conversation, and she'll be sat there just like I was, disinterested and wearing a forced smile, to make it seem like she's listening.

The comic con did not go as planned, and now I feel foolish that I ever thought it was a good idea.

I was so angry that I let my thoughts about revenge get the best of me.

And instead of making my ex jealous, I'm sitting here reading comments from people who are making fun of me, commenting on how desperate I must be to flash Dalton, commenting on my looks; in fact, it's fair to say I've spent hours reading the worst insults a human could read about themselves, something I did not envision when I thought about my revenge plan.

Hence, everything backfired on me, and now I'm feeling bruised.

Della notices I'm still scrolling through nasty comments and memes that have now been created, and she walks behind me and grabs my phone out of my hand; I have no time to react, and I so I let her take it away from me

"Stop!" Della sits down and has a serious expression on her face. "You can't sit reading all that shit about you; it's social media. Fake. Things on there just get completely blown out of proportion. It's not real, and in a couple of hours, everyone will have moved on to their next victim."

I know she's right, but I'm the centre of today's news. No matter how much I don't want to read all the hurtful comments about me, I'm twitching as I feel compelled to read them; it's an addiction I can't fight. I know anything I'm reading is for the public, and Reed is the public.

This fiasco has damaged my image, which I never even had before.

Reed will be relieved he's got rid of me, so now I'm stooping even lower emotionally, as I really thought I had a chance of getting Reed's attention positively with my plan. But I've just made the situation so much worse for myself.

"How has this become my life, Della? I've gone from being a nobody who was happy and loved up, having a secure home, a secure job, and a secure relationship, being a non-criminal, and today I sit here single, broken-hearted, with no home, no job, a criminal, and the entire world has just seen the one part of my body I wouldn't ever want anyone to see, and to top it all off, they're making jokes about me." Della leans forward, and her tone changes. "Look, I know everything is really hard at the moment, but it's a blip, a part of your life that maybe is teaching you something. You're better off without Reed, even though you don't want to hear it. You have a home here with me for as long as you want, and you'll find a new job; maybe this is divine intervention, maybe the universe is telling you to put yourself first, and I beg you, for once in your life, do! And as for the jokes, they're stupid, irrelevant people who mean nothing to you; their opinions aren't valid."

I know she's right, but everything feels so heavy on me.

I thought I was carrying a few plates before, and suddenly, I feel like I'm spinning them, and at any point, I'm going to drop everything.

I'm barely being honest with myself about how I'm actually not coping.

I don't have the heart to tell Della how low I actually feel, as she's doing her best to keep me up with her positive vibes and pep talks.

Della's caring tone comes into force: "Charity, we both know who Charity Fletcher is. Don't pay any attention to this rubbish; it's just gossip. They're trying to find out things about you and they're making most of it up as they go along."

"He's going to be glad he broke up with me, isn't he?" I sound so pathetic.

"Who gives a fuck, Charity? He's rotten, he's the rotten piece of fruit in the bowl that spoils all the good fruit. Give it time, and you'll see how good this situation is. I imagine he's seething and jealous of the media attention of you and his hero, Dalton."

"You think so?" There's an excitement in my tone. Because, I didn't think of that.

My original plan was to get close to his idol, just enough to make him jealous. I haven't considered all the media frenzy that's contributed to my plan.

"Charity, if I know him as well as I think I do, I'm surprised he hasn't reached out to you because being close to you gets him one step closer to Dalton. He's pathetic. Right I'm going for a shower."

And with that, Della leaves the room.

I sit thinking about Reed's possible jealousy, as I wasn't looking at the situation this way. Della may have a point. Maybe I have hurt him by getting close to Dalton. I got closer than expected, and while marvelling at the possibility that I may have succeeded somewhat in my plan, my phone quacks.

I look over at my phone on the kitchen counter and wonder what horrible message has now dropped into my inbox.

I've had so many sent to my social channels, and I wonder if they will have anything new to say this time. I get up and walk over to the counter, and before I even reach down to pick my phone up, I see Reed's name on the front screen.

He sent me a message! My stomach feels like it's dropped to my feet. I stand as still as the Statue of Liberty, frozen and a matching shade of green, because I'm unsure if I'm ready to see what he sent me. Then, there's another quack of the phone, and it's a number I don't have saved.

I pick my phone up slowly, telling myself I will read the unknown number message first. Because I want to make Reed wait and by doing this, I'm proving to myself that he is no longer the centre of my world, and despite telling myself this, I open Reeds message first:

Hey, Charity, I hope you're well. I'm checking in after seeing all the news stories with you. If you're free at some point, it would be good to have a coffee.

It sounds so formal, not a message I would usually get from the love of my life, but I keep forgetting I'm not his love anymore. He wants to go for a coffee? We hadn't spoken since the day of our anniversary before I discovered he'd been cheating on me. He's given me no explanation for why he broke my heart the way he did, and he now wants a coffee with me.

I'm so angry, but I feel the butterflies are still behind the anger, and I tell myself firmly that this is not a time to get all loved up; it is a time to be angry. The audacity of this man.

How dare he just casually message me about coffee?

I can sit at a table and have coffee with the man I once adored. I wonder if this is the beginning of my plan, where he realises what a mistake he's made?

It will start with coffee and then lead to us falling in love with each other all over again.

My mind races away with the possibility of this never-ending nightmare coming to an end and me getting my life back to where it was a few months ago. Before I respond, I want him to see I've read it and I will not be reacting straight away; I need to play it somewhat cool here, so I move from his message to the unknown number message; it reads:

Hello, Charity. I hope you're okay. I feel weird sending you a message when we haven't been introduced properly. Please don't think I'm weird. The reason I'm messaging you is to ask if you would you like to go for a coffee? Given all the media circus after the comic con, I wanted to ensure you're okay and maybe rewind our first introduction. I understand if you don't want to, but I'd love it if you could. Dalton.

This can't be real. How would Dalton Rivers get my phone number? I wonder who would be sick and twisted enough to send me a text like that. God, these people have nothing better to do.

Anger reminds me it's still around, and without thinking about it, I respond:

Don't you have anything better to do with your time? Come on, seriously. This is so pathetic!

That should be enough to tell them I'm not in the mood for childish games today, although I still wonder how they got my number. All my social apps are private, and my number wouldn't be listed online. Then I look down and see the bubbles going for another text incoming. As if they're responding to me.

While they're coming up with their genius reply, I flick the kettle on; I may as well have a nice cup of tea while playing this game with whoever is on the other end of these texts.

I make a tea, grab my phone, and return to the chair to get comfortable. I settle in for a lengthy response, looking at how long the bubbles are bubbling.

I take a sip of my tea. I love the first hit of a good cup of tea, that hot liquid going straight into my veins, that makes me see all problems are manageable and can be resolved. There's something about the English. Whenever there's a disaster, a problem that people don't think they can solve, or someone's just received bad news, the first thing we say is. *I'll get the kettle on.* Like this cup of tea possesses magical qualities that can fix anything, no matter how bad it is.

I feel the cup's warmth in my hand, and it feels soothing. and despite Della having nice cups, I can't help but momentarily miss my favourite mug. I realise the mystery texter had somehow made me forget Reed had messaged me. I've still left him on read, and just as I'm about to go back and respond, the message from the mystery person comes through:

I apologise if it came across in the wrong way; it would be good for us to have a proper introduction, and maybe, as we're both going through this media

circus together, we could talk about it. I'm used to this, but I'm sensing you may not be, so I wanted to help.

My message may have come across as unwanted, especially given that I was messaging you without you being the one to give me your number. I have lots to do with my time, but having a coffee with you would be better than my to-do list. Sorry if it came across as pathetic; I didn't intend it to.

I also apologise for inviting myself into your inbox without asking you first; I'm sensing you're annoyed with me as you seemed annoyed with me at our first introduction.

If I'm being honest, I thought if we had a coffee, I might get an answer about what I may have done to offend you. Anyway, if you change your mind, let me know. Sorry again, I'm off to make a start on my to-do list:)

Oh fuck!!! I think Dalton Rivers just asked me for a coffee, and I think I just shut him down…

Chapter Seventeen
Meeting Dalton – Take Two

I don't know how I'm still doing it, but I have yet to respond to Reed's message, so he's been left on read.

I'm dying to tell him Dalton Rivers invited me for a coffee. Still, Della gave me one of her excellent speeches about not replying to him. Also, she reminded me of all the shit things he's done to me, which charged my anger battery enough to hold out on replying to him. Although, I don't know how long I can hold out on this.

In the meantime, I'm on my way to a coffee meet-up with Dalton Rivers.

We're meeting in a park tucked away from prying eyes, and this prevents anyone else from capturing unwanted photos of us. And, as Della predicted, the media circus is slowly fading.

Part of me still thinks I'm being cat-fished, and when I arrive, it won't be Dalton. But some weird fan of his, and the next media headline, will be:

A crazed fan of Dalton Rivers murders a woman who's not a fan of Dalton Rivers, over an incident with a velcro skirt and a love heart shaped vagina...

But I'm looking at it this way: I've stooped so low recently that nothing could possibly feel worse than it already does, so I'm preparing to embrace any further catastrophes.

When I get to our meeting point, which seems so isolated, I feel on edge and worried I may not have thought this through.

The idea of it not being him intimidates me, and I think if these are my last moments, I should respond to Reed in case of the worst outcome:

Hello, I'm good, thanks. How are you? Coffee sounds good. Let me know when you're free.

Sent.

Della will not be happy with me, but she'll only find out after my body is found. When the crime unit is looking through my last activities.

They announce to the world, *she sent a text message at 14.02 to her ex-partner Reed, agreeing to a coffee from the last known location we have of her.*

"Hey Charity."

I jump out of my skin because I didn't hear Dalton arrive while I was drowning in the thoughts of being cat-fished, and my murdered body being found.

"Sorry, I didn't mean to scare you," he smiles.

While my heart is going faster than designed, I respond breathlessly.

"You seem to have been apologising a lot to me recently," I smile back at him, so he knows I'm being friendly.

He lifts his arm up and I see a picnic hamper in his hand. "I thought it would be nice for us to have a picnic instead of coffee. That's if you would like to, of course, as I wasn't sure if you'd eaten lunch already today." His expression looks hopeful.

"I haven't eaten yet, and that's really thoughtful; I'd love to." This now makes sense to me that we're in a park out of the way, with no coffee shops in sight.

We walk into the park's forest together, hoping to find a secluded spot where we won't be disturbed by mobile phones or prying eyes.

We find a spot, and Dalton places the hamper down and turns to me. "Hi, I'm Dalton; I don't think we've been properly introduced," he holds out his hand for me to shake.

All the memories of our last encounter come flooding back to me, and I remember the last time we were in each other's presence; that I flashed him.

With flush pink cheeks, I take his hand. "I'm Charity. It's nice to meet you."

We hold hands for a lot longer than a usual handshake, and with the silence between us, it's becoming a little awkward; I think he senses this, and he slowly drags his hand away, almost reluctantly.

Dalton takes a blanket out of the hamper, he places it on the ground for us both, and ushers with his hand for me to sit. I think about how he's a gentleman. I'm not sure if I considered before that he would be or if I assumed he wouldn't be. I watch him sit down after me, and he takes bits of food and drink out from the hamper. There is a bottle of champagne, 2 glasses, some cheese and cucumber sandwiches, Victoria sponge cakes, carrot sticks, olives and nuts, and the pièce de résistance is a bag of Percy Pig sweets.

I pick up the sweets.

"How did you know these are my favourites?" I laugh.

"Lucky guess and they're one of my favourites too," he smiles and starts pouring us both a drink.

At that moment, my phone quacks, and we both look at each other.

"Sorry, let me put that on silent."

I look down at my phone and see a message from Reed, and without thinking, I open the message:

That sounds great; I'm free this afternoon if that suits you. How about 17.00 at our favourite coffee shop?

Our favourite coffee shop, this hits close to the bone and makes me wonder if it will feel a bit too raw going together.

I sit, wondering how to respond.

Dalton reminds me he's still here.

"Nothing serious, I hope."

"Oh, sorry. It's unimportant; I just need to reply, and then the phone will go off."

I quickly reply:

Sure, sounds good. See you there X.

Sent.

I switch my phone to silent and put it in my bag, and then I realise, as I was rushing, I put a kiss at the end of the message and I cringe inside.

Why the hell did I just do that?

"Is everything okay?" I forget I'm here with Dalton and realise I'm being rude, having only said a few words to him since he arrived.

"Sorry again, yes, it's nothing, really. You have my full attention."

I realise I'm being quite ignorant towards him, and as I look down at the picnic blanket and remember Dalton reached out to me, and I see the effort he's gone to with the picnic.

"Tell me about you." I realise as soon as I said it sounds like an interview question.

"What would you like to know? I can tell you about my time in London or perhaps you want to know about my work; what would you like to know?"

"How about your childhood?" as soon as I ask, I realise it's more personal than other questions I could've asked, and I'm being ruder than I mean to be.

"Well, I wasn't really a fan of my childhood. It was almost like I couldn't wait to grow up, get out into the world, and become who I always wanted to be.

I knew when I grew up that I wanted to be an actor from an early age, so as soon as I got the chance, I went for it, and the rest is history. How about yourself?"

His answer feels pretty scripted, as though he's used to getting asked it.

No doubt he's been asked a million times when he's been on talk shows and press tours.

"I had a good childhood; I was spoilt. My dad was a tyre inspector, and my mum was an artist; she loved painting watercolours mainly. They've both passed away now, so there's only my sister and I left."

He looks sad, "I'm so sorry, was it recently?"

"No, it was a few years ago; they both died of different things. They loved each other more than life, so we always said it was because they couldn't be apart that they both died so close to each other; I still believe my mum died from a broken heart."

The conversation's taken a turn.

I wasn't expecting it to, but Dalton continues,

"That must've been really hard for you and your sister. I couldn't imagine losing both of my parents so closely together. I'm really sorry for you both."

Although I'm back to a memory that hurts me, my mind is focused on Reed's text and the fact that I'm going to be seeing him shortly.

I need to get through this date quickly so I'm not late meeting him, so I close the subject off.

"That's okay. Thank you for being sorry, but it was a long time ago, and it's life, really." But he's still not done with the parents' conversation.

131

"Did your mum sell her paintings?"

"She did; she made little amounts for them, but she didn't paint for the money; she painted because it made her soul happy. My sister and I are planning to sell some of her work at an auction in a few weeks, we have lots of her work, and we both agreed it would be nice for the legacy of her work to continue on, rather than being stored away, plus we could both use the money right now, my sister has little ones so she's saving up to take them away on holiday and me, well after recently losing my home and my job, I'm in no position to argue some extra money."

As soon as I say it, I regret it.

What am I doing?

I'm sitting here sharing all my problems with a complete stranger who, frankly, doesn't need this type of negativity in his life.

"Sorry, you don't need to know about my troubles. That was rude of me."

I raise the glass of bubbly he's poured me, up to my mouth to hide the embarrassment now creeping across my face.

I notice I'm drinking it as slowly as possible, hoping the redness fades by the time I put the glass back down.

"Don't apologise. I want to hear it. Can I ask happened to your home and job?"

There's a sincerity in his eyes that tells my brain that putting all my troubles on this man is safe. Over the next hour and a half, I share with him details about my life, including about the love of my life, how my life plan was ripped away out of nowhere, the heartbreak I've suffered, how I ended up at the comic convention, why I was a little rude to him on our first meeting, having to stay at Della's like her roommate, and how I lost my job, omitting the criminal activities out of this all.

My favourite remarks he made were that he didn't respect Reed for treating me the way he has and that he would love to meet him and tell him to his face. I also liked that he said Della sounds like a total gem of a friend. He's glad that I have her. Talking about Reed has made my anxiety set in, and I've become very nervous. All I wanted was me and him face to face, him apologising for how he's treated me and answering what I did wrong and why he did what he did.

And with that, I abruptly end the date I'm on.

"I've had a really nice time this afternoon, but I have to go as I have plans," I say it quicker than I intended and I get up and start packing up the picnic that Dalton kindly brought along with him."Oh, okay. I'm sorry. I didn't know you had plans, and I certainly don't want to make you late. I can drop you off somewhere if you like."

I look at the time and realise it would be easier for him to drop me off, but then my brain says it's weird to go from one date to another and be dropped off by one of your suitors.

"Erm, okay, sure, that would be great."

I'll let him drop me off somewhere nearby, but not at the coffee place.

With that, we head out of the park towards the car and a private chauffeur, who is awaiting Dalton's instructions on where to go.

Chapter Eighteen
Meeting the Ex

I'm nervous on the journey to the coffee shop. Not because I'm currently in the presence of a famous actor, but because I'm about to finally face Reed.

I'm excited and giddy, that butterfly feeling you experience when you're going on a first date, or when you're about to see that person you have a massive crush on or the feeling that I used to experience whenever Reed's name would pop up on my phone with a loving text message he'd just sent me.

I pause momentarily to have a check in with myself. All my emotions are mixed up because right now I should be angry, but I can't help it.

I then realise that I haven't really said anything to Dalton since getting in the car, so I start small talk.

"Thank you for the picnic; it was really lovely."

He's sitting next to me in the back of the car, and I feel him looking at me, but he doesn't respond, so I fill the void some more.

"I was impressed you included Percy Pigs in the basket; they are the number one sweet for such an occasion."

I'm doing an awful job at this small talk. Maybe I need to shut up. After a few moments of awkward silence, Dalton finally breaks the silence.

"Have I done something to upset you?"

He thinks he's done something? "No, of course not; you've been a perfect gentleman this afternoon, and I've had a lovely time with you."

The awkward silence is back.

"Why did you ask that?" I feebly say, but I already know the answer.

My behaviour hasn't been warm towards him; I just didn't realise it was that obvious.

"It's just that on the two occasions I've met you, it seems you can't get away from me quick enough, and I wondered if it's something I'm doing. It would help to know if there is something, that's all."

He's looking out the window, and I sense he's upset.

I feel bad because he's just caught in the middle of all of this mess, and he's been nothing but pleasant to me; in fact, I'm lucky to have even had a picnic with him, but the bottom line of it is I'm not interested in him, I just wanted some ammunition, something to brag to Reed about, in which I feel I've now got.

So, I try to ease the situation for him.

"No, of course not. I'm sorry if it's coming across that way. It's just that I made plans this afternoon and didn't realise how long we would talk, and I guess I'm just rushing. That's all. You've done nothing. Please don't think that. If I didn't have plans, we would probably still be talking and getting to know each other."

The silence appears again.

But this time, I don't know what to say to fill it.

After what feels like forever, Dalton turns and looks at me. I can sense his stare. It's like he's unsure about asking me something, or he's trying to work out if I'm lying from intensely staring at my face, expecting it to show what's going on underneath inside of me right now.

It becomes uncomfortable as I'm staring straight ahead at the road, but can feel.his eyes bore into me, so I turn to face him, and we just stare at each other, saying nothing.

I look at his face; it seems uncertain, like he's confused, but he also has this wonderful innocence about him in his eyes, a trusting feeling that makes me feel safe; oh no, I can't get wrapped up at this moment, because I'll become like everyone else and without warning end up becoming obsessed with him.

I'm not allowing that, so I turn to look ahead again. I recognise the street, which confirms we're nearly at the spot I've asked to be dropped off.

"Are you busy tomorrow night, Charity?" he says with a hint of uncertainty.

"I'm not busy tomorrow night," I respond matter-of-factly. I now wonder how this situation has arisen and why I feel tense on this car journey.

"Would you like to have dinner with me?" he's looking out the window. "I understand if you don't want to."

Why on earth does he want to have dinner with me?

That's a story to tell, isn't it? The most famous man on the planet not only sat with me on a picnic but also took me out for dinner, and part of me feels like it's the right

137

thing to do, considering I can't get away quickly enough to see Reed.

The car pulls up and parks at the kerb. I could text him later if anything transpires with my meet-up with Reed

"Yes, of course. I would like that."

He turns to face me, and now he doesn't look uncertain anymore. Instead, he's got a glint of happiness behind his eyes and a smirk to match it.

"How does 8pm sound? Can I come and collect you?" he says confidently.

"8pm sounds good to me. How about I meet you at the restaurant?"

This way, I don't have to give him my address. It's easy to block someone on your phone and social media channels, but not so easy to block them from turning up at home.

He looks confused again but accepts my suggestion: "Okay, I will send you the details later if that's okay. I look forward to seeing you tomorrow. I hope whatever your plans are for this evening goes well."

"Thank you, me too."

I leap out of the car and slam the door harder than I meant to, but that comes from all the adrenaline I have pulsating around my body. I stroll, allowing Dalton's car to go by me so he doesn't see me heading for the coffee shop. The car drives by slowly, and he gives me a wave out of the window; I give him a half-hearted wave, one that makes me feel awkward.

Right, it's time to pull yourself together, girl.

I stop at a shop window to ensure I look presentable for Reed. I realise I need to retouch up my lipstick, so I grab it from my bag and spray myself with some perfume that I now carry around in my bag.

It's at this moment I realise I have become more girly than I've ever been, I never would've even bothered checking myself out in a window before, but this shows how important it is to me that Reed sees this new and improved version of me, one he hasn't met before.

I throw the perfume and lipstick back into my bag. This bag could give Mary Poppins a run for her money because the amount of stuff I now carry around with me in such a small bag is incredible.

I check there's no lipstick on my teeth.

I'm all set, I tidy my fringe and hair, take a deep breath, and head towards the coffee shop.

My heart is pounding out of my chest, I'm clammy, and my mind is racing. The butterflies are doing somersaults, and I'm hoping my voice doesn't break and give me away.

I slowly walk by the big glass window and spot Reed instantly. He's already in there, sitting at our usual table in our coffee shop, just like in the old times.

It's a strange feeling, nostalgic like all the past few months haven't happened, and this is just a usual day for us, but my mind reminds me it is anything but typical.

I don't look like the Charity that used to date Reed. Reed is dating a plastic doll. I'm now a criminal, and I've just been dropped off by the most sought-after man on the planet. Hence, nothing about this situation is like the olden days, and this now instils a glint of anger in me as I slowly remember all that's happened over the past few months.

I stop at the door and think, what am I doing?

My feet hesitate. Is this the right thing?

Am I out of my mind for meeting up with him? But I can't run away as he's spotted me, and he stands up and gives me a wave. Another coffee-goer opens the door and invites me in, and with that, my feet remember how to work again.

The first thing that hits me when I enter *Roasty Beans* is the overpowering aroma of coffee, an aroma I'm so used to being hit with every single time I enter this place.

The second thing that strikes me is Reed, standing by our table, looking perfect like he always does. It's clear he hasn't had the same few months as me, and if anything, he looks better than before, which I can't believe. He couldn't be more gorgeous than he already was.

I walk over to our table and see he's checking me out. His eyes look up and down at me, making me blush because I know he thinks I look good. I could always tell what he was thinking without words.

As I approach the table, he stretches his arms out and hugs me, which takes me back as it was unexpected. But I embrace it anyway and realise he smells as good as ever. The hug lasts longer than it should and slips into an awkward phase, and we both realise, let go, and sit down at the table.

None of us says anything at first; he just sits smiling at me, and I'm grinning because he's smiling at me.

"Can I get you a coffee?" he says, breaking the silence.

"Yes, sure, I'll have a…"

"You'll have a French vanilla latte, no sugar." He smiles at me, proud that he remembered my favourite coffee.

I think about changing my coffee to make a point that he doesn't know this version of me sitting opposite him. But,I don't.

Instead, I nod yes, because I want that coffee, and I've somehow become weaker now that I'm in his presence again.

He gets up and goes to the counter to order my coffee, and I watch him, realising how weird everything feels. This is the man who tore my heart apart, cheated on me, and made a fool out of me, and yet there he is, ordering my favourite coffee. I couldn't be happier right now to be here with him, which tops all the reasons to be angry with him.

I suddenly feel his spell cast all over me once again.

I should be so angry with him right now, and he deserves to wear that coffee he's about to order for me, but there is no anger in sight. Instead, I feel content and at peace, and that giddiness is there and the love I have for him is also still very much there. While I daydream about our situation and wish things had turned out differently, he's suddenly back at the table, sat across from me, smiling.

"So, you've become a bit of a celebrity; how did that happen, C?"

And there it is. He's straight back into our pet nicknames, as though he didn't cause me any pain or heartache.

"I'm not sure. It was all accidental, and I'd love it if things returned to normal. It wasn't my most graceful moment in life." I blush because I'm reminded that everyone has probably seen my vagina. I had somehow deleted that out of my mind—well, until Reed just fixed my amnesia, that is.

"The girl at the counter just asked me if it was you who became famous for flashing the famous Dalton Rivers." he's grinning, which makes me feel like he's proud of me for my embarrassing efforts, I'm sensing he loves the fact he's sat here with the person who flashed his idol.

"And what did you tell her?" I ask, through curiosity more than anything.

"I said, hell yeah, it is. She used to be my girlfriend. She said she's giving you a large coffee for the price of a small."

He's smug right now, and it's nice to see I'm worth a small coffee; that says a lot to me.

My inner devil slips out, and I respond, "Well, it couldn't have hurt; I've just had a picnic with the famous Dalton Rivers."

Reed spits his coffee out and it goes all over the table and down his arm, he even has coffee dripping from his chin.

I sit cold-faced and serious, staring at the car crash of my ex-boyfriend sitting opposite me.

"Sorry, can you repeat that? I thought you just said you went on a picnic with Dalton Rivers."

"I did. Is that surprising to you?"

We sit staring at each other, and suddenly, the smugness on his face has slipped into what looks like jealousy.

"No, you didn't," he says in a tone that tells me he doesn't believe it.

"Okay, I didn't, but I did, so I'm not sure what you want me to say."

I sit back in my chair and realise I've gone into defence mode as I cross my arms across my chest and look at him with a squinted eye, awaiting his next insult.

At this moment, the girl who so kindly gave me a large French vanilla latte for the price of a small brings it to the table.

"One large French vanilla latte, and can I just say you're a legend? I saw everything online and in the paper and…."

I sternly look up at her, and she receives my non-impressed look, which was intended for Reed. However, she's now caught in the middle of it. She senses this and wants to remove herself from the battle that has begun across this tiny coffee shop table.

"Anyway, enjoy your coffee," she says quickly, returning to her safe zone behind the coffee shop counter.

I turn back to Reed with a look that he probably wouldn't recognise from me, and with a stern tone, I ask, "Is there some reason you find it hard to believe that I could have a picnic with another man?"

He laughs. "No, of course not; I don't expect you to be on your own forever, C. I just find it unbelievable that Dalton Rivers would want to go on a picnic…with you. That man could have anyone on the planet, and he's certainly not short of a beauty queen to put on his arm."

"So?" I ask, "Do you find me hideous, Reed? Am I not good enough?" He takes a slow sip of his remaining coffee and ushers me to drink mine; I ignore his ushering and continue sitting in defence mode, ready to attack.

"No, I don't find you hideous C, I…"

I interrupt abruptly because I want to take control of this situation.

"Can you please stop calling me C? That was a pet name when we were together, but we're not together anymore. My name is Charity."

He's taken aback by my assertiveness, and he slowly puts his coffee cup down and leans back in his chair.

We sit for a few moments in silence.

It's awkward and not how I expected this coffee date to go.

My phone quacks, so I take it out of my pocket and see that it's a message from Dalton.

144

"He just messaged me." I turn my phone around to him and show him Daltons name on the front screen.

I look at every inch of his face, which has jealousy written all across it.

"So, are you and him involved or something?" He can't hide the annoyance from his voice.

I understand how much this is bothering him, so I go along with it. "Who knows? After that embarrassing incident, he reached out to me, and we went on a picnic; it was really nice, and we're going out for dinner tomorrow night, so who knows what it is."

Reed wipes his brow; this situation is getting to him more than I expected. He's obviously thrown off by it.

"Well, who knew you had it in you C? Sorry, Charity. All those times we sat talking about him, and here we are today, you going for dinner with him. It's astonishing and somewhat hard to believe. Did you get any photos of your picnic with him?"

I didn't take any photos of the picnic, and now I realise that was a mistake, as I could've had so much ammunition to use.

"No, I didn't, actually; we were having too much fun for that."

He quickly responds, "Well, you know what they say? If there are no photos, it didn't happen."

And with that, he laughs, and suddenly, I'm sitting, feeling uncomfortable and somewhat like he thinks I'm a liar.

145

Reed takes his phone out of his pocket. "Oh, sorry, I have to dash; I would love to hear more about your adventures with Dalton; maybe get a photo the next time you're together." He stands up from the chair, and he swings his jacket on, and then heads for the door, forgetting to even be polite enough to say goodbye to me.

I sit there.

What the fuck just happened?

Where was my chance to ask him why he felt it was acceptable to break my heart?

Where was the apology he was meant to give me?

How did that meet-up all become about Dalton flaming Rivers?

Reed looked jealous, angry, like he didn't believe me, and then he left, and I'm left sitting here, my head spinning with what just happened.

The coffee girl leaves her safe zone and comes back over to the table. "Sorry about earlier. If you felt I stepped out of line; it's just I haven't met anyone famous before."

I look up, but this time, I'm not sternly looking at her; I'm confused. "Sorry, what? I'm not famous."

She snorts. "Of course you are; anyone whose in the newspapers or trends online the way you did is most certainly famous, even if only for 15 minutes. Would you mind if we get a selfie together?"

With no energy to understand what has just happened or the coffee girl's comments, I agree to the photo. I dread to think of the hashtag she will post underneath the photo, no doubt something that relates to my vagina.

But right now, I'm more concerned about not getting closure with Reed.

As I begin to leave the coffee shop, I see the girl showing everyone our photo.

I can hear the chatter from people and I sense it won't be the only selfie I'm asked for if I don't make a quick escape. So I dash out of the door.

And with that, I'm walking home; and I Daltons text, so I open it, and it reads:

Look forward to seeing you again tomorrow night at 8pm, maybe third time lucky :)

Underneath there's a postcode to a restaurant he wants me to meet him at.

Why didn't he just write its name? What's with the mysteriousness of the postcode? I don't reply.

I walk home, going over the coffee shop to meet up with Reed, utterly oblivious that I've just left the most famous man on the planet on read once again.

Chapter Nineteen
A short dress

"What on earth do you wear to dinner with the sexiest man in the worldddddddd." Della shouts as she rummages through her wardrobe.

She's already emptied the small contents of my wardrobe, dismissing every single item I own, and now she's moved to hers, hoping to find something acceptable for me to wear to dinner.

I don't want to dress up, as that implies I'm interested in Dalton, and I'm not.

I'm going to dinner because I've been rude towards him, and after Della's lecture last night, I realised she had very valid points on how Dalton wasn't the problem in my life situations; it's Reed.

She also shared how she can't believe I dared to leave him on read, not once, but twice, and then rush off from our picnic to the narcissist that is Reed.

I have concluded from this lecture that the least I can do is stop thinking about Reed for an hour and have a civil dinner with Dalton, and hopefully repair a small amount of damage I may have caused with my behaviour, along with making him aware I'm not actually as rude as I've been portraying towards him and that he hasn't actually done anything wrong to me. Despite Della's annoyance at me for how I treated Dalton, it was nothing compared to

148

how angry she was that I met up with Reed. I had the full speech about how much of a narcissist he is, how he's using me to get closer to Dalton, how far I've come and now I'm taking ten steps backwards by agreeing to see him. I tried to explain my reasoning around wanting closure from him and that I'd hoped he would at least say sorry about how he treated me, but that got lost in the red mist in front of Della.

I know she's right; can I help it?

No. I'm broken, I'm living a life I didn't choose to, and I can't help but get excited at the prospect of Reed wanting to get closer to me because that means I'm one step closer back to my life before all of this nightmare began.

I also know I shouldn't have feelings for him anymore, but I'm in control; I didn't have to meet him for a coffee; the ball was in my court, and I could've turned him down. If he messaged me right now and asked to meet me again, I would take some time to think it over, as our last encounter left me with a bad taste in my mouth.

Della throws a little black dress next to me.

"I wore this for a funeral; it's the only thing I have that isn't tie-dyed or neon pink. For dinner, you need to look less colourful, and this will suit you; you will make it look classy."

"Thanks. I better get myself ready. I find it strange that he didn't just give me the name of the restaurant we're going to."

I pick up the dress and head towards the bathroom.

"Didn't you google the address?" Della shouts through the door.

"No, I'm certain if he planned to murder me, it would be difficult for him not to be recognised on CCTV. Could you imagine a police sketch artist doing a picture of him and you think no one's going to recognise him instantly and anyway, you know I'm going for dinner with him, so if I go missing, he's the first person you need to make sure is interviewed," I laugh.

It's ridiculous how we're talking right now.

It's just a dinner, and I'm sure he has his reasons; he probably doesn't want me to announce the restaurant on my social media channels to anyone so he doesn't have floods of fans turn up; I get it; he doesn't really know me that well.

I hop in the shower, get myself glammed up, and slide on the little black dress.

I look down and realise it's shorter than expected. I wonder why Della thought this was suitable funeral attire, considering she's taller than me. I imagine she got some looks that day.

I head into the living room to find her spread out across the sofa with her pyjamas on, snacks on one side, and all the remote controls on the other. I know her plans for the evening are Netflix and chill. She loves her own company, and of course she will await all the details of my dinner date. I envy her because part of me would love to switch places with her right now."Wow, you wear that dress so much better than I did, hot Charity, perfect!"

I'm bashful. I realise this dress is short, and I hope it doesn't give Dalton the wrong impression. As I sit down and try to put my heels on as gracefully as possible without exposing myself, because I don't plan on that happening again, not at least for the rest of my life.

As I slip on the second shoe, I hear my phone quack.

Could that be Dalton ditching me, as he's realised how rude I am and he's found a nicer alternative for a dinner date?

I walk over to the kitchen counter, and as my eyes catch sight of the front screen of my phone, my stomach flips when I see a text from Reed.

I'm now breathing faster. The last thing I expected was a text from him when I was already nervous about tonight.

I look over at Della, who's scrolling through the Netflix menu, and I know she would tell me not to open the message and to go out and forget Reed even exists. I think about it; she would have a point. However, if I don't read the message now, I will think about it throughout my dinner date. I plan to not get distracted on my date tonight and to give Dalton the polite version of myself, which includes giving him my full attention.

I open the message:

Hello, sorry I had to dash off yesterday; If you fancy a catch-up again, maybe lunch together?
LUNCH?!?!?!?!

He's inviting me to lunch????

WHY DID I OPEN THE MESSAGE!

My mind is racing. Why does he want dinner with me? Not a casual coffee, not a friends chat; he said lunch; where's BOOB when we go for lunch I wonder? I'm sure she wouldn't be happy to find out he's having lunch with me, but then again, it didn't stop her, so part of me wants to accept to seek a little revenge back on her, let's see how she likes it.

"Shouldn't you be going?" Della assertively says, saving my mind from a sudden explosion.

"Erm, yes, yes, I'm just checking a few things." My voice breaks, and I have to clear my throat.

"Is everything ok? It's only dinner; there's no need to be nervous; apart from the fact it's Dalton Rivers, it's just dinner." I can't tell her Reed's just texted me, and I can't deal with another lecture before I leave.

"You're right; maybe I'm nervous; I'm sure it will be fine." My nerves feel entirely shot that my ex has just asked me to lunch. I just lied to my best friend and now I'm heading for dinner with a celebrity.

My phone quacks again, and my stomach falls through the floor. I look down and see it's just my lift outside, and with that, I feel my stomach start its ascent back up to the correct place in my body.

"Have a great night. I will message you shortly to tell you everything is good, and I'm still alive," I laugh nervously and head out the door.

I hop inside my ride, and the first thing I notice is how happy the driver is; he asks me how I am as soon as my hand touches the door.

I check his ID and see his name is Bennet.

That sounds like a name for a positive person, to be fair.

Bennet recognises me from the photos online and he puts me at ease by saying how sorry he felt for me to be in that position. I like him and immediately I feel like we're friends as we chat.

Before we've even left the street, Bennet knows more about me than I know myself.

He's really easy to talk to, and it doesn't take long for me to pour my heart out to him about where I'm going and my ex-partner's text about dinner. I omit the part that it's Dalton Rivers I'm going for dinner with; I just tell him it's a well-known person who is very well-liked by everyone, and as I won't see Bennet again soon, he seems like a good therapist right now, along with the fact we have a twenty-minute car ride together. I have no one else to seek advice from now.

Bennet seems on team Della and says Reed deserves no more of my time, especially given how he's treated me.

I then fight my corner and explain to him I need closure to move on, and he seems to understand; Della dismissed my reasonings, but Bennet seems to get me; he may agree because I have the power to tip and rate him at the end of this ride, but he looks like a trustworthy guy. We talk about how I should go to dinner with Reed. But, that I need to keep control the entire time, only going there for the closure, leave him at the table, and go home when I've got the apology I'm searching for.

Bennet also advises me to dress in a knock-out way to ensure Reed knows what he's missing out on. He comments that the dress I'm currently wearing would do the trick, and I blush.

"Do you smoke?"

"No, I've never tried a cigarette," I say, feeling like I'm not cool.

"You should; it can help to calm your nerves, even only for this situation; you seem on edge, somewhat erratic, and the last thing you need is for your date to think you are nervous because of him, unless you want to scare him off, that is?"

The last thing I want to do is behave this way in front of Dalton. I'm intending to show him a nicer version of myself this evening. I agree with Bennet that I'm all over the place; since receiving the text from Reed, I've become a mess.

REED!

I realise I left him on read.

I open my phone and text him back:

Yes, that sounds great. Let me know a time and place.

Right, that's done; I can now focus on this evening and not be an unstable mess at dinner. Bennet presses me again. "I have a smoke if you want one; it's only one; you won't become a smoker; just have a puff or two, and it will calm those nerves, trust me."

I feel uncomfortable refusing when Bennet's been the best therapist I've had today.

"I think you're probably right, and what's the worst that could happen, other than I smell like an ashtray?"

Bennet pulls up at the destination and turns around in the car. He hands me a lighter, a smoke, and his business card.

"If you ever need a lift or a smoke, here's my number. Now, have a nice dinner; you've got this."

I take a deep breath and thank him for being such a good listener. I leave the car as gracefully as I can, wearing such a short dress.

Bennet drives away, off for a night of him delivering therapy and rides to all the strangers who never knew they could find such solace in a transportation company employee.

I go on the app and rate him five stars with a quick comment:

If you're looking to steady your nerves and get a smoke, request Bennet.

Phone away, and dress pulled down as far as it will go.

I look up to see a very exclusive-looking restaurant I've never seen or been in before.

I look through the window. There doesn't seem to be anyone dining in there. I look at my watch, thinking I may be early, but I'm ten minutes late. Great, now there's a possibility I've left Dalton waiting for me; this is not the start to the night I was hoping for…

Chapter Twenty
Meeting Dalton – Take Three

I walk into the restaurant, and immediately, a staff member pounces on me.

"Sorry, we're closed this evening for a private function," says the uptight woman, who looks as though she certainly keeps everyone in line in the business, with visual similarities to Miss Trunchbull from Matilda.

"Oh, I'm sorry, I'm meeting someone here; maybe I'm at the wrong address."

I feel embarrassed. One, because I'm about to be turned away as though I'm not a part of the exclusive private function occurring here tonight. Two, because my dress is shorter than expected for such an exclusive-looking place. And three, because I'm now going to be even later than expected, and my manners couldn't get any worse when it comes to Dalton.

I need a nervous wee. I'm unsure how long I can hold it in because it's come on suddenly and aggressively. The uptight woman gives me a look as though she wants to shoo me away, like an unwanted insect hovering over your barbecue dinner.

"Would you mind if I just quickly used your toilet?" I smile at her, trying to melt away the iciness she's beaming towards me. She looks towards the toilets and says, "Yes, but be quick," and she points towards the toilets.

I do a quick walk to show her I know she wants me to hurry, and I hear her tut under her breath and make a comment about my dress; I try to piece together if she called me a tart or not. I'm sure she did, but I don't want to get into an arguement tonight, so I'm going to bite my lip and not say anything. I have the most glorious wee; it's long and relieving and instantly makes me feel less uptight.

As I go to wash my hands in the poshest toilets, I've ever seen in a restaurant before, I get angry at the woman at the front door.

A rage builds inside me because I'm almost sure she called me a tart.

I look at myself in the mirror and realise that although I look like I'm holding everything together on the outside, I'm certainly not holding it together internally.

My nerves are shot, Reed is spinning around my mind, Dalton has taken up another section of my thought pattern, and I'm acting out of character; I know this.

I pull my lipstick out of my bag and as I reach for it; I feel the lighter and cigarette Bennet gave me in the taxi. I look at it and then think about smoking it, only because it wouldn't be in my nature to do this, but mainly because the stuck-up cow at the front door would disapprove of me smoking in her very exclusive toilets.

I slowly bring the cigarette up to my mouth.

I hold the lighter at the end while staring at myself in the giant mirror in front of me.

Wow, Charity, look at you! You've become someone else. The Charity, you were a few months ago, wouldn't have even dared to get the lighter out of the bag, let alone hold it at the end of a cigarette and with that, a switch flicks inside of me when the echo of *tart* comes to mind and almost in unison the lighter gets lit and I pull the cigarette up to my mouth and light it.

I inhale it quickly and it tastes disgusting; , it also smells disgusting and I choke out the first lot of smoke.

It quickly becomes apparent this is no ordinary cigarette. I've walked past people before who smell like this and my eyes examine the cigarette and now it becomes very clear this is a joint, marijuana, not your average smoke. So instead of stubbing it out, I quickly take five more long drags, just to confirm it to myself and then I run it under the bathroom tap to put it out.

I waft away any remnants of smoke, realising I could set the restaurants fire alarms off.

I go to throw the evidence down the toilet, but then I think about the awful woman at the front door and I decide to let her know what I actually think of her exclusive restaurant, so I lay it neatly on the side of the posh marble sink. I doubt Trunchbull will ever see me again, considering I'm leaving the restaurant in seconds and so, I check my hair; I apply my lipstick and I walk back out to the restaurant.

As I'm walking towards the door, I see the uptight cow staring at me and she appears to be tapping her foot. I feel so glad I broke the law in her toilets, just to stick my metaphorical middle finger up at her.

"Charity." I recognise the voice instantly, and I turn around to see Dalton standing behind me.

"Heyyyy," I'm completely taken aback that he's in the restaurant.

"I was wondering if you were going to show up," he holds his hand out to lead me into what looks like a back dining area.

"Oh, the woman at the door told me they were closed for a private function this evening, so I was just leaving, as I thought I had got the address wrong."

As I say the words, I question myself as to if I actually said the words, or did I imagine I'd said them?

So I repeat everything I just said.

Dalton turns and looks at me, "Are you ok?"

"I'm ok." "I'm ok." "Did I just say that twice to you?"

Everything feels really heavy to me right now, even saying words and I can't recall walking through the restaurant, but somehow I'm now seated at a private table, with Dalton sat opposite me.

"The private function is our reservation. I wanted a nice, quiet dinner with you, so I hired the restaurant out."

Dalton pours me a water, and it pours really slowly.

My eyes are completely fixated on it. When Dalton stops pouring it, I realise my mouth is open, and it takes all if of my energy to close it. I look down at the table and see the cutlery. I pick up a fork and it feels weird, so I scan it over, observing how it feels to hold a fork, like it's the first fork I've ever held, and after an extended period of me observing the cutlery, Dalton interrupts by slowly lowering my hand and the fork, and placing them both back down on to the table.

"Charity, are you stoned?"

"Stoned!!!! me?" I say, delivering an Oscar worthy performance of being shocked by such a question. I try to hide my guilt with a little laugh, but this huge hollering of laughter starts. Laughter that feels like it's been inside of me trying to escape for years, that deep belly laughing that hurts.

Dalton has no control over helping me to stop laughing, and I have no control over it either. Whilst hysterically laughing, I notice the uptight woman has come over to the table, and she's having a quiet word with Dalton. She doesn't look happy, unlike me, who's relieved to be laughing as I'd forgotten how to do it.

The conversation between them both seems quite heated, and I realise I've never seen Dalton look annoyed before, but he looks annoyed at Miss Trunchbull right now, and whatever is wrong, she isn't backing down. I think she really is the most uptight restaurant worker I've ever come across before.

The next thing that follows is Dalton takes my hand and frog marches towards the restaurant exit, but not in a rough way, but more a let's get out of here way.

As I get towards the front door, the uptight monster is standing there with a disapproving look on her face, and before I can even speak to my mouth about not saying anything, I say "We need to get out of here quick, or she'll put us in THE CHOKEY."

I catch sight of her gob smacked reaction as Dalton pulls me past her, while I'm still laughing like some deranged coyote.

Dalton's car pulls up to the kerb like he's *Batman*. I want to know how he gets his driver and car, where he needs them, when he needs them.

Dalton opens the car door, and he slides me gently into it. I realise that if he wanted to murder me, I've just willingly helped him to take me.

Dalton gets in and leans forward to his driver, whispering something to him, which makes me feel unsettled and without thinking, I say, "Is this where you murder me, would have I been better off in THE CHOKEY?"

Dalton looks at me with an astonished expression.

"Why would you say something like that, Charity?"

The awkward silence fills the air in the car and for a small space, the silence is deafening.

I stop laughing, and I look out of the window, watching the world go by, unaware of where I'm going and feeling idiotic for my embarrassing behaviour tonight.

After about what feels like fifteen minutes, the car stops and the driver gets out.

"I'm sorry." I'm still looking out of the window, as I'm too embarrassed to look at him.

"You don't need to apologise to me, but you could open up a bit and let me know what's going on with you. That could help."

He sounds so sincere, like he actually cares about what I'm going through, despite not actually realising what I'm going through.

"Did you smoke a joint in the restaurant toilet?" His voice is calm for such a question. I feel ashamed hearing those words, and even though he said it in a kind way, I can't help feeling like I'm being told off and scolded.

"I did." I say quietly.

"Why?"

"I'm not sure. I've never smoked anything in my life, but the woman in the restaurant upset me. She called me a tart, and I know my dress is short, but what right does she have to call me that? My driver on the way to the restaurant gave me it. I thought it was a normal cigarette. It's all a mess and more complicated than I'm explaining." I slouch back into the warm, heated leather seats of the expensive private car I'm in.

Dalton's thoughts seem loud, despite him not saying anything, but I can sense he's thinking about a lot of things, one being what a mistake it was to invite me for dinner no doubt, and I think back to how he hired an entire restaurant to have dinner with me, and I ruined it. The driver opens the door and I assume it's to haul me out of the car and make me walk miles back home alone as a punishment, but instead of removing me, he hands me a big bag and closes the door.

I look at the bag confused and then I look over at Dalton, who has a suspicious look on his face, with a hidden smile

"Dig in."

I don't want to look inside of the bag as I feel like a child and it's my birthday and everyone's watching me open presents and I'm cringing.

I slowly peek into the bag and I can see it's filled with snacks, from doughnuts to crisps, to boxes of chocolate to cakes.

"In case you have the munchies."

Dalton smiles at me and with that, the driver starts the car to take me home. It feels weird to me I've just ruined our night, and as a reward, I've been given a bag of treats.

I have mixed emotions on the drive back home, mainly about my behaviour tonight.

Chapter Twenty-One
New Day, New Charge

The last thing anyone wants is a voicemail from one of your favourite police officers telling you to come into the station to make a statement about the drugs you consumed on a restaurant's premises last night.

But there we have it, the start of a new day and another criminal charge for me.

Rupinder's message was not what I was expecting today. Still, I guess if I'd answered the door earlier instead of shutting the world out, then no doubt I would've been arrested again, and instead, it's now on me to face the music and go down to my favourite police station again.

I'm sure Rupinder is sick of seeing me. Still, I guess I'm keeping her in a job as I'm sure there's plenty of paperwork for her to do with regular criminals like me keeping her busy; I see it this way: I'm doing something positive for her, even if she's ungrateful and she can't see it.

What was I thinking last night? Who am I?

Dalton must think I'm a complete car crash of a woman. I don't expect him to contact me anytime soon, but on the plus side, I achieved a lot more than I expected, trying to get close to him while getting revenge on Reed.

I've done an excellent job putting Dalton off me, and let's face it: I'm not in his league. The only explanation I can come up with is that he was looking for an easy booty call while in London, and I'm not booty call material.

After a quick browse online, it appears no one has discovered my little incident from last night.

So my plan for the day is to head to the police station, face the music, and prevent them from coming back here, because the last thing I need is Della on my case about my stupid behaviour. Sometimes, she's more of a mum than a friend, and I don't need anymore lectures from her, so I need to make sure she doesn't find out about the latest incident.

I will tell her the dinner was ok last night and leave it at that.

I know Della is desperate to hear all about it. She will press me for every tiny detail of the night because she wants to go on a date with a celebrity through me, but I'm going to have to make this one up; I can't exactly tell her Dalton hired out a restaurant for me, and then I smoked an illegal substance in the toilets, which then got us both kicked out of the building before we even saw what kind of food was on the menu.

The Police wouldn't have even known who I was if it wasn't because I've recently gone viral, and no doubt they recognised me instantly on the CCTV—I see being well-known works both ways.

I check my phone and see that Reed has sent me a morning message, just like he used to. My heart skips a beat, and that one message makes today much better. It shows he's making more of an effort to contact me. Maybe he's realising he's missing me. Perhaps our coffee made him think about what we had. I think this could be the start of us getting close to each other again. First it was coffee, then it's lunch, then it will be dinner and before you know it, we will live together again.

I grab some clothes and get dressed; I pop into the kitchen, make a quick coffee in my flask, and realise I've left my phone in my bedroom. As I walk back in to grab it, I get punched in the face with an overpowering smell of pot.

I pick up my dress that I was wearing last night. Ugh, it stinks of it, Della must've noticed this smell; it's more overpowering than I realised. I frantically grab all the evidence of my crime from last night and throw everything into the washer, putting it on at a scorching hot temperature to ensure the evidence burns away.

I grab a bottle of Febreze from under the kitchen sink and spray the floral scent on every inch of my bedroom, attempting to mask it.

I look at the time and realise I need to get to the police station. I quickly spray myself with Febreze, in case I smell of it but don't realise, and I grab my coffee flask and head out of the door.

On the walk to the Police station, I text Reed back:

Morning, how are you? :)

I then notice a text from Dalton sitting in my box:

Hey Charity, I hope you're ok and enjoyed the snacks last night.

Then, a second message:

It's a shame we didn't get the chance to have a proper dinner; if you'd like to try again, let me know.

How on earth can he want to meet up with me again? What am I missing? Maybe he's used to crazies, and I fit the bill perfectly.

I take a large gulp of coffee and give it a minute to hit my veins while thinking about how to respond. Should I meet up with him again? He is sweet. He did get me a bag of snacks last night, and he wasn't angry despite what I did; I mean, what harm could it do meeting up with him again? It could benefit me with Reed if he finds out I'm spending more time with Dalton.

I'm now fuelled on coffee and the fumes from the Febreze; I over-sprayed myself with, and I'm ready to do the walk of shame into the police station to answer to my crimes.

But before I answer to my crimes, I answer Dalton:

Hey, sorry about last night. Are you sure you want to meet me again? I'm sure I'm costing you a fortune on Percy Pigs :)

The bubbles go immediately.

He replies: **I can afford it ;)**

Well, I'm going to meet up with Dalton again, unless the Police detain me and send me straight to prison.

I leave him on read until I know if I'm free; it would be rude to make plans and not show up.

Chapter Twenty-Two
Invitation

So, I got the third degree from Rupinder and Derek on arrival at the Police station, where I had to give a statement and admit to my crime.

I wasn't forthcoming with the details of the driver. I didn't see the point in dragging his name through the mud; after all, I was the one who took it and lit it and smoked it and then put it where it could be found.

However, Rupinder, being so good at her job, located the review I'd left for Bennet and then questioned me as to what I was getting out of promoting Bennet's drug selling.

When she read the review back to me, it sounded like I was telling people to go for him for good drugs. On this occasion, I've given myself idiot points.

Rupinder told me to expect a prison sentence at my court hearing, especially if I keep going the way I am by adding new charges to my ever-growing list of criminal activities.

I know she has a point, but there's no point in explaining why I keep messing up; she wouldn't understand.

She also handed me a leaflet about talking to some man about my drug problem on the way out, I'm sure he's called Frank. I won't be calling him as I don't have a problem. So far, Della hasn't mentioned the pot smell, so

I've got away with an additional lecture from her. I made up a story about my dinner date. It was casual and romantic, Dalton was a gentleman, and the food was lovely. I was surprised at how easily I could lie when she asked me questions about what clothes Dalton was wearing and what dessert I had.

Dalton and I have been messaging each other a lot today, and for me, it's filling the void of when Reed and I would message one another constantly throughout the day.

That's the thing when a relationship ends: all the things you're used to suddenly end as well, and I've felt a huge loss at no longer texting anyone.

Dalton never shares personal things while we're texting each other. I sense this is because people may have used this against him before, so I don't press questions when I'm trying to get to know him, and I also understand when he changes the subject on why he's doing it, so our messaging is very lighthearted and straightforward.

I love how most of our language is in the form of emojis, from a zombie for rising in the morning to Dalton sharing the person in a lotus position as he's doing yoga. I used the unicorn emoji when discussing Della because it's the most mystical and colourful creature I could compare her to.

Dalton uses the grey wolf emoji a lot; he said it's because he likes wolves; it feels like his sign off signature and that there's more to it than he's sharing, so I've made a mental note to ask him about it the next time I see him.

Despite not sharing personal things, we've found a lot of time to talk to each other, alas, electronically. Whenever my phone quacks, I know it's a message from him because Reed seems to have gone quiet, somewhat off the grid.

A conversation we stumbled upon earlier was about all the things we hadn't done before. Dalton asked if living in London meant I had visited all the famous landmarks, and ashamed, I had to say no. I never seemed to go near Buckingham Palace or Big Ben, and Dalton was mortified that I hadn't at least attempted to see them in real life, even just once.

I explained that I never felt like I was missing out on it; after all, I knew what it looked like, and I also knew that if I wanted to see it, I easily could.

Dalton explained to me about living in the moment and grabbing things while you can. He talked to me about how he's seen people make plans in life and create bucket lists, and sadly, they've never got around to actually doing them.

He explained he doesn't live like that, as he wants to experience everything now and not leave it to a chance where he may never get to do it. I understood this, and I agreed it made sense to do it if you can.

However, I also felt like there once was a time when I, too, wanted to grab everything with both of my hands, but somehow, I lost that adventurous side of me somewhere in life. Dalton asked me to list off all the landmarks in

London that I hadn't seen, so I did, and I was embarrassed while admitting them because it was all of them.

I was glad he couldn't see my face or how disappointed I felt in myself, given that it's taken someone I've not long met to make me know I live on the doorstep of these iconic landmarks that people travel from all around the world to see. I'm minutes away from them and haven't even made the effort.

After a shower and a tidy-up of the flat, the doorbell rings, and I answer it to find a man with a delivery addressed to me. That's strange; I haven't ordered anything.

I switch the kettle on to make a cup of tea while constantly looking at the mysterious-looking box. Before the kettle has even finished boiling, I open the box.

Inside, I'm surprised to find an outfit in the form of Luigi from Mario & Luigi, and I'm now more confused than before I opened the box. I pull the outfit out, and I notice it's my size. Sitting neatly at the bottom of the box is a card.

I'll pick you up at 18.00 tomorrow. Wear the outfit and the moustache; the moustache is very important. I'm going to show you all the things you've been missing, Dalton x.

Moustache?

Sure enough, the most ridiculous-looking moustache I've ever seen is taped to the side at the bottom of the box. It's so ridiculous that it looks like Dr Seuss's Lorax and

Bill the Butcher from Gangs of New York had a love child.

I'm not sure about this outfit, and I'm surprised he got my size perfectly.

As I sit drinking my tea, I keep looking at the same line on the note from Dalton, where he said it's very important that I wear the moustache.

Chapter Twenty-Three
Man Under The Moustache

I feel somewhat ridiculous standing in front of the mirror dressed as Luigi from the Mario Brothers.

But underneath the uncomfortableness, I feel intrigued to find out why I must dress up, and I can't wait to hear Dalton's explanation.

I stick the ridiculous moustache on and laugh at myself because I can't get over how stupid I look with such a huge moustache.

But after exposing myself this year, nothing could be worse than that, so I grabbed my bag off the bed and head into the living room to show Della.

Della, who is knitting, looks up and gasps, completely surprised.

"What the hell, you scared me?" Della laughs. "I wasn't expecting the moustache; it's huge; I can barely tell it's you underneath it."

"I told you it was ridiculous. This situation is ridiculous, but I'll ride it out, as I'm sure whatever Dalton has planned will be fun."

"Yeah, I get dressing up, Charity. Maybe you're going to a fancy dress party or something, but why is the moustache so important, and why does it have to be so big and stupid-looking?" My phone quacks, and Dalton tells me my carriage is waiting outside.

As I head towards the door, Della shouts, "You best put me out of misery as soon as you know your plans for the night, please."

"I will. Have a good night, I'll catch you later on."

With that, I slam the door and enter the world—well, London as Luigi.

As soon as the car door opens, I burst out laughing when I see how ridiculous Dalton looks with the moustache on dressed as Mario.

I now understand how taken aback Della was when I came into the room.

When I can control my laughter, I climb into the car and I can't wait to hear the reason for the ridiculous moustaches.

"Can you recognise me?'" asks Dalton.

I know it's Dalton, but I look at him and say, "No, I wouldn't know it was you unless you told me it was you, with the outfit, the hat, and the moustache covering your face so much, it would be difficult for you to be recognised."

And then the penny drops for me.

He doesn't want to be recognised, hence the ridiculous moustache.

"I want an uninterrupted evening with you, and this will ensure the paparazzi or fans don't follow us around; it can be difficult for actors, who just want to experience things, but without everyone wanting to say hello and asking for photos, because once you do one, other people notice and before long you've got a crowd of a hundred people wanting autographs, and it gets out of hand quickly."

I suddenly don't feel ridiculous wearing the outfit or the moustache because I sympathise with Dalton, realising he can't just be a normal person, going about doing everyday things, and that must be difficult and draining for him.

"So Mario, what's the plan?"

"Well, Luigi, I have a list of places and things that we will tick off together tonight, and our first stop is Buckingham Palace."

I get comfortable in the seat, as I know what London traffic is like.

This will give me time to see the sights out of the window while also enjoying the company of Dalton.

"What sights do you have on the list? Have you seen them all?"

"Yes, I've seen them all, but I'm determined to ensure you've seen them all, so for each landmark, we're taking a photo to mark the special occasion of Charity seeing it for the first time." Dalton pulls out a Polaroid camera and a scrapbook from next to his feet and he hands them to me.

I flick open the pages, and each page gives away the night that is ahead for us:

Buckingham Palace

Big Ben

Houses of Parliament

St Paul's Cathedral

Trafalgar Square

Covent Garden

Tower Bridge

The Tower of London

Westminister Abbey

The London Eye

"That isn't the whole night; we have lots planned."

"Why have you put all this effort into me, Dalton?"

"Well, I want to show you how to have fun again because I feel you haven't experienced it in a long time. So buckle up and prepare to get crazy. Tonight will be a night to remember. Do you trust me?"

I'm taken aback by him asking this question, especially as I have a broken heart from a man I trusted completely, and only a fool would get back on the saddle and put their trust straight back into a man again.

I think to myself that Dalton hasn't given me any reason not to trust him, and I know, despite how broken I currently feel, it's unfair for me to tarnish everyone with the same brush; It takes a lot to admit it to myself and even more to say it, but I do.

"I do trust you."

"Good, that's the correct answer, just remember I'm not here to hurt you, I'm here to help you, and it will be my pleasure to show you, the person who lives in London, all the iconic sites of London." I smile because I know how ridiculous it must sound to someone to say you live in the capital surrounded by all these places. Yet, you've been living underneath a rock for years, letting these beautiful buildings go unseen by you.

I'm starting to understand that I need to look at life differently because I feel like I've been paused for a long time. I've let opportunities and experiences go by me, and I know it's because I put all of my time and energy into Reed, but I don't understand why loving Reed meant missing out on things in my life; surely you can love someone and still love life.

I know I wrapped myself around him and forget about all of my daydreams, and I'm now regretting it because I've walked away broken-hearted, with no home and no achievements.

Along with sadness, I'm also battling with self-pity and guilt for how I've treated myself over the years.

I push the negative feelings aside because right now, I'm sitting next to the most famous man on the planet, and he's putting all of his energy into a night that's mainly just for me.

You can't make this up, I think to myself, and I know I have to text Della immediately to tell her what the moustaches were for and the night that is ahead for me.

After texting Della, a text that contained barely any words but around a hundred of the shocked face emoji, I sit staring at the scrapbook on my knee, and I'm not thinking about the landmarks that we're heading for; I realise that I'm experiencing a feeling inside of me I forgot I had; it feels like joy, like a warmth inside of me, I can't remember the last time I felt it, it feels so long ago, could I be feeling happiness right now and as I look across to Dalton who is staring out of the car window, I have a revelation.

This man is incredible.

Damn it!

Chapter Twenty-Four
London

The car pulls up as close to Buckingham Palace as it can, because even as a worldwide megastar, there are no exceptions to where someone can park around this area of London.

Dalton requests his driver not to open the door to prevent unwanted attention from people. He isn't taking any risks tonight.

Getting out of the car in public dressed as Luigi now has me on edge; it's not so much because of the outfit itself, but because I know how silly I look with the giant moustache across my face.

After recent events, I've learned I dislike drawing attention to myself.

I've also learned that I care about what strangers think about me despite always believing I'm one of those people who didn't."Give it thirty minutes, and you'll forget about the moustache." Dalton says with a reassuring tone.

"Don't you feel silly right now?" I quietly ask

"Have you seen some characters I've played? A moustache is a small price to pay for peace tonight," he laughs.

I know he has a point, and I remind myself of the reasons that we're currently dressed this way. I tell myself to shake it off, get over it and remember it's about having fun.

"Yo, Mario and Luigi," shouts a random person from behind us. Which startles me.

As we both turn to see who just yelled at us, we see a man with a group of friends, all wearing matching tracksuits and lots of heavy-looking jewellery. They finish their attire off with the latest neon-coloured Nike high-tops. They look like a dance crew, but one you wouldn't want to bump into in an alleyway very late at night

"You look, sic, guys," says the man who initially yelled. "Can we get a selfie?"

Dalton gives me a look that suggests he maybe shouldn't have picked such fun and iconic characters to dress as, but he's willing to have fun tonight because no one knows who's underneath the outfits.

"Of course, it would be our pleasure," Dalton says in a perfect English accent.

I laugh while holding on to my moustache for dear life, as I'm not sure how much movement it can withstand.

"That was an impressive accent," I remark.

"Well, I am an actor, darling," he pretends to flick his hair. We huddle close to the group, ready for our first selfie of the night.

After a brief chat with the group, I feel terrible that I misjudged the group as potential thugs because they turned out to be a friendly group of dancers from East London. They shared their very cool business cards, suggesting we drop them a follow on Instagram and TikTok, which we promised we would.

As we wave goodbye to our new friends, Dalton takes my hand, which catches me off guard, but I don't resist. He then leads me on a walk towards the most famous landmark in London, Buckingham Palace.

The front gates of the Palace is flooded with tourists from around the world, all there to capture an iconic photo of themselves in front of one of the famous homes of the British Royal family.

I know that despite people marvelling at the grand building in front of them, they still have time to side-eye Mario and Luigi, and I know they're probably wondering why we're both dressed up. I embrace the attention we're getting and try not to let it distract me from the night ahead.

I look at Dalton, and I can see he seems calm and almost enjoying his newfound freedom for the first time since I've been in his presence. The impact it has on him by being able to do something that everyone else on the planet manages daily without being ambushed by strangers; it's such a small thing, the freedom to walk among everyone. I realise how much I take for granted being a nobody.

We find a spot together and capture our first photo of the night with the first historical landmark.

While waiting for the polaroid to develop, people ask if they can take a selfie with us, which, surprisingly, Dalton doesn't seem to mind.

"Is it not annoying you that everyone wants a selfie? Isn't this like a normal day for you?"

"Not at all, they're asking for a photo with the famous Mario and Luigi and as soon as they get the photo they happily leave us alone, now if I took the outfit off, it would be a different matter, people would follow us, the paparazzi would come out of nowhere and stalk us for the entire night, and it would be chaos, so no, I don't mind. How are you holding up with your newfound fame? Does it bother you, Charity?"

I'm forced to admit that I'm actually enjoying it because being a nobody, I rarely experience this type of attention, and the recent attention I've got has been negative, so this is a new experience for me.

We agree that selfies with strangers are a go for tonight. "Do you know what I want to do?" Dalton coyly says. "I want to go on the underground, are you ok with that?"

I'm surprised by this request.

"You want to go on the London underground, crammed up against strangers in this outfit? You know you'll overheat down there with that moustache?"

"It'll be fun. I know tonight is about you, but I never get to go on public transport as a member of the public. Could we squeeze this one request in for me? I understand if you don't want to."

How can I possibly say no? I surprise myself as I take Dalton's hand. This time, I lead the way, heading towards the public transport system, that is the famous London Underground.

Through the barriers, down the escalators, a walk through a tunnel, down more escalators. Walking through the station to get on a train on the underground can sometimes feel like walking from England to France, but Dalton seems to enjoy every minute.

We take selfies on the escalators together and await the tube's arrival on the platform.

I wasn't lying about the heat, as I can see Dalton is now experiencing the warmth of being stood beneath the city of London with hundreds of fellow tube goers, all squashed onto a thin platform.

We both squeeze onto a packed train and get cosy together. Despite not seeing Dalton's full expression, I can see in his eyes that he's having a great time, and I feel happy that something so small that I take for granted every day can bring such happiness to someone else. I feel a sudden attraction towards Dalton as I'm pressed up tightly against him, and I cannot turn around due to how many people are squeezed up against us.

His dreamy eyes seem to pierce through me.

His eyes are so full of emotion, and I've noticed I can sense his mood just from his eyes. I also experience how good he smells this close-up and whatever aftershave he's wearing; it's an aphrodisiac, and I feel giddy over this man dressed as Mario.

The train doesn't take long, and we arrive at Westminster, ready to see sights two and three.

We stroll together out of the station and Dalton subtly takes my hand while we talk about how excited he got riding on the underground system undetected as the global superstar he is.

The Westminster area is clean and tidy and has a calmer feel than where we were minutes before.

Visiting Westminster, Big Ben would be very hard to miss; this beautiful, tall and elegant clock tower watching over the area, and a recognisable image on the latest news broadcast, seen in hundreds of TV shows and films and another iconic landmark that people flock to see, coming from every corner of the earth.

We grab a photo together with Ben in the background, and while waiting for it to develop, I ask Dalton, "Do you know the name of Big Ben?"

Dalton looks at me, confused. "It's not Big Benjamin, is it?'" not wholly believing that himself.

"The Elizabeth Tower, it was renamed in 2012 to mark the Diamond Jubilee of Queen Elizabeth II, but everyone will always refer to it as Big Ben, and it suits it, to be honest."

With more history lessons and photos added to the scrapbook, Dalton and I visit the Houses of Parliament,

Westminster Abbey, the London Eye, Tower Bridge, the Tower of London, and Trafalgar Square.

"Want to do something crazy?" Dalton raises an eyebrow.

"Crazy how? Is it legal because I do not want to spend the night locked up? I'm becoming too much of a regular at a certain police station."

Dalton raises his eyebrow again, like he's wondering if it's appropriate to ask me to expand on this.

"Am I spending the evening with a master criminal?"

"Remove the master part, and you'd be right, according to the criminal record I have."

I now have a sudden rush of embarrassment surge through me. Why did I mention that.

We both sit on a bench in the garden of St Paul's Cathedral.

It's quiet, and this gives us some time alone, away from all the hustle and bustle of the city.

I take this opportunity to ask Dalton if something happened to him in the past because I sense he's pretty closed off from letting people know about him.

Dalton explains on several occasions, people he thought he could trust have sold stories about him, hurting him. He's used to betrayal, but in a different way to me. He tells me personal stories about friendships he's lost over the years. He explains why he's careful about what he shares with people, including through texts and emails, because when it's written, it makes it easier for people to share it as proof. It's heartbreaking for him to see his words splashed across newspapers; he explains how this has created his trust issues and it's all so someone can make a quick buck.

He shares that had those people needed money, if they'd have asked him, he would've helped them out, but they went behind his back, and it made him feel used and proved to him there was no friendship there. He said not everyone behaves this way, but separating people from this behaviour is tricky because sometimes the dollar bill signs get in the way, and people can't see past the money signs to see the damage they will cause to make some cash.

After his honest sharing, I feel it's time I was a bit more honest with him.

I share the disaster of how I became a criminal overnight.

"Can I ask you a personal question?" Dalton's tone has shifted to one of concern.

I nod yes.

"I know you have a broken heart, and I'm sorry you're going through this, but can I ask what made you love Reed? You don't have to answer if you don't want to; I understand it's a personal question."

I look up at St Paul's Cathedral, gathering my thoughts, while Dalton gives me space, not pressing me to answer.

I take a deep breath. "I love…I loved the way he made me feel. He was funny. It was like hanging out with your best friend. It always felt fun and easy, and it was always just us," my eyes sting, but I hold the tears back as I refuse to allow Reed to have this affect on me whenever he's mentioned.

"It was the way I thought I knew him. Like, I never worried about him cheating on me. It never came into question, where I felt like he would do that, because he never seemed the type of man to break someone's heart."

Dalton sits listening; he listens to the heartbreak coming out with the words I say, and he has this look on his face that says that all he wants to do is hold me and tell me how sorry he is, that another man could treat me this way, but he doesn't, he continues listening to me and puts his hand gently on top of mine.

"I just wasn't expecting it; there were no signs…oh, who am I kidding? Maybe there was, and I didn't notice because I wasn't looking for them. I felt hoodwinked when I found out, and the most challenging part for me was how stupid I feel."

Dalton looks upset; I feel he knows this feeling well because he knows how betrayal feels.

"You can't feel stupid; it wasn't your actions. He did all of this."

"Well, the part I feel silly for was I thought he was going to propose to me; it was our anniversary, I'd been reading the wrong signs, I thought he was being secretive because he was hiding the proposal, and I don't understand how it could've turned out in the worst way

189

possible, Why not on another day? Why that day? I'll never get closure on that or understand the reasonings behind it."

I realise I've started droning on about Reed, and I don't want the night to become about him.

"I'm sorry, please forgive me; I'm bringing the mood down." Dalton tells me he doesn't think this. I think he seems to understand my situation and he thanks me for being open and sharing my personal feelings with him.He grabs my hand and pulls me off the bench.

"Where to next?" I ask.

"It's time to do something crazy. It's time for the fun bus," he laughs.

"The.......what?"

Chapter Twenty-Five
The Fun Bus

You can hear the fun bus before you can see it.

It's a head turner for the people of London as they stop to look around to see where the sound of a party is coming from.

A party on wheels is the best way to sum up the fun bus. Music booms from it, and it's all lit up with neon lights.

As the bus pulls up, the song by *The Vengaboys - We like to party* is on full blast, and it's loud enough for people two hundred miles away to hear as everyone on the bus is singing in time to every word, while jumping up and down.

"We're not going on that, are we?" I nervously laugh.

"We certainly are, and why wouldn't we?" Dalton bops up and down.

He's itching to get onboard. His dazzling white Hollywood smile is in full view, and he has a cheeky glint in his eyes. It's almost as though he knows he's pushing me out of my comfort zone tonight and he looks like he's loving every minute.

The bus halts in front of us, and I expect the doors to open and to be greeted by Ernie and Stan from the night bus from Harry Potter, but I'm surprised when instead I'm greeted by Kylie and Jason, both fierce looking contenders for a shot at Ru Pauls Drag Race UK.

The music is lowered temporarily as Dalton and I are welcomed onboard, and as soon as we step on the bus everyone shouts out Mario and Luigi, and I feel overwhelmed with the attention we're drawing to ourselves, but it's not a bad feeling of being overwhelmed, it feels like a good overwhelmed, as though I'm important to people, and this sits ok with me, as I've quickly realised that the characters of Mario and Luigi seem to bring a universal happiness to people.

In less than 30 seconds, Kylie and Jason have broken down the rules of the fun bus. In a quick summary, the fun bus is about:

Having fun

Having more fun

Having even more fun

And with the summary confirmed, the Vengaboys is turned back up as loud as it can go and Dalton and I are handed our first shots to drink.

As we cheers to each other, the first alcoholic drink of the night is consumed.

I feel a hand on my shoulder and I'm quickly spun around as Kylie shouts 'selfie'.

Everyone quickly scrambles together, cocktails and shot glasses held up in the air and then everyone shouts *FUN BUS*, while smiling at the camera.

I sense they've done this before, as it was very well organised when the camera came out. Dalton hands me a light up cocktail and as the music's so loud, my attempts to discover what it is in go unheard, so I sip what resembles a purple rain cocktail having a rave.

I look over at Dalton, who's in such high spirits. He's dancing away on the fun bus, with a cocktail in hand, and he looks as though he doesn't have a care in the world. I can see how much this night means to him, for him to let his hair down and be someone other than Dalton Rivers for the night. He's dancing with a couple and if only they knew who was under the outfit, they would be screaming right now. Even though the bus we're on is fun, I feel a little left out now that I no longer have all of Dalton's attention to myself.

Robbie Williams, *Rock DJ* starts and everyone screams in agreement that they love the choice of music on the bus. Everyone's shouting out the words in time, and Dalton is no exception. He's got the moves and the words going on. As I watch him, I feel warm inside. I realise how lucky I am to be the only person on this bus that knows who is currently underneath the Mario outfit and I find this very exciting.

The purple rain looking cocktail is kicking in and I join in with the rest of the crowd on the bus, I start off gentle with a tap of the foot and a nod of the head and before long I'm in the middle of the bus dishing out the dance moves on the dance floor that is centre stage of the bus.

I'm happy, and temporarily I don't feel like a brokenhearted woman seeking revenge on her ex partner, I'm merely a woman having fun on the fun bus, with the best company, enjoying the music and the lights, all while dressed like a cartoon character.

A tray of more shots is passed around, courtesy of Kylie, who's doing a great job of being the host. I gladly take one and neck it.

Despite Jason being the designated driver, they too are having fun as they dance in their seat at the front of the bus, and it's clear to see every single person on the bus is happy, as laughter fills the air, but it's about to be ramped up as *Cotton Eye Joe* by *Rednex* starts and the bus erupts into organised chaos of everyone linking arms with each other, moving in and out to find the next partner, and despite it being difficult in such a small space, everyone's laughing and it feels as though every person is enjoying being alive, dancing, drinking, singing and everyone's in this moment together.

Dalton links arms with me, but instead of swapping on to the next person, he keeps me where I am, looking at me and gently swaying my arms from side to side. He's choosing to dance solely with just me.

I get goosebumps from getting his undivided attention back on me once again, and I don't want him to let go of me. I'm hoping he can't see how red my face is as I blush under the thrill of him touching me. I wonder whether it's the alcohol that is heightening my feelings for him right now. As we dance together, holding hands, close to one another, I look at him and I don't see a cartoon character, I also don't see a famous actor, I see a man who is enjoying every minute of being on this bus, a man who knows how to have fun, and be in the moment and a man who I quickly realising that I'm crushing on.

The moment is quickly interrupted when the loud shout from Kylie comes "next stop Covent gardennnnnnnnn."

"This is us." Dalton drops one of my hands, but keeps a hold of the other and starts to lead me off the bus.

I feel a little disappointed this moment is ending, because I'm certain that with a few more shots and some more dancing together it could certainly lead to other things between Dalton and I, but I'm also happy that I'll now have him all to myself again.

As Mario and Luigi leave the bus, everyone shouts goodbye to us and it's a nice feeling. As soon as the bus pulls away, we can both now hear properly once again, and all the sounds of Covent Garden surround us.

"Are you hungry?" Dalton asks.

My immediate thought is *for you Dalton, I am*, but I don't reply with that. Instead, I say, "I am a little, you know."

The truth is, I'm famished. I haven't eaten a lot today, because nerves and excitement about tonight got the better of me.

Dalton takes the lead once again and escorts me through the crowds of people, who all double take at us as we pass by them and he leads me down a quieter street towards a local patisserie that he likes.

Chapter Twenty-Six
Cake

The patisserie window is filled with the most gorgeous looking cakes, created by a dedicated artist of the dessert world and my mouth waters at the delicious sights.

While in the queue, I look out of the window and see that across the road, are a group of people who look homeless. They're standing in front of cardboard boxes, wearing tattered clothes, and they look unwashed. At the side of them are a few carrier bags that have what looks like their small possessions in and I feel guilty.

Dalton sees me looking out of the window.

"Shall we do a good deed?" he indicates to the people outside of the window.

We approach the counter, and there's a young girl behind the counter who looks us both up and down and she smiles at our outfits.

"Hello, what can I get you?"

"Well, can you put your best ten cakes in a box, and times it by…"

Dalton looks over his shoulder out of the window.

"Times it by eight, please," he confirms.

"Sorry, you want ten of our best cakes in a box and you want eight boxes of them?" she confirms.

"Yes, please."

"So, you want eighty cakes?" she reconfirms.

196

"Oh, no I want more than that, but if you can start with those first please." Dalton walks away, heading for a fridge that has bottled water and sandwiches in. He grabs a handful and ushers me over to help him.

"Can you grab loads of these?"

"Are these for the people outside?"

Dalton nods yes.

The girl shouts to request help from the back of the shop as the queue inside is building up.

Dalton drops a pile of sandwiches and water on the counter. "I will also pay for everyone's orders that are in the queue, as an apology for holding everyone up."

The girl stands with her mouth open. Her expression says she didn't expect such a huge order from a generous man dressed as Mario on her shift this evening.

I pop a pile of sandwiches and water on the counter and it's now stacked with items, leaving no room for anything else. Another staff member helps on a second till and I look up to see several more staff come from out of the back of the store to assist, they start by taking orders from people in the queue, which is now out of the door and down the road.

"Oh, no, that's ok, your order is being paid for, by Mario. Sorry, I meant this gentleman here," says one worker.

A storm of chatter now erupts in the cake shop as everyone in the queue learns they're about to have their delicious and not very cheap desserts paid for, courtesy of a man dressed up as a game character.

People pat Dalton on the back and say thank you, while others ask for a selfie with him and I. We happily oblige and I'm now getting used to posing for photos, something I never thought would happen.

A very expensive bill totalled up and paid for and the only way for us to leave the shop, is for Dalton to ask if some people would be kind enough to help us carry the cake boxes, sandwiches and bottled water out for the people stood across the road, who're completely unaware they are about to be given a mountain of delicious food and drink.

With an army of helpers, people carry items across the road and hand them to the people that I'd been looking at.

They all seem appreciative and grateful that they're being given the items and they thank everyone for their help and there's a spirit in the air of neighbourly help, and I love that Dalton's done something kind for so many people this evening.

The thing with being kind, is it has a ripple effect and the people that entered the cake shop not only received free items, but they also got their oxytocin topped up as well, feeling like they'd helped others and it's all thanks to the generosity of Dalton Rivers, who without them even realising was the man behind the mask.

It's probably a good thing they're unaware, because if they'd discovered who he is, it may have sent their levels over the top. I'm feeling content and happy that we've done a good deed for the evening, and I'm surprised at the Dalton I've seen tonight.

Every second I spend with him, I'm discovering that I'm becoming a new member of the Dalton Rivers fan club.

Armed with a box of goodies and some bottled water for us, Dalton leads me to the main square in Covent Garden.

There, we find a quiet spot to sit down, which is in front of a busker, who's currently performing magic, and we get to enjoy the delicious cakes and entertainment together.

We both soon learn how difficult it is to eat cream cakes with a giant moustache on.

I turn to Dalton.

"Do I have anything on my face?" I know I'm covered in cream, and he laughs.

"No, you're good."

He rubs the cream off for me, and gently taps my nose, which sends shivers down my spine.

Embarrassed and flustered, I pretend to be enthralled with the street performer, hoping this will distract Dalton from seeing the redness on my face or seeing straight through me, to know that I'm developing feelings for him.

Content and happy, we sit together and people watch, talking about people's different professions and we try to guess what job everyone in the crowd does.

Some guesses are funnier than others and more ridiculous as they go on.

"If you could do any job in the entire world, what would it be, Charity?"

I don't need to think about the answer to it.

"An author of children's books."

"How come you aren't currently doing it?"

"Maybe I'm not good enough, or maybe I lost my imagination somewhere. We don't all have drive like you," I smile at him.

"Have you written any stories before?"

"I have a box of stories that I did when I was younger, with lots of different characters that I created. I just haven't ever done anything with them all." I feel regret as I say this, because I know I've wasted opportunities in my life and I have little excuses why I haven't pursued my dreams.

"You said you lost your imagination. We're all guilty of doing that. Can you remember being a child and not having a care in the world? You could pretend to be a princess or a doctor or a vet or even an astronaut, and no-one laughed at you, because you were a child and children can dream. But when we become adults, it shifts. People then laugh when you tell them you want to be an astronaut, because you're a grownup and you're meant to have it all figured out. But, you don't Charity, that's just what the system has made us believe, you can be whatever you want to, at any point of your life, this is your life and if you want to write children's books, then the only person stopping you from doing it, is you."

I look at him, this man with a jawline that other men would kill for, whose full of passion and motivation, and something switches inside of me. He's right, the only person who is stopping me is me.

"Maybe you could read them to me sometime. I'd love to hear them."

"Maybe," I can't believe that he would be interested in hearing my childhood stories and I feel embarrassed at the thought of sharing them with him, in case he thinks they're rubbish.

"Good, that's settled then. Fancy a walk?"

I think that's a great idea, considering the amount of calories I've just stuffed into my face. A good walk is just what I need.

And together we head off towards Leicester Square, hand in hand.

Chapter Twenty-Seven
Run

Dalton pulls me across the road in an excitable way. "I need to show you something."

I'm trying to keep up with his pace, wondering what's so important, then we come to a halt outside of a shop—it's a book shop.

Dalton stands behind me and moves me in front of the window, and it sinks in.

It's a window full of beautifully designed books, from thrillers to self-help books to children's books.

"You could have your book in this window."

I see what he's trying to do.

He's encouraging me. It's something I've been lacking: the belief in myself that this is something I can do.

As I look at the books displayed, I envy the authors who've achieved the goal of not only pursuing their dream and creating their books but also having them displayed beautifully in this shop window.

"Wouldn't you like this to see your characters come to life? Your books being the choice of a children's bedtime story, you could be responsible for that magic, Charity."

I don't need convincing. I recall the days when I was younger. I would spend hours daydreaming about seeing my books in the front window of all the bookshops, and I'd play scenes through my head, where I'm sitting doing readings, with all the children sitting on the carpet, intently listening to me. They're brimming with excitement over the adventures the characters I created are on, and they cheer, gasp, and oooh.

"Why do you think I have it in me to achieve this, Dalton? Millions of people dream of publishing books; it doesn't mean they can achieve it."

"Nothing is impossible. Everyone has to start somewhere, and with hard work, encouragement and determination, you could have your story in lots of bookstore windows. I believe you could have your books in this specific window. Think of your younger self and how she would want you to do this because she dreamed of it, and it's now your responsibility as an adult to help the younger version of yourself achieve it. Still, the question is, why would you think you don't have it in you to achieve this?"

"I'm not sure. I'm scared because I've never tried to pursue it. It's the fear of not knowing if it will work out, perhaps, along with what if I'm not good enough to do this, too? If I'm no good, then my daydream will be crushed, and sometimes I think it's easier to have still the dream than to fail at it." Dalton turns me around so I'm facing him. He puts his hand up to my face and strokes my cheek with his finger.

"It's the hardest things that are worth fighting for; if something doesn't terrify you, it shows it doesn't mean much to you. What will you lose if you try it and it doesn't work out? Now look at it this way: what will you lose out on if you never try to do it? Do you want to be an old lady regretting never giving her dreams a go?"

I look at his face. He never seems to get a five o'clock shadow. He's always perfectly groomed, and he's always perfectly nice as well.

"Why are you so nice to me?"

"You're a good person, and I need you to know that I enjoy your company. I also firmly believe that a person can be the master of their own destiny, so if there's something you want, then only you can stand in the way of getting it. And I kinda like you."

My face goes to a shade of cherry red within a second. I wasn't expecting him to say that he likes me. As if the famous Dalton Rivers just told me he likes me. I'm over the moon about it, because my feelings have grown immensely tonight for him.

I noticed earlier when he first held my hand; it felt like I was cheating on Reed because Reed's hand was the only one I'd held for years.

But throughout the evening, Dalton's hand is feeling familiar, like I've always held his hand.

I've also recognised that being in his company and getting to know him it somehow feels like we've met up dozens of times and that we've known each other for a lot longer than we have.

"Thank you," I look at him thoughtfully.

"For what?"

"For the pep talk and the motivational speech, I needed to hear it, despite not thinking I did."

Dalton holds his hand out, and I willingly take it once again.

We walk together hand in hand through Leicester Square, with the lights flashing and tourists from all over the world marvelling at the sights and sounds. We see the queues outside the Lego store and people smiling as they leave M&M World with their bright yellow bags full of chocolate.

I feel at ease and so comfortable with Dalton. It just feels so right, and despite being brokenhearted, it feels manageable, because the more I speak to Dalton or spend time with him; I heal a bit more.

Some people might call this a rebound, but it's not because I'm doing my best not to like Dalton that way, despite failing miserably at it.

Maybe it isn't even the physical attraction helping to heal me; perhaps it's the fun Dalton brings and how everything seems so easy when I'm around him.

Nothing needs much work; laughter flows, conversations are easy, and everything feels calm.

I can't decide if it's because he's such a laid-back man and his aura brings this, or whether it's just the two of them together that help to combine that easiness. It doesn't take long until some tourists request a photo with us again, and as we have all night, we once again happily oblige.

As we both crouch down to kneel in front of the group, Dalton's moustache gets caught on a strap on one of the tourists' jackets. The photo is taken, and as Dalton stands up, his moustache is ripped clean off his face.

As the group members look at him, laughing that he's lost his iconic moustache, unexpectedly, and out of nowhere, we hear a loud shout of *Dalton Rivers*.

Daaaaaaaaaalton comes the screams, and within seconds, it's like bees in a hive: we're both swarmed with people wanting photos and autographs. Out of all the places this unfortunate encounter could've happened, it just so happened to be in the middle of one of the busiest areas of London.

Dalton looks at me and laughs. "You ready?"

"For what?" I'm panicking, because I'm unsure how to act in situations like this; I'm not media-trained and I'm certainly not a security guard.

Dalton grabs my hand and shouts, "RUN!"

With that, we're both running through Leicester Square and up towards Piccadilly Circus while being chased by a mob of fans from the 'I love Dalton' club.

Dalton drags me in and out of people, manoeuvring here and there. I look over at him briefly, and he looks gorgeous.

The Mario outfit suits him, and now that hideous moustache is gone. I can see the man underneath, and I really like what I see. I did not expect tonight that I'd be dressed as Luigi, running through Leicester Square, with

Dalton Rivers holding on to my hand for dear life. This night has earned the top slot of the most unexpected events that have happened to me.

Why did it have to be in Leicester Square?

For the love of God, everyone in London seems to be on the streets, making it nearly impossible for us not to push people while we run.

A car swiftly slams its brakes on ahead of us, and Daltons' driver shouts for us to get in.

Frantically, the mob is catching up with us, and the adrenaline that's going through me is unreal. We leap towards the car like stunt performers, lunging straight into the back, and with that, the driver slams the door and dashes to the front seat.

I hear the doors lock, and I feel I can breathe again. I look out of the window, and people surround the car screaming; I see women crying while they're pushing their breasts against the windows, and I look over at Dalton, who is looking straight ahead; he seems in a zoned-out phase, like he's frozen, but not in a good way.

I gently place my hand on top of his, asking, "Are you okay?" I rub my thumb across the top of his hand, and it looks like he releases a breath he'd held in. I sit wondering how he had any breath to hold. I'm completely out of it after that run.

"I'm good," he says, looking at me. "It's part of being a celebrity. I'm not a fan because I've seen situations like that get out of hand, and it can be quite scary when you're outnumbered in that way, and people are frantic and emotional; they don't mean any harm, I know this, but for me, I find it very intimidating."

I don't understand completely because I'm not him, but my adrenaline is going crazy, and they were chasing Dalton, not me. I just got caught up in it all. I feel bad for him because I can see why it's so scary: the shouting, the crying, the overwhelmed people. After all, they want to meet their idol.

I realise I'm still rubbing his hand, and I quickly move it away, feeling a little embarrassed. Dalton looks at me, and then at my hand. He takes my hand back and places it in his, with our fingers intertwined together.

I blush and realise that I'm starting to believe in love at first sight.

Stop it Charity, you're being ridiculous tonight, I say to myself.

I pull off my moustache as I realise it's still attached to my face, surprisingly considering the sweat that's just run down it.

"I had a great night tonight, thank you."

Dalton looks at me, smiling, "It's not over yet."

"It's not?" I'm surprised. I thought that would be enough for one night.

"Not even close," he grins and turns to look out the window.

"I need to change out of this outfit. Would you mind coming to my hotel?"

Would I mind coming to his hotel?!?!?!?

I think we both know what he really means.

"No, of course not," I'm embarrassed by how quickly I agree. I look out of the window and think to myself, of course, I want to go to Dalton's hotel, even more so after tonight.

I sit watching people going about their lives from the car window. I wonder if they've got a broken heart or if they're happy and in love. I wonder if they'll ever get the chance to experience a night like I have tonight or if they'll ever spend an evening with a celebrity this way— probably not; I think. These situations are what dreams are made of for us average people.

The car pulls up outside the hotel, and as I look up and marvel at the building, I see the sign that is Claridges.

Of course, he's staying somewhere exclusive. He's not exactly going to be booked into a Premier Inn Hub, even though I'm a fan of them, because even Claridges would be up against stiff competition to beat their quilts and pillows.

The driver opens the door for me, and I step out, suddenly extremely nervous.

I'm going into Claridge's dressed as Luigi, and I'm about to be invited into Dalton's hotel room, and I think we all know what's going to happen once that hotel door is closed.

Chapter Twenty-Eight
Bathroom Dilemma

Fuck =*a word used to express impatience, annoyance and anger.*

Fuckkkkkkk…fuck, fuck, fuckity fuck!

How is it possible that the most sought-after man on the planet—no, the most sought-after man in the entire galaxy—is sitting in the room next door, waiting to lead me by the hand into his bed?

Millions of people would give their souls for a bed to spend just one night with this godly specimen of a man.

And here I am, the least sought-after person on the planet—no, the least sought-after person in the entire galaxy—wearing the most inappropriate underwear for this occasion.

These are the knickers I pulled out from the back of the drawer because they looked comfortable, knowing full well no one would see them.

I chose comfort over sexiness, but truthfully, even I find them off-putting.

However, if the choice of underwear tonight wasn't a big enough problem, problem two is that I didn't even bother tidying up downstairs.

So if the sight of the knickers isn't enough to put him off, then what's lurking behind them will seal my fate.

I frantically ransack the bathroom, hoping to find a razor. I open a cupboard, and I see an electric shaver; oh fuck! If I switch this on, there's no way he's not going to hear the buzzing coming from the bathroom, and how the hell can I walk out after that, without having to explain the dilemma I've found myself in and then share the embarrassing explanation for why he's just heard buzzing in his bathroom, like I've just opened a pop-up barber shop.

I could make an excuse. I've drunk too much. I feel a headache coming on. I'm suddenly tired.

I could get Della to ring me in an emergency, telling me some relative has been rushed to the hospital. To be honest, Della is that best friend that would save my soul in every situation in life, except this one, because she wouldn't ever let me ever pass up the opportunity of spending the night with the sexiest man alive for four consecutive years in a row now.

Oh, who am I kidding? I can't do it, because I know the moment I open this door, his eyes are going to seduce me, those goblin-green perfect eyes and my body will let me down and be begging for it, despite my brain screaming out to remind me, that there's a car crash of a mess going on downstairs.

Fuckkkkkk! I panic; here come the short, sharp breaths, and now, on top of everything else, I'm sweating; oh dear lord, I'm going to leave this bathroom a stinking, bushy mess. I'm running out of time when it's acceptable to be in the bathroom before the other person wonders what's going on there.

The man next door is a god to thousands, no, millions of people on the planet. I do not doubt that he's made sweet love to goddesses, those women who're always prepared. Clean and tidy, with their perfect-looking vaginas, Della and I call them car wash women because they look like they've just walked out of a car wash, smelling fresh and all shiny and waxed.

I can't let him see this monstrosity of a female sex organ. I can't do it. I'm panicking, I have no choice. I have to bail.

I look frantically around me; of course, there's no bathroom window, fuckkkkkkk again!

I sit on the toilet seat and put my head in my hands, dragging my hands down my face in a WTF moment, I run my fingers up through my hair, and then yank it as tight as I can, as punishment to myself, for being such a tramp, I only have myself to blame for this mess.

The time has now elapsed. I'm now in the category of what the hell is she doing in the bathroom? I wonder if she's okay, while I'm just making things worse for myself, adding problem after problem on top of more problems.

A knock at the door startles me. I drag my hands down my face, my mouth agape in shock. I'm being summoned out of the bathroom. Oh, fuckkkkkkk, I don't even have time to decide what to do. I stop breathing momentarily and freeze like a statue; I don't even move my eyes in case he hears; maybe if I stay as silent as possible, he will leave.

"Are you okay, Charity?" comes the seductive and caring tone through the strong oak wood door.

"Uh-huh, yep, it's all good in here," my voice is feeble, and my eyes are frozen from the fear of this situation.

"Are you sure? Is there anything I can get you?"

And then, without thinking, I reply, "A razor and a new vagina, perhaps?"

Oh fuckkkkkkkkk!

What follows is an awkward silence that lasts longer than the time I was frantically in this bathroom, trying to sort out all of my life's problems.

It feels like forever. I need him to say something. Please say something, anything

"Come out, your wine is getting cold."

I know I wanted him to say something, anything, but I wanted him to at least make sense.

"Eh? Isn't wine meant to be cold?"

I realise the muscles in my face are no longer frozen as I sit with a confused frown.

He laughs behind the door. "That was a joke. Please come out." Oh fuck it, what can I do?

I can't exactly turn the buzzing on now. I'm going to fess up on my dilemma; I'm already looking like an idiot behaving this way. Locked in a bathroom, I wonder if I have it to painfully pluck out hairs with a pair of tweezers I clocked earlier in his cabinet.

I slowly get up, and it feels like walking into the dentist's room when you know you're about to have teeth pulled, and your feet don't seem to want to work; they're hesitating, and your inner self tells them to sort themselves out.

I don't want to open the door, and I don't want to explain myself, but I have no choice.

I unlock the door quietly, allowing myself a second or two to quickly change my mind; I mean, I could live here and never surface again; there's fresh running water and toothpaste that I could eat when things get rough in a few weeks.

There are towels to keep me warm and a bath to use as a bed, and during this time, I could make myself look like the goddess he's so used to.

Oh, who am I kidding? I slowly open the door.

Dalton stands looking at me, mouth wide open. "What's wrong?" He swallows, and has a concerned look in his gorgeous I can make you do anything, eyes. "Are you okay?"

"Who me?" Trying to play it down. "I'm great, never better. Why do you ask?"

He puts his hands on my shoulders and slowly turns me around. He walks me back into the bathroom, where it appears I'm doomed to stay, despite being brave and plucking up the courage to open the door.

Dalton turns me around, and I see my face staring back at me from the mirror. If I thought I had life problems ten minutes ago, I'm now faced with red lipstick all smeared down my jowls and mascara all wiped down my face, with my hair standing up to attention.

Oh fuckkkkkkkk! Sitting to contemplate my downstairs dilemma on the toilet just added to my ever-growing list of problems.

"For fuck's sake!" I don't even apologise for my language. I quickly reach for toilet paper and put it under the sink tap to wet it to rid the crazy version of myself staring back at me in disappointment. I'm even more frantic than my first visit to the bathroom. I wipe my face aggressively while trying to hide my cheeks, which are now a scorching red tone of embarrassment.

"Let me help you Luigi."

He takes the toilet paper from my hand and I feel the gentleness of his skin although I'm frantic, and I'm having the biggest panic attack internally; his touch seems to set off a calm emotion inside of me.

He throws the toilet paper in the bin under the sink and grabs a cotton pad out of his cupboard and some micellar water, and I think to myself, of course, he looks after his multi-million-pound face; I seemed to have missed all his expensive face products in his cupboard while looking for garden shears and power tools to sort out my poorly kept garden.

He drips the water onto the cotton pad and gently rubs it on my face, removing the disaster scene I've just created

"How is it possible that you came into this room looking more beautiful than ever, and minutes later, you've recreated the Joker? Don't people go into bathrooms to tidy themselves up?"

He looks at me with caring eyes that tell me he is trying to make this situation lighter for me.

If only I was brave enough to be honest and tell him my dilemma, where we could just laugh about how much I have built up this situation and how I've created some sort of monster in my mind about how I won't be good enough physically for this god of a man.

Without thinking, I open my mouth and say, "I didn't shave."

My face is on fire; it's not the micellar water or the lipstick; it's the fact my brain has once again just let me down and allowed my mouth to say what I was thinking.

Now, my embarrassment is on an entirely new level

"Why do you need to shave? I see no beard?" He scans my chin and under my nose with a playful grin.

I look at him with hope, hoping that he doesn't make me explain what I just said to him because I don't think I have any more embarrassment to give to myself tonight; it's exhausted itself.

My eyes look into his, and without words, they say, please don't make me say it.

"Ohhhhhhhhhhh," he's clocked on.

The penny has dropped, and then there's that awkward silence again; I seem to be a master at creating these recently.

I quietly respond, almost in a mumble of words and avoiding eye contact with him.

"Yeah, sorry, I panicked; I'm not exactly on form tonight, and I didn't think this would be how the night ended, and I know a man like you.." I slowly lift my head and catch sight of his face, looking puzzled.

"A man like me?" he slowly lowers his arm from wiping my face. It rests mid-air in front of us both.

"Yes, a god like yourself who would have had so many encounters with goddesses."

Oh fuckkkkk, this is the worst conversation I've ever found myself in.

He slowly raises his arm back up and starts gently wiping my face again while tidying strands of my hair at the same time with his other hand; he's trying so gently to get me back to a respectable vision of myself.

"Tell me what you're trying to say, Charity," he softly tucks my hair behind my ear and runs his finger down the side of my cheek as though he's reassuring me he doesn't bite and this is a safe space for me to be honest with him.

I say nothing.

I watch him intently as he fixes up the rest of my face. I can sense the hurt in his eyes, and I realise my comment could mean so many things and be misconstrued so quickly. Still, I keep putting my foot in my mouth tonight, and now my mouth has gone on strike, and it's refusing to say anything.

I look at every inch of his face, and my eyes become fixed on his strong jawline, which could be made from diamonds, making it completely unbreakable. I look up at his perfect brown chestnut-coloured hair, which he constantly sweeps off his face, and I think about how he has so many beautiful qualities. And then here's me looking like the definition of unstable.

He throws the cotton pad in the bin, puts away the water, and then gently turns me back around to face the mirror. I now stand utterly vulnerable to him, with no makeup to hide all the flaws I have now learned to cover.

"You look even more beautiful than you did before the first time you entered this bathroom."

I blush.

He stands behind me, and we look at each other through the mirror.

"Why does it feel you don't believe what I just said?

He gently puts his arms around my waist.

My mouth still can't remember how to work, and I stare at him in the mirror.

His arms gently slip away from me, and he turns and walks back into the other room. I stand looking at myself, feeling foolish and somehow unkind. I saw the hurt in his eyes when I made that comment, and now my mouth won't let me talk to him to explain what I meant.

I take my freedom back, show the bathroom I'm in control by leaving it, and head into the room.

Dalton is sitting with a glass of wine in a giant, comfortable chair that looks like a chair where all life decisions should be made.

He looks sombre, so I pick my wine glass up and sit on the chair opposite him; it's not as big and as comfortable looking but nice.

Everything in Dalton's room is lovely and costly, but friendly.

Behind him are the views of London, a city I've called home for many years since finishing university and deciding I never wanted to leave.

It's evening, so all the lights of London are his backdrop. It's a perfect vision, him, this beautiful man, sitting in a big, beautiful chair, with a stunning view behind him. Yet the atmosphere doesn't match the scene because I've said something that's hurt him.

I take a large mouthful of wine, one where you swallow that much liquid, It almost feels like your throat has been punched, and it helps to restart my mouth working; it's a bit like a car running out of petrol. Pop the petrol back in, and hey presto, it runs; I'm learning my mouth is the same.

"When I said a man like you…" Dalton looks at me. He has an expression of hope, like he wants me to confirm that I didn't mean it insultingly, which I certainly didn't mean.

I take another mouthful of wine and it hurts my throat again. "What I meant was, you're so famous, you're the most known person on the planet, and everyone wants you or to be you, and there's not a single person on earth that wouldn't chew their fingers off to spend a night with you. You could have anyone you choose because you're so beautiful, and yet here you are stuck with me, the person who has the worst possible underwear on right now, who's just spent god knows how long searching for a razor in your bathroom to sort out the mess of her downstairs, and I'm embarrassed because you're too good for me. The minute I remove my clothes, this will confirm it."

And release, all the stress and breath exhales from me at once. I take another large mouthful of wine, finishing my glass.

"You think I'm beautiful?"

He now has a smile on his face. I sit stunned that after everything I just said; he took the word beautiful out of it.

"No one has ever called me beautiful before and meant it the way you just said it." He looks at me so sincerely, and I believe he means what he's saying.

He stands up and walks over to the other side of the large living room, while I go over all the things I just said to him in my mind.

He turns around with a fresh bottle of wine, which is probably not a good idea for me tonight. Still, he opens it and starts pouring me another glass, which I don't verbally decline.

He places the bottle on the table and sits back in the big, comfortable chair. "Can I be honest with you?"

I nod, while drinking more of the freshly filled glass of wine.

"I'm not stuck with you; why would you even say that? I can't imagine anyone else I would want to be sitting opposite me right now, badly groomed garden or not."

This makes me laugh; it was only a matter of time before we both started seeing the lightheartedness of this ridiculous situation; I felt I was in.

"I don't know if I ever told you, but I'm quite a dab hand at gardening," he says through the cheekiest grin.

I didn't think it was possible, but once again, tonight, my embarrassment is on point. We sit staring at each other, not saying anything, but the atmosphere feels somewhat more relaxed; I'm not sure if it's what we both just said to each other or if it's the wine that's kicked in.

"Do you know what's so endearing about you, Charity?"

I shake my head slowly from side to side because I didn't know I had any endearing qualities. I brace myself as I'm about to learn something new about myself.

"You have no idea how beautiful you are. You have no idea how I'm the one that's lucky to be sitting here right now with you…"

I'm bashful, and I interrupt him because i can't take anymore embarrassment this evening. "You've been with goddesses; I'm not anywhere near being a goddess; I can't match up to that level; that makes me not good enough to be sitting here with you."

I didn't realise tonight would be about sharing so many truths. I wasn't prepared for any of this.

He picks up his glass while looking at me and he takes a drink from it, not moving his eyes away from mine. I'm so attracted to him and the confidence he has. He puts his glass down and asks me, "What do you think defines a goddess?"

I shift uncomfortably in my seat, knowing I'm about to describe someone who is the complete opposite of me. This will surely make it clear to him and myself that I'm not worthy of being sat here right now, with this man, having this conversation.

"She's perfect looking, beautiful to everyone's eyes, she's a head turner, she walks in a room, and everyone's drawn to her. She owns the room, and yet she hasn't even opened her mouth yet. But she knows that everyone in the room wants seconds with her to talk to her, to know who she is. She's visually stunning from head to toe; everything is in the right place, she is in the right proportion, and every single part of her is the visual image everyone wants to have."

Dalton shakes his head in a disappointing and disagreeing way. "You're wrong; you are describing an unrealistic vision of beauty, a vision that you think everyone thinks is beautiful, but everyone has different visions of what beauty is, and your biggest mistake in that description is that it seems all about looks. What if that beautiful woman opens her mouth and is entitled and rude? Would she still be seen as beautiful as you've just described her? How about when she starts shouting insults and demands because she knows she's beautiful, and this arrogant personality has grown from it? Is that beauty? Is that how a goddess would be?"

He's made a good argument, and I know he's right, but I don't want to be wrong; nobody enjoys being wrong.

So, I say nothing; I awkwardly play with my wineglass, twirling it in my hands in the hope I'm spared a comeback.

He leans forward and quietly asks, "would you like me to tell you what a goddess is?"

I'm intrigued to see what he can come up with that doesn't match the description I gave.

This new conversation is now making my bathroom dilemma seem like yesterday's news, so it's welcomed. "I would like to hear your definition," I say confidently in my tone.

223

He takes a deep breath, looks me straight in the eyes, and whispers, "You."

He smiles and sits back in his chair, leaving me bewildered as to what he means by me, and he opens the floor to my response, like we're playing a game of verbal tennis.

"I'm confused, me? I'm not a goddess; I'm far from it, Dalton, and we both know that." I take another drink, mainly because it's in my hand, and it feels like the only deflection I have.

"Do you know what one of the most beautiful qualities is about you, Charity? You described yourself when you described what you think a goddess is; you're gorgeous, and you light up rooms, whether or not you mean to, and whether it's positive or accidental, you do it. The best part is that you have no idea how beautiful you are, so you have no arrogance or entitlement when you open your mouth. You're too insecure if you want my opinion, and I'm trying to understand where it comes from. Still, I'm piecing it together. You're one of the most honest and down-to-earth people I've ever met. You're honest and kind, you swear more than you need to. I heard the F words coming from the bathroom. Oh, and you're a little self-destructive. I can't decide if it's your brain or mouth that gets you into the most trouble. Still, the bottom line is I love spending time with you, and I want to get the most time of yours when you enter the room; I know you're hurt because of your ex, and I get where this crazy behaviour comes from. I'm glad he messed everything up with you. We wouldn't be sitting here, drinking wine and conversing, if he hadn't."

And there it is, my Kryptonite, Reed, who's pushed straight to the front of my mind once again when I try so hard to forget about him.

Everything he did to me, even if it was for ten minutes of respite and with no control over this situation, the sadness and anger have once again invited themselves back inside of me, and my life rewinds to four months ago.

Sitting across from Dalton, I wonder how we got here, metaphorically anyway, because we got here in his car.

A few months ago, this man was the topic of conversation across the breakfast table with Reed, excited about a new film that Dalton had signed up to star in, and now here I am, no longer with Reed, and sat drinking wine with his idol instead. My bathroom dilemma is a minor issue compared to my current most significant problems. I'm sure there are people out there who could only wish that their most important problem in life was not having a tidy lady area while sitting drinking wine with a god of a celebrity, who's giving me the eyes that he wants to sleep with me, messy garden or not. I'm stuck between some heartache and torment, trying to get closure from Reed while also spending time with whom I saw as the enemy, and now I realise I was wrong about Dalton.

Since I've met him, he's looked past my stupid behaviour and actions. He hasn't judged me on things I've done or said. He's said nothing but nice things to me, complimented me frequently and been a complete gentleman.

He even gave me a sightseeing tour of my city when it should have been the other way around.

He has a nice way of making me see significant issues aren't that big, and he makes me laugh about things I should be serious about.

He's shown me kindness, politeness, and gentleness, sometimes making my heart feel a little less broken.

He always makes me smile and surprises me in ways I didn't think were possible.

"Do you think it's weird for us to sit here drinking wine together?" I ask the beautiful man sitting across from me

"Why would I find it weird? I meant what I said. I love spending time with you, and I look at it this way: sometimes the universe steps in and helps people along their way and had you and Reed not broken up, I wouldn't have got to know you, so the answer to your question is no, I don't think it's weird."

I believe him.

I believe every word this man says, and it's not because I'm naïve; I know I'm naïve, but there's something about Dalton that is so sincere, and I don't think he has it in him to lie to my face.

"Can I ask you another question?"

He smiles at me and nods yes.

"Have you ever cheated on anyone before? I understand if that's too much of a personal question." I know this question is personal, but I couldn't stop myself from asking him it.

He doesn't even hesitate. "No, I honestly don't believe in it. What's the point of causing hurt towards another person in that way? Betrayal is awful to be on the receiving end, and trust me, I know I've experienced it many times, and I'm not prepared to be the one dishing it out to others."

I believe him again. "Sorry, if that was too personal, it's just… I wasn't ever really insecure before, you know, before I found out what Reed had done. It wasn't something that even crossed my mind, and now I feel like I was stupid…stupid not to recognise it or see the signs of being cheated on, and I don't want ever to feel how I feel now again, so I guess my guard is up."

"You don't have to explain this to me, Charity. When I said I've experienced it many times before, I meant I've experienced betrayal in all different forms. From friends stabbing me in the back to partners cheating to managers stealing from me, there are lots of different ways people can betray your trust, and I just want you to know, I get it, I understand."

We sit looking at each other in silence. There's no need for words; we both know how it feels. We're connected because we've both experienced betrayal, and we get each other.

I have this overwhelming urge to kiss this man. To hold him. To feel every part of him. To embody him.

And then something unexpected happens; I open my mouth and say.

"Dalton…will you kiss me".

I swallow hard because the moment just took over me and I notice my throat is still hurting. I'm surprised at myself, but the words just came out.

It's not like me to be so forward, although I know the wine has given me a small amount of Dutch courage with this.

My eyes are fixed on him, waiting for his response.

"I thought you'd never ask."

He puts his wineglass on the table, his eyes still fixed on mine, and he slowly walks towards me; my heart is thumping like a woodpeckers trapped inside it.

He comes over and sits down next to me, and I get a wave of his scent covering me; and I'm melting from the inside out.

I fear my legs would give way about now if it weren't for the fact I'm already sitting down.

He gently puts his hand under my chin and tilts my head slightly so our eyes meet.

He tucks a loose strand of my hair behind my ear, and I'm so close to losing it; I'm so weak for him. He traces my cheek with his finger right down to my lips, and I think how his fingers are so soft and gentle.

The woodpecker inside my heart is determined to break through, and I need Dalton to kiss me; I'm desperate for it, more than I ever thought possible.

"You're so beautiful, Charity," his finger gently strokes down my nose.

I have now lost the ability to speak; my words are stuck somewhere inside my sore throat.

"Can I ask you a question?"

I smile and nod slowly to indicate yes to him because I fear my voice will break if I try to speak.

"Can I make love to you?"

"I thought you'd never ask."

I can't hold back any longer. I put my lips on him with a sudden urgency.

Kissing Dalton Rivers is what dreams are made of. Not because he's the sexiest man on the planet, but because kissing him is like all of those romantic scenes. You watch in films when the two main characters finally declare their love for each other.

There's been a significant build-up to the moment, and it's passionate, loving, hot, steamy, and simply mind-blowing. I've never been kissed like this before in my entire life.

I feel a surge of electricity shooting through every part of me, and I never want this moment to end.

But it does, and as we give our lips a short rest, he gently pulls back away from my face and says, "Wow.

And I realise that while I'm experiencing heavenly bliss from his kiss, I didn't stop to think about how it felt for him. He confirms he feels the same way from the one word he just gave me.

He stands up and gently picks my hand up to get me to stand up. As I do, he swoops his arms under my legs, and in a split second, he's carrying me. With my arms wrapped around his neck, we look at each other; it feels like trying to look through each other's eyes to see what's in our souls.

And it's at this moment that Dalton Rivers carries me into his bedroom.

Chapter Twenty-Nine
Surprising

I experienced something tonight, something new. I learned the difference between having sex with someone and making love with someone.

I've never experienced making love with someone the way I just did with Dalton.

It was gentle yet passionate; I felt strongly connected to him throughout, and I couldn't have been more turned on.

He was tentative and a gentleman, and my disastrous garden issue quickly became a distant memory because, at that moment with him, I didn't have time to worry about how I looked or how well-groomed I was. It was all about the strong emotional connection I felt with him.

It didn't take long for me to climax because I was weak for him before he carried me into his bedroom, and as we lay in his bed, both spent, I think to myself how incredible that just felt.

He rolls over and leans on his elbow, looking at me, and I gently turn onto my side to look deep into his eyes. Despite us both just getting so personal with one another, I feel a little embarrassed looking at him. Mainly because we've just taken our relationship to a new level, and he's now seen me naked.

He says nothing; he just smiles at me, and I smile back. We stay here for a while this way.

The world is always full of noise, and everyone always has something to say; constant noise all the time, and it's moments like this where you connect with someone, and you don't need words; there's just silence between you both, and you speak to one another through your eyes, and it's deep and it's rare.

Dalton climbs out of bed, and I look at his entire body, this gorgeous, perfect-looking specimen of a man.

He's so confident, if it was me getting out of this bed, my hand would try to find my underwear, and I would shuffle down the bed to put them on uncomfortably, gripping the quilt while I lean off the bed to grab a long top I can slip on to cover my naked body, giving me my dignity back, because I am the opposite to him, I'm not that confident; I wish I were, but I'm not.

I'm too good at seeing my flaws and I certainly don't want to share them with anyone else.

I envy his confidence, and I hope that one day, I can find myself in his position and climb out of bed stark naked with tremendous confidence that says, *this is me, and this is who I am.*

"Be right back," he grins and walks out of the bedroom.

While he's out of the room, this gives me the perfect opportunity to gather all of my clothing that's strewn across different parts of the bedroom and put them next to me on the floor so I have easy access, I can't believe I'll be getting back dressed as Luigi again. I look at the clock on the bedside table, and it's the early morning hours;

tonight has flown by. I lay back in Dalton's eleven out of ten bed, with his cloud-like mattress underneath me and his cloud-like pillows resting underneath my head and I replay the lovemaking we've just done, It excites me, and the surge of electricity is back; although the woodpecker seems to have fallen asleep, it's good he's taking a break. It was getting a lot to take him and his hammering. What the hell is happening to me? What just happened and how did that happen? I blush. I can feel my face getting redder and redder the more I relive everything. Della is going to freak out when I tell her about tonight.

Dalton enters the room, he's carrying wine glasses and a bottle of wine. He places a glass next to me on the bedside table with the bottle, then he scoots around the bed and places his glass on his table. Then he dashes off again and out of the room.

The next time he returns, he's carrying a tray with different items on it and he puts it in the middle of the giant bed.

There's a bowl of strawberries and a pot of cream, and there are nuts and nibbles galore.

"Oh, I nearly forgot," he holds his finger up in a thought moment.

He dashes out of the room again, and I sit there looking at the after sex picnic he's just made me and this beats a breakfast god any day.

He comes back into the room and he's holding his hand behind his back, which is a sight I never thought I would see. Dalton Rivers, naked, standing in front of me with his hand behind his back as he has something to give me.

"What have you got?" I playfully ask.

He teases me by not answering, and I look at him and think how beautiful he is and how lucky I am to be here at this moment with him. I also think he could have anything behind his back right now, and it wouldn't surprise me as much as he's surprised me tonight.

Well, maybe an axe that would be a weird surprise and a very different vibe from what I'm feeling.

He smiles at me, and I melt inside; like I've instantly fallen in love, and he pulls his hand from behind his back and gives me a bowl of Percy Pigs.

"Ma, ladies favourite, we can't forget these," he says in a medieval English accent.

I'm about to burst. I feel so overwhelmed. While I'm carrying so much sadness and anger around with me, I'm now experiencing happiness and love, something I'd forgotten what that felt like, and it's counteracting all the bad feelings, and it feels like a war going on inside of me.

But it's short-lived as Dalton climbs back into bed, and we share a bed picnic.

"Can I ask you a question?" I look over at him, biting into the reddest and most fresh-looking strawberries I've ever seen; they must be from Harrods.

He nods yes to be polite because he's too much of a gentleman to talk with food in his mouth."Will you tell me about the real Dalton?"

He turns and looks at me, and that's when I can see the pain in his eyes.

Chapter Thirty
The Real Me - Dalton

People look at you, and they think you've got it all.

By all, this usually means a flash car, a lovely apartment, an expensive shiny watch, women, cash in the bank, the latest tech—you know, the usual materialistic things.

If people can see what you've got, then they assume you've got it all. But the people on the outside, looking in at the materialistic things, don't seem to understand that those people look back at them, and they know they're the ones who have it all.

They may not have a watch covered in crystals or a car that drives faster than you could ever throttle it to, but they usually have family, and that's priceless. You'd think everyone would have a family because everyone came from somewhere, right?

Wrong.

I envy those people who have a family. Especially the type of family that always has dinner together; everyone gets to talk about their day and what they're doing.

A family that all gets together on summer days and shares BBQs and fun memories, with days at the beach.

A family that pulls crackers and shares turkey at the table with everyone around it they love at Christmas because that's what Christmas is all about: family. A family that picks up the phone and helps you when you're in a crisis or need a check-in moment with someone.

A family that's proud of you when you achieve things and always encourages you to keep aiming for more because they know you can do it. You're unstoppable, they say.

And a family that attends a red carpet event for your latest movie or comes along to the awards shows with you. They're the first people you ring when you get the call and you've landed the part.

Or maybe even a family that's there for you when you finish therapy because of all the trauma you've had to deal with, and they're there to support you as you get your mental health back into a better place, because they want you to be the best version of yourself.

Or maybe, even a birthday card every once in a while, or a text message to see how you are, or they come and visit you when you end up in hospital from a stupid accident you had skiing.

One thing I know is that there are some things in life that cannot be bought and family is one of those things.

So what use is having lots of money if you don't have a family to share it with? I used to have a family long ago when I was a child. But it broke. My mother and father realised they didn't love each other anymore. So, instead of doing what's right for me and each other, they strung it out, and the hate grew day by day until it got to the point where they resented each other so much, they couldn't even bear to breathe the same air as one another. They lost respect for each other and became full of hate for each other. It broke them both. They should've separated a long time before, so they could've prevented it from getting to this point.

After my father left and found solace in a new relationship, my mother hit rock bottom. She turned to the bottle because she felt like she'd failed, and she also didn't want to take any responsibility for the breakdown of their relationship. She changed, and she started going to the local bars and clubs; it wasn't uncommon for her to bring the worst types of men back home with her, and they were usually the violent kind, only after one thing. She was trying to fill a void inside of herself with meaningless sex with strangers, which never worked.

I hated my childhood; I felt utterly alone and had no one to talk to about what was happening at home. I just remember feeling scared all the time, scared of the breaking glass, scared of the shouting, scared of the house getting smashed up, scared that they would bring violence into my room.

I was scared I would get hurt, and mostly, I was afraid that my mum was getting hurt and I was too little to protect her.

Once she looked at the bottom of that bottle, there was no turning back. It wasn't uncommon for me to go days without eating. It was important that the little money my mother had was to get alcohol.

During the purchases of the bottles of vodka, she didn't consider that she needed to feed her only child. I don't blame her for this; I know the drink made her make those decisions.

Watching a parent self-destruct in front of your eyes is one of the most challenging and cruellest things a child can have to deal with, because you blame yourself for their behaviour; you think it's your fault that you're not big enough to stop them, you're not strong enough to help them.

You don't have a loud enough voice for them to hear you.

But all the time I spent blaming myself, I never considered that it was my parents' responsibility to look out for me, especially at a young age. When adults have children, they are agreeing to protect, love and nurture the child, and a parent's love for their child should have no expiration date on it.

Eventually, I was removed from my mother's care because it was clear to the authorities that she wasn't looking after me; I was underweight and had bags under my eyes from not sleeping; I was wearing unwashed clothes and wasn't the picture of health, and my father wasn't interested in having anything to do with me, he had moved on with his life, and I wasn't a part of it, so I became a part of the system, and I went into foster homes. Some homes were okay, and some I never want to talk about, so while the other kids were outside playing cops and robbers, being astronauts and putting out fires as firefighters, I was alone in my room making up my characters. Naturally, I would become an actor because I used that as escapism.

Do I speak to my family now? No, I'm estranged from them. They didn't want me before I found fame. Why would I invite them into my life now, knowing they didn't want me before?

My demons are that I come from a background of not feeling loved, and yet here I am, walking around, bubbling over with love that I desperately want to share with someone. Ironically, my career has brought the takers out of the woodwork, and I don't attract the right people. My heart hurts because that's all I want, and the truth is I would give up all my money and this fame for that any day.

I want a real family, a family that's mine. One that loves me as much as I love them. So, when people think I've got it all, that's up to them to believe it because I don't have it all; those people have a real family, and that's something I don't have.

I want the Cinderella story, and I can't wait for the day when she comes along, slides that glass slipper onto my foot, and we can live happily ever after together.

Chapter Thirty One
Lunch Date

As predicted, Dalton and I are all over the newspapers because of our night of sightseeing, and social media has blown up again.

Everyone we had a photo with shared posts about it. It was funny to see one headline that read: **Dalton Rivers and Charity Fletcher sneaking around London together dressed up**.

No doubt Reed will be seething with jealousy over the news coverage.

Dalton has meetings today regarding a new film he's working on later this year. When I woke up, I saw a message from Reed asking if I was free today.

I responded yes, so Reed is meeting me for lunch at one of our favourite sandwich shops, *Everything in Bread*. We've been going there for years, and the name is accurate because there's nothing they won't put in two slices of bread for you. One of the most ordered sandwiches is the crisps sandwich. Some people may find it weird to have cheese & onion crisps inside two slices of bread. But you shouldn't knock it until you've tried it.

I'm on my way to the lunch date, and I've observed that I've been making a lot of effort recently with how I look. I certainly didn't look this well-groomed a few months ago. My nails still look perfectly manicured, my make-up has improved, thanks to discovering YouTube tutorials. My dress sense is much smarter than before. I actually put effort into my dress sense. I look at what matches my outfit, from the jewellery I now wear to the handbag I choose. My savings have taken a significant hit recently with this new version of me, but weirdly, it's made me happier. I never really understood retail therapy until Reed and I broke up, but I get it now; and I don't think there's anything wrong with wanting to treat yourself and pay attention to a new version of yourself that you've become, because if it makes you feel good, then where's the harm in it?

Della keeps nudging me about looking for a new job. She sees the spending I'm doing, especially when someone is knocking on the door every five minutes with my recently purchased items, and the room I'm staying in at Della's is quickly filling up with all my new possessions. I like the new version of myself.

I've discovered a side to me I didn't know even existed because I was never interested in makeovers, fashion, or even waxing. But now I've tasted these things, I want them.

I can see that my time was always consumed by making Reed happy when we were together, and maybe I should've spent a little more time on making myself happy.

I just didn't realise I was missing out. As I arrive at the sandwich shop, I can see Reed isn't here yet, so I enter and find us a table in the corner; it's out of the way and more private.

I sit down, wondering why I chose more privacy. It's not like I need to hide from anyone. But a part of me knows that meeting up with Reed is deceitful towards Dalton, especially given we've taken everything to the next level.

My phone quacks. It's a text from Reed. He's on his way. At that moment, a text from Dalton comes through asking me how my day's going.

I walk up to the counter and order a vanilla latte. I may as well start on the coffee while I'm waiting for Reed.

I head back over to the table. And I sense someone's talking about me. As I turn around and see three of the staff talking to each other, while looking at me and smirking. It appears I can't even go out for coffee without being recognised.

Maybe I am famous.

I text Reed to let him know I've got us the little corner table and that there's no rush; there's plenty of bread still available.

As I take a sip from my coffee, another message pops up from Dalton:

Was that meant for me?

Oh Fucccccccckkkkkkkk!

As I look at the messages, I realise I've accidentally texted Dalton instead of Reed. I panic. How could I be so stupid as not to check that I was messaging Reed first?

I message Dalton back:

Sorry, no, my mistake; how's the meetings going?

Sometimes, you just need a quick deflection to escape a sticky situation. Hopefully, it works. Why am I such an idiot?

Dalton messages back:

Meetings are going well, although I'd rather be doing something with you; what are you up to?

My adrenaline is going wild. How can I message him back and tell him I'm having sandwiches with my ex-partner, but how can I lie to him about where I am? I mean, we're not exclusive or anything. We've just spent some time together and maybe some adult time together, but why do I feel like I'm doing something wrong to him?

Fuck!

I can't text him back and say I'm with my ex; who messages someone they spent the night with that?!?

So instead, I message back:

Just meeting up with someone for a sandwich.

I frantically await his response. I don't think he's going to leave it without knowing who it is, and as predicted, he messages back:

Who is someone?

He puts a laughing face at the end, but I know this is because we're both dancing around trying to get an answer about who I'm meeting up with, and I'm not helping as I'm being secretive about it. Reed walks through the door at the moment I figure out what to reply. He rushes across to the table and apologises for being late. He bends down to kiss me on my cheek, and I pull back in surprise. So he awkwardly looks at my coffee and asks if he can get me another one. I oblige.

I message Dalton back:

Can I see you tonight, and I will explain everything? It may be better than texting.

My message has been read, but the bubbles aren't going. He isn't responding. Have I just offended him? What does my message come across as? I'm now going to overthink everything.

And the worst part about this all is, Dalton has left me on read…

Chapter Thirty-Two
Wasted Sandwich

I'm not sure why I bothered having a sandwich with Reed today. I hoped to get closure, but it was the Reed show instead.

Everything was about him as usual: the prospect of a job promotion on the horizon and how life was going for him. He only asked about me when he wanted to know about Dalton and whether I'd seen anything of him lately. I relished responding yes and even dropped several hints that Dalton and I were closer than he'd realised.

It was brushed aside, though, as Reed only hears information about himself. So, despite my many hints, he didn't seem to get any of them.

Something I realised today was how irritated I felt watching Reed eat.

I sat wondering how I'd never noticed how much of an annoying eater he was until now. He doesn't close his mouth when eating and then he talks with his mouth full of food. I wondered how I had never noticed this trait in him before. It put me off from eating my sandwich, so I filled myself up with coffee instead.

On top of this, the Reed show is grating on me; I've never realised how self-obsessed this man is in himself. All he did was talk about himself; it was all me, me, me, me. When I left, he went to kiss me on my cheek, but I didn't realise because he moved in so quickly, and as I turned my head, he ended up kissing me on my mouth. It took me aback. I wasn't expecting it, and I'm not sure how to feel about it; it's been months since I felt Reed's lips touch mine, and despite his lips being all I knew for nine years, today when they met mine, our lips felt like strangers.

I immediately turned a bright shade of scarlet over this mishap.

I left exhausted, my head spinning about everything to do with him. It felt like I'd been overloaded with information my brain didn't want to keep. The most poignant part was that his life seemed on the up, and it's more significant now without me. I also feel guilty that I'm meeting Dalton later, and he does not know that Reed put his lips on mine today.

As I head back to Della's, Dalton finally replies to me:

I will pick you up at 8 pm.

I feel nervous reading that he's picking me up later because I will have to tell him I met up with Reed today and I hope he understands why.

Chapter Thirty-Three
Sunset

I feel like I'm going on a first date; I'm a bundle of nerves tonight.

Part of me knows meeting up with Reed is weird, given the circumstances and because of the time I'm spending with Dalton, so I know the conversation with Dalton tonight will be tricky.

My phone quacks, and it's Dalton letting me know he's outside in the car.

Della's out at yoga. I could've really used some advice from her on the conversation that's heading my way, but then that would mean admitting to her I've been in contact with Reed, and I know I'll get a lecture from her about it all, so I'll have to go without my best friend's advice tonight.

I leave the flat, and the first thing I see is Dalton standing by the car door.

He's such a gentleman. I'm not used to being treated this way, and every time he does something small, like pulling out my chair or opening the car door, it makes me like him even more for the way he treats me and his manners.

"Hello beautiful," he smiles, and instantly my stomach faints into my feet.

"Hello you," I respond, and we both stand smiling at each other. He kisses me gently on my cheek.

"How would you feel about a sunset and a glass of wine?"

"That sounds perfect." I want to add a problematic conversation to the plans, but I refrain from making the remark. After a glass of wine, I'm sure I'll get my words out better.

I've practiced what I want to say to him, and hopefully he'll understand why I'm having a lunch date with my ex-partner.

Dalton tucks a strand of hair behind my ear and his touch wakes up the woodpecker inside of me.

He whispers "Shall we?" into my ear and I melt inside.

We drive to an area outside of London, and while on the ride there, Dalton and I share small talk about our day, with me omitting the part about the sandwich date.

Dalton tells me about his meeting with the film production company and how his next role is playing an action hero, and it's going to be filmed in London, so this would give him plenty of time in the city.

While he shared his news, I could feel him analysing my face to see whether I was pleased with the news that he would be close to me for several months.

I obviously would be and I couldn't hide my face lighting up at this news even if I tried. I'm so happy to hear the news, but also riddled with worry over the conversation about Reed. The car pulls up, and Dalton gets out and right on queue; he opens my door for me. It shows the type of man he is when his driver is paid to

249

open the doors for him, but he refuses to accept this and does it himself; he's very humble and not what you would expect of one of the most famous people in the world, because he isn't egotistical at all when it would be very easy for him to give in to it all and be an asshole.

He grabs a wicker hamper from the boot of the car and holds out his hand, which I happily take.

Then, he leads me to the perfect spot for a sunset and some wine together.

Chapter Thirty-Four
Wow

Dalton and I get seated on a lovely soft blanket with the beautiful sun displayed in front of our eyes.

He pours us both a glass of wine and, as usual, there are plenty of nibbles for us to eat, which are scattered all over the blanket.

I take a sip of my wine and feel I need to talk with him because it's eating away at me.

I know the sooner I speak to him, the quicker I can get rid of all the stress and anxiety that has built up inside of me.

"I met up with Reed at the sandwich place I went to today."

I look at him to see if he seems disappointed in me.

"Reed? Oh," he sips his wine and then asks, "How did it go?"

I can't hold it in any longer, and an explosion of words shoots out of me.

"It was quite terrible, actually. You see, I've been trying to get some closure from Reed since the break-up on why he did what he did to me and why he felt I deserved to be treated that way, but he dances around the conversation and somehow always avoids answering me, and then talks about himself, to be honest, I felt deflated today meeting up with him again, and I'm not sure why I'm bothering."

Dalton looks at me, "Again?"

"Sorry, I don't understand."

He now looks at me without blinking.

"You said again, how many times have you met up with him?"

"Oh, a couple of times, he messaged me after the comic con and asked if I wanted coffee, but that conversation ended up being all about me meeting you and me exposing myself and how it had gone viral and again, he never seems to want to answer me about our relationship."

"Can I ask you a serious question, Charity?"

Oh no, what is he going to ask me? I nod yes.

"Do you want to get back with him?"

The silence between us is deafening. I fiddle with my shoelace because I haven't thought about this recently.

"It's complicated. He was my home. He was all I knew for years."

Dalton puts his hand gently on my chin and lifts my head up so our eyes meet.

"Be honest with me. Do you still love him? If he asked you to get back with him tonight, would you?"

I look over Dalton's shoulder, and I can see the sun is setting.

Without even thinking about my response, my mouth runs wild as usual.

"No, I wouldn't get back with him; I wanted to. After we broke up, that's all I wanted. I wanted him to beg for me to get back with him; I had a makeover to make him like me more; I met you to make him jealous; I didn't know life without him; it's like oxygen being taken away from you. You have no life without it, and that's how I felt without him, but…"

"But?"

"But, then I met you, and the way you treat me is something unfamiliar, and the more time I spend with you, the more I like you, and it's not because you're famous or because you're hot because you are hot, but take the money and the fame away, I would still like you the same, because of how you make me feel."

Part of me feels like this whole situation is wrong.

This isn't fair to him and my baggage is for me to deal with. Then, out of nowhere, anger erupts from my stomach and straight out of my mouth.

"I'm sorry, this is wrong; I shouldn't be here with you."

Dalton looks at me, surprised by the anger that's come out of nowhere.

"What's wrong, and why shouldn't you be here?"

"It feels wrong that I'm here with you because a few months ago, I was in love with Reed, and we would sit talking about you and your films, and I used to loathe it. I never told Reed because I knew how much he loved you, but I couldn't bear another conversation about you; I was sick to death of hearing about your films and what you were doing in your life; I wasn't a fan of you then."

253

A smile forms on Dalton's face, which is not my expected expression.

"Why are you smiling?"

"Because Charity, you said you weren't a fan of me then."

"Okay? But isn't that an insult?"

"No, because you used the past tense, which tells me you're a fan of me now," he smirks. We both know he's right; I'm his number one fan now.

"Don't you think this is somehow messed up? Me being here with you?"

"No, why would I think that? Whether or not you loathed me, I'm happy we met; I like you, Charity, a lot."

"But I'm not being fair to you, Dalton; I've used you to make Reed jealous; my actions were selfish, and now I've got to know you and I can see how wrong it is. I always complain about being a pawn in Reed's chess game, and yet here I am treating you the same way, and you don't deserve that."

My eyes well up because the realisation has set in on what I've been doing; I didn't think about the consequences of how my behaviour would ever make Dalton feel because I used him as a pawn as Reed used me.

Dalton moves closer to me and takes my hand; he looks at me profoundly, "Look, Charity, sometimes we all act out of character. I knew you weren't a fan of me initially, which intrigued me; no one usually treats me the way you did, and ironically you stood out because of it. And if you hadn't been that way, you'd have probably been just another fan having a photo with me. I believe everything happens for a reason, including you coming along to seek revenge and make your ex jealous, because here we are today, getting ready to watch the sunset together."

"How are you so positive about things Dalton?"

"Life's too short; we all worry about the small things, and we allow those small things to become big problems, and then we use up so much energy on it, and it isn't worth it; we have limited time in this life, why waste it on small things, focus on making the bigger moments count, when I was younger, all I ever wanted was the small things that people take for granted, it gave me a different perception on life I guess."

"What were the small things you wanted?" I hope he tells me because his perspective on life is beautiful, and I could learn from him.

"I wanted a safe home, somewhere I knew no harm could come to me, where it could be as loud or as quiet as I wanted it to be, somewhere that no one could move me from and pass me to the next place. I appreciate having warm clothes and food in my stomach and access to medical care if needed. The simple things that people are just used to having, along with anything else I have in my life on top of this, are bonuses. Having money is a luxury; it allows me to travel the world, which is a dream for some people. I can go out and buy any car I want and buy an apartment with the click of my fingers, but all of it is materialistic; I want what money can't buy."

"What do you want, Dalton?" I'm so enthralled by this man.

I hope whatever he wants is something I can give him.

I sit, hoping and praying, while waiting for his response.

"This right here. I'm sitting here with you, this beautiful woman, and we're having a heart-to-heart; she's being open and honest with me, and I appreciate how hard it can be to be so honest, but I love honestly from people. There are too many people in the world who are dishonest, so when you find people who can speak the truth, even if they know it may hurt the person hearing it, that's a quality I love in people because having morals like that is something money can't buy."

"Can I ask you a question?" now seems like the right time to get an answer to a question I'm curious about.

"Sure."

"Why do you use the wolf emoji when texting? I kept meaning to ask you, but I kept forgetting, but it's come to my mind again."

He smiles at me as though he's been waiting for me to ask him. "Do you know about the wolf, Charity?"

"Not really," I say, feeling a little uneducated and wishing I knew more about wolves right now.

"Well, they're loyal; they only have one partner in their lifetime, to which they're always faithful, and they would do anything to protect their family and loved ones, even if that means sacrificing themselves. They live in tough environments, but they survive. They also only take what they need in life; they're not like humans who always want more and they also understand how important rest is; humans don't. Sometimes we forget to preserve our energy, and it can be wasted on those small things I was telling you about before, and we end up running ourselves into the ground. But a wolf knows how important it is to keep their strength."

I look at him, and I understand the way he is and why he's the way he is, and it makes me feel like I have a deeper connection with him. "You're a wolf, Dalton."

He smiles at me. "Yes, I'm a wolf, or I at least share their morals, Charity."

"I wonder what I am? I mean, if you're a wolf, what am I?"

Dalton looks at me with his beautiful elixir green eyes, eyes that have the power to make people do anything he asks of them. He picks his wine glass up and instead of drinking from it; he swirls the wine around the glass, thinking and then he looks at me and smiles.

"Everything that's yellow."

"Everything that's yellow?"

"Yeah, you're everything that's yellow. You're the worker bee who's loyal and protects the hive at all costs, never betraying it. You're the tall standing sunflower in the garden. You think everyone wants a rose in their life, but they don't. Yes, roses are nice to look at, but don't forget they have thorns. Sunflowers always bring a sunny disposition, day in and day out. I mean, when do you ever see a sad-looking sunflower? You're that little rubber duck bobbing along in a bubble bath, not really sure where they're going or what they're doing, and that's okay. You're a bright yellow dandelion, a flower that some people see as a weed, but other people see as a wish. You're a beautiful singing Canary bird. You're like the sun, Charity, you bring a warmth to the world. So, yeah, you're everything that's yellow."

If there's going to be a point where I fall in love with this man, I think it's probably this moment, right here, right now.

Dalton takes a drink of wine, looking through me as he tilts the glass up for the liquid to slide down his throat, and it feels like his eyes see deep into my soul. He puts the glass down, raises his hand up to my chin and tilts it, so his lips can meet mine, and we kiss. It's a kiss full of passion, and despite us missing out on the sun setting, I never want this kiss to end.

But the kiss is only the beginning as our hands touch each other, and the heat between us ramps up. Dalton strokes his hand through my hair, and gently tugs on it, and lightning bolts shoot through me. I take off his shirt, and then he slowly unbuttons my top.

Within seconds, our clothes become thrown on the grass beside us, and within a minute, we are making love. I don't care that my toes are dipped inside a tub of olives or that we came here to watch the sunset, and that we're now missing it; or that I think I'm laid on a pile of sausage rolls and there may be some Percy Pigs stuck to the back of my hair. I'm just glad to be here, making love to a man who's woodpecker approved.

This is certainly not how I expected this conversation to go, and suddenly, all the stress and anxiety I'd built up inside of me gets released in a way I least expect, but very much enjoyed.

Chapter Thirty-Five
Turning Point

While I was frantically worried about how to approach the fact I'd met up with Reed to Dalton, something I didn't consider was that he might understand.

We spent a long time last night talking about the breakup, and Dalton told me he understands why I'm looking for closure; he said it's only natural to want to close the chapter to write a new one for myself.

He gave me advice on Reed, though, and said he wouldn't ever be forthcoming with admitting he was in the wrong, so if that's what I'm waiting for, I'll be waiting for a lifetime.

My biggest problem with everything is that I feel I'm owed an explanation, even if I'm acting like a dog with a bone over it all.

But why shouldn't I have an answer?

I need to know if I did something wrong and how I can write my next chapter if I don't know what I did because I may make the same mistakes again.

I was shocked that I told Dalton that I didn't want Reed back because it's true.

I wanted him back before, but now seeing how he's treated me with the breakup and the cheating, I'm now seeing a different side to him, one that's not so attractive or appealing to me.

I can't believe I've turned a corner on how I feel about him; I thought I'd pine for him for the rest of my life, if I'm honest.

I look at how disastrous my life has become since the breakup, and I know it wouldn't have become this way if we'd still been together, but the chain of events that has stemmed from the breakup all began with Reed and his actions.

When I've met up with him, he doesn't seem to care about me or what he's done to me; there is no remorse for me, but thankfully, meeting Dalton has helped me begin the healing process for the end of this relationship. Some people would say Dalton is a rebound, and I've thought about it myself occasionally, but there's more to him than him being labelled as a rebound.

He listens to me, and he's opened my eyes to how little attention I've given myself over the past few years. He's got me thinking about my dreams, which I had forgotten about while I was so wrapped up in the love bubble that was Reed.

I can't recall the last time I'd thought about turning a dream into a reality and becoming an author of children's books, but something has sparked inside of me, and I think it's the belief that I can do it, which came from Dalton telling me I could.

He's made me feel like a woman again; he's gentle and kind, attentive and loving, he's interesting and fun, and not to mention he's incredibly hot! I feel 100% myself when I'm around him like I don't have to pretend to be someone I'm not; I'm just comfortable, and if I'm not comfortable, he sees that, and he somehow makes me feel relaxed.

There is so much more to him as a person than the actor people watch on the giant cinema screen.

I'm still shocked he even has the time of day for me because this is what fairytales are made of. I've never asked him why he keeps wanting more dates and to spend more time with me because I thought it might not be rude to approach it, but I think the next time we meet up, I might just ask the question.

I'm sure there are millions of women he could call up who would give their kidney to spend an evening with him, and instead, he's meeting up with me, an obsessed, broken-hearted woman who, by day, is having sandwiches with her ex and, by night is watching the sunset with him.

If someone had told me a few months ago that this is how my life would be, I would've thought they were crazy because it's so unrealistic. I wake up most days and can't believe how much my life has changed, and the strangest thing is that I've changed, too, which is something I don't think anyone saw coming.

Chapter Thirty-Six
Morning Text

Weirdly, I awoke to a message from Reed this morning asking if I'd like to meet as he wants to give me my favourite mug back.

I find this strange, considering he's had months to provide me with my things that are still currently in my old home, so I'm not sure why now, all of a sudden, it's become critical to him to drip-feed me my missing items back.

He's been messaging me a lot recently, and although this is something I wanted, he's becoming annoying because I'm ready to move on.

Still, his getting back in touch with his text messages and offering a coffee or a meet-up seems to be slowing down my grieving process, and I can't close this chapter off while I'm still in touch with him.

I messaged Dalton as I wanted to be transparent with him, and he agreed as it's my favourite mug, the meet-up would be worth it to get it back.

He offered to buy me many new mugs if I did not meet Reed. I love how he can see the humour in everything, even a situation like this, where a broken-hearted woman has to meet up with her ex-partner to get her mug back because she's finding it even harder to let go of the mug now than her ex-partner.

Della is currently knitting in the front room as I enter to make a coffee.

"Hey you, how did last night go?" she looks up at me with eyes that say give me every detail.

I grab a cup from the cupboard and switch the kettle on.

"Oh, it was great. We had a picnic," I give her a wry smile, and she knows immediately that there's more to the picnic than the nibbles of fruit and breadsticks. I feel giddy putting a spoonful of coffee into the cup as I relive last night's passion with Dalton.

"Charity Fletcher, you dark horse, I never realised you had it in you and I love this new version of you. What's your plans for today?"

I slowly stir the coffee in the cup while I put on my lying voice.

"Nothing much; I'm going to pop out and grab a couple of bits and then meet up with Dalton tonight; what about you?"

"I'm going to finish knitting these little booties; they're for Joan downstairs, her daughters expecting in the next month, and then I'm going to go for a swim; you could come along if you fancy it."

I feel guilty as I realise I've spent little time with Della recently, but today I need to meet Reed and then meet up with Dalton. "I'd love to, but maybe another time. Do you fancy a movie night tomorrow or a night of Netflix documentaries?"

Della smiles. I know she's missed us spending time together. "I'd love that, when you're out grabbing a few bits, maybe grab some popcorn and snacks, we could watch a proper marathon of 90s films and you can give me every detail about what happened at your picnic last night; what do you think?"

"Yes, of course. That sounds great. I can't wait."

I take a large gulp of coffee, ashamed I've just lied to my best friend.

Chapter Thirty-Seven
Favourite Mug

I'm walking to *Moo Shakes*.

This used to be a place Reed and I used to frequent, mainly because it has my favourite milkshake, the Dimeamite, which is milk, ice cream and several Dime chocolate bars crushed into it, then it's topped with a mountain of squirty cream, and then finished off with another Dime bar sticking out of the top.

It's filthy.

Delicious on the lips and an enemy of your hips.

Weirdly, he suggested meeting up here; we seem to always meet in our favourite places, which I find hard as it's almost like stepping back in time in your life, only your life is no longer how it used to be; it somehow feels like watching someone else's life play out.

I see Reed is already in the shop as I get to the door. He's sitting with a milkshake, tucking in to it. He obviously couldn't wait for me, which is a little impolite.

If it were Dalton I was meeting, he would've waited because he had manners. I walk in, and Reed waves me over, saying hello, although he still doesn't get up because he's too invested in his milkshake.

Next to him on the table is my favourite mug.

"Hey, I see you started without me," I try not to sound annoyed by his lack of manners.

"Yeah, it's good, try it. This one's full of chunks of Mars bar and it's out of this world."

He continues slurping his milkshake, which grates me because, again, I never realised how rude Reed is; and at this moment, part of me wishes he got a chunk of Mars bar stuck in his throat so I can sit back watching him choke while indulging in my Dimeamite milkshake. I realise this is quite menacing, so I shake off the thought.

Reed pushes his nearly finished milkshake to one side and slides my mug across the table with a smug look.

"I knew you'd be missing it, so I thought it was time you had it back where it belongs, well that and Bea thinks it's tacky."

He has this grin on his face that I really want to punch off and it feels like this is all a game to him.

"Thanks, I was missing it, but why now?"

"Huh?"

"Why are you giving it to me now? You've had months to give it back to me? What made you decide to hand it to me now?"

I lean back in my chair and realise that my arms are crossed and my tone is one of annoyance. Defence mode activated.

"I just saw it in the cupboard, and I thought you might like it back. How are things going with you and Dalton? I hear rumours that you two have been spotted together occasionally." The words coming from his mouth make my blood boil, and the way he said Dalton so casually, as

267

though they're friends, and before I can even stop myself, my mouth runs away with itself.

"It's going great; he's a lovely man with manners, kindness, humour, intelligence, he's caring, and attractive. I mean, what's not to like about him?"

Reed looks taken aback; he picks up his milkshake and drains the last part, making an annoying slurping sound while keeping his eyes fixed on me.

"Well, you have me to thank for that then, eh?"

"I'm sorry, could you repeat that? What exactly do I have to thank you for?"

The blood is rushing to my head, and my anger has built to a point where I'm about to erupt."Well Charity, if we were still together, you and he wouldn't be anything really, so you're welcome. Does this mean I will get free tickets to his films now? What with me giving him my ex partner an all."

I want to take my favourite mug and clock him around the head with it, but I certainly do not need another criminal charge on my record. And this is not me; I'm not a violent person, but there's something about Reed at this moment that makes me want to dip my toe in being a violent person.

"Are you jealous, Reed?"

I scan his face to see if he can show emotion. It appears not as he laughs, but it looks forced.

"The only part of me that would ever be jealous would be the part where I would get to spend time with the legend that is Dalton Rivers; apart from that, he's welcome to you."

"You're a fucking piece of work, Reed; in fact, that's too much of a compliment to give you. You're a narcissist who spends every minute of every day in love with himself. Dalton is worth so much more than someone like you."

"Oh, calm down, Charity, you're talking as though you know the man," he sniggers.

"I do. We've spent enough time together to get to know each other, and he's a decent man; considering the upbringing he had been passed from foster home to foster home and having to manage his mother being an alcoholic, I think he's turned out amazingly, what's your excuse for being a pathetic excuse for a man?"

It's in this moment that all I can see is red...

What follows is a heated exchange of words between Reed and me, where I defend Dalton to the ends of the earth, and Reed pushes every one of my buttons.

A worker in the milkshake shop comes over to the table and calmly tries to intervene in our heated argument. "Erm, sorry to interrupt, but could you take this outside?" The young man looks about twelve years old and also looks worried about having to challenge us both.

I look around the shop and observe everyone else's faces, looking at us in shock. Who goes to a milkshake shop to air their dirty laundry?

I feel embarrassed.

"I'm sorry." I look up at the worker. "I'm just leaving."

I get up from the table and walk towards the door, but I'm stopped in my tracks. I turn back around and go back to the table and snatch my mug off it.

"You're an awful person, Reed, and I'm glad we're no longer together."

And with that, I leave the milkshake shop, with everyone's eyes boring into me

I walk home, angry and frustrated with Reed's words; they cut through me like a knife; who does he think he is?

I look at my favourite mug. I've always thought this mug is pretty, with all the little ladybirds scattered across it. They say ladybirds are a sign for good fortune, and I've always loved ladybirds, because my mum used to paint them all the time. She loved them too. This was something we both shared, our love for these little insects.

I think of all the times I would wake up first thing in the morning and start my day by filling this mug to the brim with hot coffee.

In times of crisis, this mug would be full of tea, and I would sit cupping it to keep my hands warm in the winter with soup inside of it. I love this mug.

But then I look at it again and I don't see it the same way. This mug is a part of my life that I no longer have; this mug is something from when I was the Charity before the Charity I am now. She was weaker than me and delusional in a relationship that wasn't real; she was naïve and used by the man she thought loved her. She took no time for herself and forgot what it was like to have fun;

she was a well-behaved and submissive partner, and she is not the person I am today.

This mug isn't my favourite mug; it's all the things I thought I loved about my life before.

As I continue walking down the road, I see a rubbish bin and I throw the mug into it.

I don't want this mug anymore, and I don't want anything to do with the life I used to have.

I continue walking home, grieving the mug I just threw away

Chapter Thirty-Eight
Time Out

I was going to meet Dalton this evening, but I feel mentally drained after my run-in with Reed.

I decide to take some time out and get an early night. It's been a roller coaster lately, and I need to stop and breathe.

Della is out swimming, and so I take some time to think about everything: Reed Dalton, the fact I'm unemployed, the criminal charges.

I'm feeling optimistic that Reed has shown this side to me because, frankly, it's not what I want in a man, so I'm moving away from him; no more meeting up for coffees and no more morning text messages. I need to sever him out of my life completely.

I also need to sit down and apologise to Della. She deserves to know exactly what's been going on. I haven't been as truthful with her as I should've been, so I'll explain everything to her tomorrow and prepare myself for the 'I told you so' speech and then a lecture about meeting up with Reed.

And then there's Dalton. He deserves more than how I'm currently treating him.

He was so understanding over my meeting up with Reed, and from where I'm standing, everything he does is for my benefit; his actions show me he cares about me, and it's about time I started showing him the same kindness and respect that he's given me. I need to tell him about my run-in with Reed because I may have said some things I didn't mean to, so I need to be honest about this because I know how Dalton feels about people sharing his personal life.

I know I shouldn't have said what I did to Reed about Daltons' childhood, but I was so angry, and I know this isn't an excuse because I feel awful that I gave any information to that idiot. He didn't deserve to know anything about Dalton.

I know what I want now…

I want Reed out of my life, and I want Dalton in it.

Chapter Thirty-Nine
Extra, Extra, Read All About It

I wake up feeling completely refreshed from a great night's sleep, and I feel full of the joys of spring, as they say, and ready to take on the day where I make amends with everyone.

Today is going to be a beautiful day.

I have plans to see Dalton later; he messaged me late last night and invited me to visit the Zoo with him after hours together. It's a private tour, which is very exciting, and it will also give me time to explain everything to him and apologise for my recent behaviour, not to mention how excited I will be at getting to see a giraffe.

Every day that I spend more time with him, I feel closer to him, and I love being around him because he's so good for my soul. I also know that the more time I spend with him, the quicker I'm getting Reed out of my system, and it's helping me heal my heart. I didn't fall into Dalton's arms; my feelings towards him grew the more I got to know him, and I've realised recently just how much he means to me.

It's strange to think of a time when someone wasn't even a part of your life; you didn't even know them; they were just a stranger to you, and then out of nowhere, they suddenly became so important to you overnight and you could never imagine your life without them in it

"Charityyyyyyyy!" Della shouts, interrupting my happy thoughts about Dalton Rivers and the zoo later.

It sounds urgent, so I jump out of bed, quickly flip on my dressing gown, and I head to the living room to see what the disaster is.

Della stands open-mouthed and points to the newspaper on the table. She still has the daily newspaper delivered as she uses the paper afterwards when she's painting.

As I get closer to the table, I can already see the big picture of Dalton spread across the front page, and as I stand looking down, the headline reads.

From Pauper to Prince

The story of an abused child who rose to stardom.

Before I can even read the story, I run back to my bedroom and grab my phone. I see missed calls from Dalton, and as I open my inbox, his first message reads:

How could you, Charity?

Followed by more messages, and I can sense he's mad at me.

I told you that in confidence it wasn't to be shared with the media!

I honestly didn't think you would be that way

I thought I could trust you

This is why I have trust issues

I was the fool who fell for it again

We won't be meeting today, which is a shame as I was looking forward to the zoo

275

We won't be meeting anytime soon

I wish you the best with your future; I'm sure you had your reasons.

My instant thought is how devastated Dalton must be feeling. I can understand why he's so mad at me.

My second thought is I may well add murder to my criminal record when I get my hands on Reed, because where else would that story have come from!!

I've messed up……big time

I go into my texts and message Reed

HOW COULD YOU DO THAT?!??!?!

I KNOW IT WAS YOU THAT SOLD THAT STORY

As I'm frantically typing a significant speech about the person he is, I see the bubbles going, and I think to myself I'd like to see how he's going to explain this one.

I stop typing, awaiting his explanation for how he could betray me again, although this is all my fault because of me and my big mouth; my adrenaline is going ten to a dozen. I feel like a volcano ready to erupt. I'm so angry.

Reed's text comes through, and it's the laughing emoji; three of them

Followed by:

It's a good story, and I got a good price for it

Followed by a wink face

I throw my phone on the bed to prevent myself from throwing it at the wall, and I scream into my pillow

Fuccccckkkkkkkkkkkkkkkk!

I spend long enough with my face stuffed into my pillow to know that any longer, and I'm probably going to suffocate myself, and even I'm not getting off the hook that easily.

I feel my face, and it's soaking from the tears falling from my eyes; they happened so suddenly that I didn't even realise I was crying.

I get off the bed and walk back into the living room. I sit at the table while Della stands with her coffee in the kitchen, saying nothing, and I read.

I'm furious, furious Reed would do this, furious poor Dalton is all over the front page with such a personal story about his life that he hasn't shared with the media, and the worst part is, after reading the story three-quarters of it sounds made up, it contains stuff I didn't say to Reed, so he's just made most of it up, which I'm sure is illegal.

"Do you want to talk about it?" Della has suddenly moved to stand behind me.

"It's all my fault."

"How is this your fault, Charity? Did you sell this story?"

"I might as well have. I told Reed some personal stuff about Dalton, and most of this story is absolute nonsense, but some of it's true, and it was personal stuff he'd told me."

"Why would you do that, and why are you even talking to Reed, anyway?" her tone has now changed towards me; she's annoyed with me.

277

"I didn't mean to; it just slipped out when I was arguing with him in *mooshakes,* and when I realised I shouldn't be saying anything, it was too late; his stupid brain had captured it all anyway, like a bloody personal dictaphone."

I swipe the newspaper off the table, and it scatters all over the floor.

"Why on earth are you were you having milkshakes with Reed? He's a creep."

Della gets the brunt of my anger. "I know we're best friends, Della, but since when was it up to you whether I have a milkshake with my ex-partner or not? God, you can be so interfering? Have you considered this is why I didn't tell you in the first place?"

"No, you didn't tell me because you know I would've talked some bloody sense into you; it's been months since you broke up; get over it!!!!"

And like every argument, unless one of you walks away, it just gets more and more heated, and you both end up saying things you don't mean, but neither of you can see clearly because of the red mist in front of you.

"Get over it? How can you say that to me? You know I love Reed, and I've been trying to fix myself. Don't you think if I could click my fingers and have all of his go away, I'd click them? Do you think it's just so simple to just…..GET….OVER….IT?" Della slams her coffee cup on the kitchen counter, and I know I'm about to get some home truths because she rarely gets mad enough to slam anything down.

"From where I'm standing, Charity, you're holding on to something that isn't real. Your relationship with Reed was a lie because he was cheating on you, and there's no question he's probably been doing it since you both got together. I've never liked him; he's always come across as an arrogant mummy's boy who only has room to love himself. You've lost your job because of him, you've lost your home because of him, you've got a criminal record now because of him, you had the chance to find real love in the arms of the most wanted man on the planet, and you've now lost that because of him. He's got away with it all, scot-free because you haven't even challenged him about how he's treated you and what do you do? You run to have coffees with him. I never took you for stupid Charity; I really didn't. Who even are you, Charity? When are you planning on waking the FUCK UP?"

I want to respond to her, but even I no longer know who I am. Her words cut through me, mainly because everything she said was true. I have no response to throw back at her because she's right, so I stay silent.

I sit silent and still, I don't move from the chair for hours.

I sit there, replaying everything repeatedly in my mind.

Reed, BOOB, Dalton, everything.

What have I done…

Chapter Forty
Running Away

Thanks to the wonderful creation of smartphones, this morning's news was a photo of Reed and I arguing in the milkshake shop, where I've been accused of being aggressive to the person who worked there.

Considering it happened two days ago, that's old news and untrue, but the media printed it, anyway. They had a great run with Dalton's story yesterday. It was everywhere, and I imagine he's been hounded non-stop.

I've taken a strong dislike towards the media recently; where have the days gone when it was about real news?

Now, it's all about everyone's lives, and it feels like living under a microscope; I can't even leave my house without someone getting a photo of me and creating some ridiculous story.

My least favourite photo I've seen online was where I popped into the shop. I sneezed, and someone got a picture of it and put a headline underneath, suggesting I was angry and aggressive towards them, all lies and wholly fabricated;

I didn't even see the person who took the photo, let alone speak to them.

I'm starting to hate camera phones and the people that use them. I need a break, so I'm sitting on a train because what does everyone do in times of crisis?

They run away, which is precisely what I'm doing.

I'm going back home to see my sister because I need someone who won't judge me when I'm already judging myself.

The train manager announces the train is delayed because of a fault with a signal, so we will wait here until that's resolved, which I think couldn't have been any more perfectly timed when all I want is to not be in London right now.

Even the universe is stopping me from leaving by breaking a signal.

The carriage I'm in is quiet; I look across and see a couple who don't have any issues with public displays of affection; they seriously need to get a room. No one needs to see their tongues in that way.

I recall the times Reed and I used to be like that, the honeymoon stage, where you feel you're walking on air and forget how to keep your hands to yourself. I watch them, and the man looks at his partner with such admiration that his eyes say, "You're so beautiful" to her. He gently strokes her face, and she's glowing from the love he gives her.

I'm becoming fixated on watching this couple, and I recall how this love can quickly turn into a heart that hurts.

I think about how happy I was once upon a time. I felt loved; but was it real love? I doubt that, although the love I felt towards Reed was true. I wasn't faking how I felt towards him; although now that love has turned to hate. I despise him for what he's done to me and Dalton.

Dalton, I try not to let my head be filled with him, but I find it hard to think of anything else. Why was I such an idiot?

I messed everything up with him.

He hasn't spoken to me since the morning he texted me and wished me a promising future, which was still a nice thing to say, especially after a news story had just come out about him, all thanks to me and my big mouth.

Even in bad times, he can still be nice.

I didn't deserve to get to know him; I realise this now.

But, he helped me, and for this, I will always be thankful to him; he helped me heal from Reed, and he's also helped me in other ways, like seeing how someone can treat you, and how different he was to Reed, all in a good way. I wish I could thank him for helping me, but I won't get that opportunity and I don't deserve it.

Della has stayed angry with me.

I haven't ever really seen her angry with me before, but I'm not surprised by how she's acting; she only wants the best for me, and I did not take her advice; I was deceitful to even her about everything, sneaking about behind her back and meeting up with Reed, and also not telling her about further encounters I had with the police. My running away today is down to a massive blowout Della and I had last night, where I told her everything, and it was clear she was disappointed in me and my behaviour.

Going to see my sister will allow a bit of time for Della and me to calm down because we've never fallen out like this before, and the saddest part about this situation is the idea of losing her, which is something I couldn't ever come back from. Men are one thing, but best friends are irreplaceable.

I look out the window at the train station, and on any other occasion, I would enjoy people-watching, but now I'm not in the mood. When I look at everyone, I imagine their lives are perfect, and they don't have to deal with the endless mistakes I keep making; I'm such a fool.

The best way to get through this train journey is tanked up on wine, so I get up and head towards the cafe bar, walking by Romeo and Juliet, whose faces are still stuck to one another. I hope I don't have to watch that for the next few hours because I'm trying to get away from disgusting lovey-dovey behaviour. I certainly don't want it forced down my throat.

Chapter Forty-One
Snapped

I get to the cafe bar, and the train manager makes a second announcement, saying the signal should be fixed shortly and then we should be on our way.

I stand at the bar and ask the train host for a white wine and a KitKat; alcohol and sugar should get me through this journey.

As the host gets my order together, Romeo walks up to the bar; he smiles at me and shuffles through the small space we have at the bar, to stand behind me.

As I'm getting my card out of my wallet, I suddenly feel a hand on my buttock. I quickly turn around and see Romeo standing there with a massive grin on his face.

"Excuse me, what are you doing?"

Adrenaline is shooting through me as I demand an answer from him.

"You're the woman who flashed, aren't you? Nice love heart," he licks his lips, ignoring my question.

He has an arrogant look on his face as though he has every right to touch me because he thinks he's god's gift to women, like another man I know very well.

"That's £4.80, please," the host interrupts.

I turn back around, flustered that I'm in this situation. I go to tap my card on the card reader, and I feel the jerk touch my buttock again, and that anger that keeps sitting in the pit of my stomach erupts.

Before I even have time to speak with myself, I take a deep breath, drop my card on the bar, and turn around, swinging in his direction.

I hit him in the face with all the anger that has been building up inside of me, from everything that happened with Reed, Dalton, and Della, and the heartbreak, and losing my home and losing my job and losing myself somewhat.

The force of my fist hitting his face was something I never thought I would see in my lifetime.

I watch my hand hit his face, and then I watch his body hit the floor, slumping down the side of the cafe bar.

I look up, and I see the host shocked. He picks up the train phone; most likely to call the train manager to report the assault they've just witnessed.

I pick my card back up, tap it on the reader, wait for the beep that tells me 'you've paid' and then I pick up my wine and KitKat and head back towards my seat.

I await the train manager's third announcement; I don't envy them, having to apologise for a new reason everyone's going to be delayed.

I'm sure the police will be here in no time, but before then, I'm going to enjoy this wine and chocolate, that's for certain.

Chapter Forty-Two
Finding Out Who Charity Is

Sometimes, you have to take a step back. You have to remove yourself from the eye of the storm because you won't see the destruction being caused until you step back and take a look from the outside.

I've messed up big time; I know this, and I firmly believe that you reap what you sow.

Dalton wants nothing to do with me, and I must accept this.

I would be lying if I said that was easy; it isn't. It's hard because I'm now grieving for him and losing my relationship with Reed, but Reed has sown his seeds, and his behaviour has shown me the man he really is. A man I don't respect.

I've had to learn the hard way.

I've had to mess up myself to realise how devastating people's actions and words can be towards someone's life, and I'm no longer pining for the day that Reed comes back to me because that is not what I want anymore.

I've deleted him on all the social media channels I use and I've taken a break from them, so currently, all of my accounts are not in use, and when I go back on, they will at least be Reed-free.

It was too easy to look in on his life, and it became an obsession, and I realised how toxic it was. How can I move on with my life when I'm constantly watching my old life?

I've stopped location sharing with him, so I can no longer see what he's doing or where he's going, and I've blocked his number to prevent any contact with him, not that he would message me.

Still, it's more to stop me from messaging him, and not in a desperate please come back to me way; angrily way, where I want to tell him how much I've learned to loathe him through learning who he is.

Watching his social media posts and having access to his location was a waste of my time and unhealthy, and I realised after the first day of not using social media how less stressed I feel about everything.

I no longer have those angry red notifications popping up on my phone or the random unwanted messages from people asking about Dalton Rivers, and I see now how much more time I have from no longer being glued to my phone or laptop.

So, now my social media obsession has been dealt with, I may have moved my obsession elsewhere, as I have been re-watching Dalton's films.

It's so weird because I watch them in a completely different way; now I know the man behind the character. It makes me sad to see him, even if it's on the TV screen, but I also get comfort from it. Because I have so much to thank him for; as he helped me in ways, I never knew he could.

He helped me to see that not everyone out there is looking to cheat and betray their partners. There are good people just looking for love and wanting to settle down.

Unlike Reed, Dalton was so kind and gave me time and attention. I woke up to the realisation that Reed and I were coasting along in a comfortable relationship; where I was naïve and blind, and he was living a double life as a Casanova. That isn't love.

I will always think of the time I spent with Dalton as a crazy period where I had a broken heart and wasn't acting clearly, but I will also look at the time with so much fondness.

I look at him in his films, and I marvel at the man he is, when I think about where he came from and where he's gone, and that's a miracle in itself.

I have discovered I have so much respect for him, and I know I will always be a fan of his films.

And I will always be first in the queue for his films when they're released.

I will always miss him and regret my decisions because I will never know what could've been between us.

But one thing I know is that he deserves to be treated much better than the way I treated him, and I will always feel bad about how he got caught in the middle of mine and Reed's break-up and how it was Dalton who came off the worst from it.

Della and I made up; I had a lot of making up to do towards her because I didn't listen, and I also mistreated her, which is appalling considering she's always there for me, and she, too, did not deserve the way I treated her.

She's been helping me look at what jobs I could do, one that will allow me to contribute towards the bills while I stay with her and one where the company doesn't mind someone with a criminal record.

Surprisingly, there are a few great companies out there that don't judge someone on their past mistakes, but help them shape a different future.

My mother's paintings that my sister sent to the auction house all sold, and we got £30,000 each from the proceeds, which surprised us both because neither of us expected 3 of my mum's paintings to sell for that amount. I'm sad that we no longer have the three paintings, but I'm happy they will be displayed on someone's walls. I know my mum is looking down on us and happy that she's still able to help us both in times of need.

I've cleared my credit cards and given Della some money to help while I'm living with her, and I now have some money saved in my account to tide me over until I find a new job.

I've done a lot of soul-searching recently, and I've focused time on what I want out of life.

I've never really put myself first, and talking to Dalton about the children's books I always dreamed of writing inspired me. Especially coming from someone who doesn't fit the profile of one of the kindest and sweetest men on the planet.

He experienced such cruelness as a child, and yet here he is, being kind to everyone he meets, and to have someone with such a success story in life tell me to chase my dream was inspiring. He made me feel like he believed I can do it, even if I don't believe it myself.

Recently, I've found all the old stories I used to write when I was younger and I've started creating plans for them.

I'm working on my first-ever children's book and I'm excited about becoming a writer.

I've been looking at how to self-publish because what's important to me is getting my work out there and sharing those magical stories with children; it's not about becoming a best seller and earning lots of money from it; for me, it's about doing something that I love and proving to myself that I can do it.

Now I've stepped out of the chaos that I was surrounded by, I've had time to focus on myself and do the things I love; remembering how much I used to love cozying up on the sofa and reading, so I bought myself a new throw and some new books, and I've been taking time every day to read.

I've also got my Netflix and chill nights back, although no longer with Reed. I now share this with Della and we both love a good true crime documentary to binge together. I actually look forward to the evening knowing we have an episode to watch with snacks and tubs of Ben & Jerry's that I paid for.

Della has also been teaching me about fashion, and I like it. We recently went to a vintage warehouse and purchased a few cool items from the 1960s and 1970s. I'm now falling in love with particular styles.

Despite everything that's happened, I'm slowly getting back up on my feet and feeling better every day. I can now see aspirations for the future, and I'm learning to be kinder to myself as I think I've been unkind, putting all the blame from Reed onto my shoulders when, in fact, it was he who started this chain of events.

I still have a court date looming over my head and the possibility of a prison stretch, but I've realised that as an adult, you have to face up to mistakes you make because there are always consequences, and if I have to do time, then so be it.

I'm focusing on myself and getting on the right path in life once again. One of the most important things I've learned recently is that sometimes you have to lose a version of yourself in order to find the version of yourself that you're destined to become. I wasn't grieving Reed as much as I realised; I was grieving, losing the life I had, but that life had everything that shaped the older version of me and sometimes you have to let go of the things you think you love in order to find the things you're actually destined to fall in love with.

Chapter Forty-Three
An Unexpected Invite

Whilst popping to the shop for a jar of coffee, the last thing I expected was to bump into my arch-enemy, BOOB.

"Hello Charity."

I have played this situation over many times in my mind, the moment I finally faced BOOB, and it always escalated to violence very quickly. A close representation would be a reenactment from a scene from *Kill Bill*.

Where I'm a martial arts master, and after an exhaustive fight with BOOB, I'd walk away from a smashed up derelict building, covered in head to toe in bruises, scratches, cuts and my blood.

My clothing ripped and patches of my hair missing, while carrying the severed head of my enemy, with BOOB's not so perfect looking blonde hair extensions dragging along the floor smothered in blood.

But now, faced with my enemy, I'm speechless.

There is no fight, no planned battle or even any hateful words to come from my mouth.

Maybe it was because it was a shock bumping into her today, or perhaps it was because I had no fight left in me, or maybe it was because deep down, despite all the violent fight scenes I'd played out in my mind, I was not a violent person. BOOB looks down at the jar of coffee I'm clutching, where my knuckles are snow white, ensuring my hand doesn't take an unexpected swing at my enemy, knocking her off her feet, which is then followed by a lengthy hospital visit.

There, a poor nurse would have to spend a lengthy amount of time delicately picking out the glass shards of the broken *Kenco* coffee jar I embedded in BOOB's face.

"I could do with a coffee. Would you like to grab one, perhaps?"

I'm stunned by the audacity of the woman who stole my man, and is now standing before me, asking if I'd like to grab a coffee with her.

"Sure," I respond.

I know Reed will never be forthcoming with any answers to the questions I have, but maybe BOOB can shed some light on the whole disaster for me instead.

I put the *Kenco* coffee jar back down on the shelf, removing any temptation for me to use this on BOOB, and together we leave the shop.

We find a local Starbucks, and I get my first real insight into the type of woman BOOB is when she orders a Venti, iced latte with coconut milk, no cream, one pump of vanilla, one pump of hazelnut, 0.5 pump of chia, 0.5 pump of nutmeg, a drizzle of caramel sauce, an additional drizzle of caramel sauce around the cup, a dash of soy milk and extra ice.

I feel somewhat intimidated by BOOB's order and completely uneducated on drinks with Starbucks, and sheepishly and quietly, I order a French vanilla latte…in a cup.

We find a table in the corner and sit down opposite one another.

I scan every inch of BOOB, from her hair to her shoes, thinking about how this woman has things I don't possess, hence the reason for Reed's betrayal.

I agree with myself that BOOB looks like a woman who takes care of herself, from her perfectly manicured nails to her perfectly applied makeup. She's wearing a fitted blazer suit, which shows off her figure, and heeled shoes I know I couldn't ever walk in, and I slowly realise that I'm no match for this woman. Going on looks alone, BOOB wins this round.

"I like your shoes," I say, then kick myself mentally, because the first thing I've said to my enemy is a compliment, and this woman does not deserve compliments from me.

"Thanks. They're Kurts."

"Oh, they look like women's shoes." I apologise, feeling stupid. I didn't realise she was wearing some man's shoes. BOOB looks confused at me.

"No, the brand is Kurt Geiger. They're not men's shoes."

"Oh, I knew that," I reply, feeling completely and utterly stupid. Maybe it's the nerves of being sat here with her,

We sit in silence momentarily, and it's broken when the barista shouts our orders. It sounds strange to hear the name Beatrix called, because I've never referred to her as her real name.

Armed with our drinks and no further interruptions scheduled, I decide to take the lead."You could say sorry to me; that would be a good start here."

"What do you want me to say sorry for?" BOOB swirls the ice around her drink, looking dead in my eyes.

"Hmmm, for stealing my man, perhaps?"

BOOB's expression changes suddenly to surprise.

"You can't steal a person; a person strays when they want to; I'm not a witch; I didn't cast a spell on him. He came to me; he was looking for something else, and for that, I can't apologise, because it was his actions and not mine. I was single. I don't need to explain my actions. He, however, does."

I think carefully about how I want to play this situation; I don't want an argument with BOOB in public, but I need some information on what happened between them, so the last thing I want to do is back her into a corner or for it to get heated between us.

"Don't you live by the girl code? Do you even know what the girl code is?"

I pick up my coffee, allowing BOOB the floor to respond.

"I know what the girl code is, but we aren't friends, so I don't feel I have any loyalty to you."

Back to me again. I understand and consider it, but I push it further.

"How about loyalty to women? Does it matter if we're not friends? What if your partner was cheating on you? Wouldn't you want to know? Instead of finding out the way I did on our anniversary night, I thought he was going to propose to me, but I had no clue he was going to dump me."

BOOB stares across the table at me, looking like her brain is processing the information it's just taken in.

"I didn't know it was your anniversary."

And for the first time since sitting at the table together, I see a tiny glimpse of remorse on BOOB's face.

"How's your Venti, Mocha, Latte, iced drink or whatever it is? I've never seen anyone order a coffee with that much detail."

BOOB smiles at me, and I smile back.

What follows are several more coffee orders, where BOOB teaches me all about the different drinks you can make, she also gets me to try different ones, and while indulging in ridiculous drink orders, we talk about our childhoods, jobs, dreams, my recent debacle in the press with a famous actor and of course Reed.

I learned Reed said nothing nice about me to his colleagues.

To BOOB, he'd fabricated a version of me I wasn't, which made it look as though he was in an unhappy relationship with a slightly demonic and possessive girlfriend. He came up with excuses about not inviting me to work do's by telling his colleagues that I didn't want to come, and things started making sense to me, because he always told me no plus ones were allowed to their work events.

I got to set the record straight, and we both laughed about all of Reed's annoyances, sharing his flaws with one another and realising we actually get on well.

I also realised that BOOB has a great sense of humour and is a lot smarter than I would've expected.

I had one answer I needed; Reed wasn't the man I thought he was. To portray me as someone I'm not hurt me. He could've broken up with me instead of betraying me, which is unforgivable.

I didn't know the man I was sharing my heart with.

BOOB being my new frenemy, shared that she's ready to ditch Reed, she's bored with her toy, and she's had her eye on Justin, a dashingly good-looking man whom she works with, and he seems to have a bit more substance to him, that and he has a higher paying salary and he's going places.

A few weeks ago, this would've been music to my ears and would've been all I'd ever wanted.

That day, Reed would come crawling back to me with his tail between his legs, begging for my forgiveness.

But everything had changed now. I didn't care about Reed anymore; I didn't want him back; my head and heart were all about Dalton and wanting to make amends with him. I talked to BOOB about the betrayal I'd dished out to

Dalton and how much I had regretted sharing anything with Reed.

BOOB had given me tips on how I could win Dalton back over, and it started with another makeover, a saucy outfit and a killer pair of Christian Louboutins (I wonder if all of BOOB's footwear are men's names).

I kindly decline the help BOOB offers in yet another transition of my image and explain I'd accepted the reasons Dalton wouldn't want to talk to me again.

Leaving the coffee shop hours after entering it, BOOB and I had now become friends, which is something that happens with women. It usually turns out that the woman you dislike most at work or through a circle of friends usually happens because you both clash, which comes down to you both being similar. And after a blowout, a disagreement or being trapped in a lift together, it's usually found that these women make great friends for one another.

After exchanging phone numbers and a promise to meet up for another coffee-tasting session, I leave Starbucks feeling like a small part of the weight I've been carrying has been lifted. I have one less villain to take down and one less fight ahead.

I edit the phone number I've just put in my phone, and under the name section, I type Beatrix.

Chapter Forty-Four
Pointless Dates

I drop my lipstick into my bag and check how I look in the mirror.

My mind wanders to the fact that I'm about to go on yet another date, which I don't have high expectations for.

I've been on several dates over the past few weeks, and all have hit lower expectations than I originally predicted.

What is it about dating now?

People putting up the best photos of themselves and then allowing others to judge whether they find the person attractive enough to want to date. It seems completely superficial.

Dating apps terrify me. Since becoming a member of this new era of dating, I've had to block several people, and that's just from the first message I've received from them.

Who in their right mind thinks they will score a date by not even saying hello but going straight in with, *You're gonna need a wheelchair by the time I've finished with you.*

And If I get one more message about pineapple on pizza, I swear I will delete any trace of dating apps from my phone, laptop, and memory forever.

Dalton was right about some people. I believed him when he said it. It's just now I know how it feels and I wish I could tell him he was right, but that's never going to happen.

I have spoken to Della about Dalton because I trust her with my life. I've admitted the mess I've made, but even she agrees there's no going back from what I did. I want her to lie and tell me there's a slight chance, but that's not Della. She doesn't lie to me, and I value that about her more than anything.

So, tonight, I've concluded that dating via apps and trusting people to look like they do in their photos is deceiving.

It's like going to the supermarket and buying a key lime pie, and then when you open it at home, ready to tuck into it and feel that zesty lime on your tongue, it turns out to be an apple pie.

Now don't get me wrong, I have nothing against apple pie, but that's not what I picked.

I picked the key lime pie, but I've somehow been duped into meeting up with an apple pie.

The date tonight isn't filling me with confidence; it's a blind date, where you don't see their photo, and I'm not sure if this will be any worse because I do not know who it is I'm meeting.

It's a new feature on the app where you both go by fake names, and no photos are shown. What you know is each other's age range, and that's if everyone is telling the truth. You meet at a specific place with a particular table reserved for you both, so to save any further disappointment, I'm giving this a try. The person I'm meeting tonight seems nice; we've both been exchanging messages over the past few days, and despite not seeing each other visually or knowing each other's name, he looks like he may be better than the other dates I've been on; I mean, it couldn't get any worse if I'm being honest.

If this date doesn't work out, despite what Della says, I'm getting rid of any dating apps and I will not be doing this again for a while.

I miss the days when you met people in libraries, coffee shops, the supermarket, or even on a night out, but that was a long time ago for me, before the likes of Reed.

The times have changed, and this is how dating is now.

I grab my bag and drag myself towards the front door, my attitude saying, *I don't want to do this*.

"Oh, it's the blind date one tonight. Eeeeeeeek." Della is enjoying every minute of my dating because she gets the horror stories afterwards and finds them all amusing, so at least one of us is getting something out of it.

She's painting in the corner of the living room, she's been painting flowers in vases a lot recently, and they're great; I think she's found her niche, and she's hoping to sell them online. Tonight, she's painting sunflowers and giving Van Gogh a run for his money by the looks of it.

"That looks great; I love it; we should keep that one; maybe I will buy it from you and put it up in my room."

Della flashes me a wry smile. "You need a new job first; maybe I will gift you this one, just because you're my best friend and you need something cheery in your room to take your mind off a certain Mr Rivers."

I haven't spoken to Dalton in weeks now and I feel a huge gaping hole inside of me.

It's strange, because although I'm still somewhat grieving about my relationship with Reed, I'm now entangled with feelings for Dalton, but I blew it and I know there's no coming back from that one.

I let him down and broke his trust, and I wouldn't want him to forgive me because it's unforgivable in my eyes.

He's better off without the likes of someone like me; he's far too good for me. I'm surprised he even gave me the time of day in the first place; why, who knows? That will always be a mystery to me.

"I swear, Della, this will be my last date. If they turn out like the last ones, there's no negotiating on this," I say this statement firmly to Della, who's flashing a devilish grin. It's almost as though she knows I'm headed for disaster, but she's enjoying it all too much and I guess sharing my horror date experiences with her is the least I can do, considering how I treated her over the whole Reed and Dalton debacle.

My phone quacks; it's a message to let me know my ride is outside.

Long gone are the days I would see both of the men in my weird love triangle flash up on my screen.

It feels eerie now that neither speaks to me anymore, so I'm feeling double the loss. However, Reed doesn't deserve my time. I'm glad he no longer speaks to me, and I'm in the mindset that karma that will come around on him, so revenge will head his way at some point. It just won't be sent his way from me.

"Gotta go, wish me luck."

"Good luckkkkkkkkk." Della shouts as I head out the door.

Chapter Forty-Five
Blind Date

I enter the restaurant, which looks like a cool place to have a date.

It's colourful and loud, with floral prints covering the back walls and several neon signs scattered around, giving it that edgy urban feel.

It has cosy booths and plenty of tables, and it's busy with people, which tells me the food must either be delicious or the menu prices are low.

The waiter who greets me, recognises me straight away.

"The famous Charity Fletcher, well, well, well, it's nice to welcome you here, you won't be losing any of your clothes this evening will you?" he laughs.

I smile because I'm too tired to argue with people who don't seem to understand I'm a nobody.

I show him the code you get sent by the dating site; he smiles when he sees it, because he knows I'm on a blind date. I wonder if he uses the dating site, and he leads me to my table.

I slide into the bright orange booth, and he asks if I want a drink. That is precisely what I need right now, so I order a vodka and coke because why not tonight?

I texted Della to let her know I was at the restaurant and that the mystery man I'm meeting seems to be running late. She hasn't seen it, so I can only imagine she's engrossed in paint and flowers, which are far more interesting than my updates.

My vodka and coke arrive, and I'm feeling awkward because I'm sat alone, not knowing if I'm about to be stood up. It wouldn't be the worst thing; it would be a blessing after the string of recent dates. But I feel awkward because the waiter keeps looking over, and I wonder if he, too, thinks I'm about to be stood up. He must've seen this often working here, especially if the dating site uses this restaurant frequently.

I look around at couples in the restaurant and wonder if they're also on dates. I watch their body language toward each other to determine if they look like they're on a first date or if they look comfortable with each other, a telltale sign that they've probably been together for a while.

As I browse towards the door, I see the waiter speaking to a man.

The waiter looks at me, and this tells me the mystery man has arrived.

I can only see the side of his head, so I can't decide if I need to be making a quick escape or not.

The fear that this man has lied about his age and that I'm about to have dinner with someone centuries older than me is still there.

I quickly swivel back around and put myself into a casual position so it doesn't look like I was sitting here feeling awkward and people-watching everyone else. And then he approaches, and as I turn to look at him, I'm not sure what I'm going to get, but I certainly didn't expect to get what I see.

"You've got to be kidding me??" my tone is one of shock and annoyance.

Reed stands, looking back at me, just as shocked. He seems to want to say something but can't seem to manage it.

"You?!?" finally comes his response, which sounds full of disappointment as it passes his lips.

"Well, I can't say I'm pleased to see you. I would try lying, but that's not me; it's more up your street.

Adrenaline is pulsating through me, and I've become angry far quicker than I realised was possible.

"I'm not doing this." Reed turns to walk away.

"Yes, you are." I respond bluntly.

He turns to look at me, shocked that I even have a tone like that within me.

"What?"

"I said you are; sit down, or I can send a quick text to your current girlfriend to tell her exactly what you're doing tonight."

I feel proud of myself for being more assertive than I've ever been, and the vodka and coke was a good choice.

I wave over to the waiter, who's watching us. His expression suggests he's senses we're not a perfect match for a blind date.

He comes over to the table. "More drinks?."

"Yes, please. I'll have another vodka and coke, can you make it a double and he will have…"

I look at Reed, ushering him with my eyes to choose his drink.

He's changed recently, so I have no doubt I will order the wrong drink if I try to take the lead.

"I'll have a Jack Daniels and coke."

"Please…" I say to him, forcing him to remember manners.

"Please…" His expression is one of someone who looks and feels uncomfortable.

We sit silently for a minute, looking at each other and trying to comprehend how we've got ourselves into this situation.

"I will have one drink with you, Charity, and then I'm leaving."

"No, we both know the ball is currently in my court, Reed, so you'll sit here for as long as it takes me to get answers."

He looks at me, and he knows there isn't much he can do about this situation.

He pushes his hair back from his head because the perspiration has set in.

Before he did this, it would get me going because I found it attractive, but now I look at him and think the opposite. The only thing that is going on is the rage burning inside of me for his cheating, his lying, the way he betrayed me and dumped me on our anniversary, his spreading stories with the media about Dalton, and his currently sitting here cheating on Beatrix.

I think to myself, *he'll never change* and when I look at him, all the qualities I used to see in him have long faded. He's not the man I once thought he was. He's emotionally immature and incapable of caring about other people's feelings. Now is my chance to get closure from him, or at least I will try.

"Did you ever love me?" I go straight in because Reed isn't someone who can take being backed into a corner, so I need to get answers quick.

"Define love Charity"

I laugh, because of course he won't give me a straight answer. "Love is something I don't think you're capable of giving someone else Reed, because you're too much in love with yourself."

I take a large drink because even I'm shocked at how quickly I'm going for his jugular.

Chapter Forty-Six
Hello Karma

Everything that's happened over the past few months has now led to this very moment, and as I sit opposite the man I thought was once the love of my life, I'm now thinking he never was.

I take a large drink of vodka, and it's not because I need dutch courage to face this situation; it's because it always looks cool in the movies in scenes like this.

"There was a time when I loved you more than I thought I loved life."

Reed's body language tells me he looks like he's trying not to yawn, and it also says that he would rather be anywhere than here right now.

"But, over the past few months, not being with you has allowed me to see the man I thought I loved, and I can assure you I do not love you anymore."

Reed takes a drink and sits up in a firm and straight position.

"Am I supposed to be upset by your revelation, C?"

"Don't call me that!" "You know I recently had a lovely coffee with Beatrix; she's a nice woman, too nice for you."

Reed looks taken aback by this news.

His expression tells me that Beatrix didn't tell him about our little Starbucks date, and now Reed is tasting a bit of his own behaviour of not being honest with your partner

"Oh, she didn't tell you? Why would she? You're not as important as you think you are. Look, I don't want to sit here with you any more than you want to be here, but I need some closure, so can you at least give me that?"

His thinking face has always been so loud, but I can see from his expression that his brain is asking what's in it for him.

"What do you want from me…Charity?" he says through gritted teeth.

"Why did you cheat on me and then break up with me on our anniversary?" The words feel like a massive weight off my chest, weight I've been carrying around for far too long.

"What difference does it make? No matter the day, you wouldn't have taken the breakup well. It was just bad timing because Bea wanted to take things to the next level, so…."

I feel like I'm a chess piece in his game of life; he has no attachment to me at all, and it doesn't bother him he's hurting me with his words or the actions he's shown.

I can't show him how much he's hurt me because he will bank that sadness and gain more power from it.

"Why book a table for dinner, if you never intended to turn up?"

"Well, it's easier to break up with someone in public. They cause less of a scene, so my intention was to come along and do it, but then I got a better offer from Bea." I drink the rest of my vodka and coke.

I see the waiter looking at me, waiting for my signal to put in another order.

I give him a gentle no-head shake because I don't want to be here longer than necessary.

"Did you ever care about me, Reed?" as soon as the words pass my lips, I dread the response because I'm not sure I'm strong enough yet to hear what I think he will say.

He sits in silence, looking at me, trying to evade being honest, so I press him further.

"I thought you were going to propose to me."

He clucks his tongue and rolls his eyes. "C, I had no plans to marry you. I don't want to get married to anyone."

Hearing the words makes me feel like I've been sucker punched, but surprisingly I think deep down I knew this all along.

"Why were you so good at pretending to love me if you didn't. The flowers, the food, all the ways I thought you were showing me you loved me."

"You've gotta play the game Charity, don't get me wrong, there was a time I enjoyed being in a relationship with you, but I realised I wanted more and it was convenient to stay with you until I got that."

"Why did you want to meet me for coffee and lunch and milkshakes? I thought you wanted to spend time with me, like you'd realised you missed me and wanted me back." He looks across at me, and whispers, "Oh sweetheart, I didn't want to get back with you; I wanted something from you."

If we were in a movie, right now my character would launch across the table and rip him to shreds, but this is not a movie; this is real life, and I need to stay composed because the final act is approaching.

I sit thinking about what he wanted from me. And then the penny drops.

"Dalton, you wanted to know about him; I'm right, aren't I? All this time, you were trying to get closer to him through me." He raises his eyebrows to confirm I'm right.

"Urgh, you are a desperate, obsessed fan, aren't you? I always had you down as a little sad about your fan-boying with Dalton, but this is on another level."

"It worked, though. It gave me a great story; he now knows who I am." He sits back, looking like the cat who got the cream.

"Yes, you're right. He knows who you are, but he doesn't have any respect for you. Can you imagine having to stoop that low to get noticed? It's pathetic?" I laugh because I can see how desperate this man is.

My phone vibrates, and I know the final act is about to begin, but I want to say one more thing before then.

As Reed goes to take a drink, the timing is perfect.

"He's 20/10 in bed, much better than you. I'd probably give you a 3/10, but Dalton, woah, he is a god, a sex god, to be fair." And with that, Reed chokes on his drink. I see the waiter looking over; he's waiting for a signal to come and help defenceless Reed from choking, so I give him a gentle no-head shake again.

Reed stops choking, and he looks across at me with disdain.

"You've changed," his tone is cold towards me.

"I have, and certainly for the better. You see Reed, it's taken a broken heart, delivered by a spiteful, self-centred, egotistical ex partner, to wake me up from the love coma I've been in. I gave you everything: loyalty, honesty, friendship and love, and look at how you've treated me. I thought I deserved it. I needed closure from you on what I did wrong, so I wouldn't ever do it again and that shows what kind of person I am, that I assumed this was all on me, when all along it was you. I've had to meet different versions of myself recently. The one I struggled with the most was the broken version of me. She couldn't see the light at the end of the tunnel, she's not felt this low in life in a very long time and she's been the hardest one to work on. But the version of myself I'm glad to have met was the resilient version of me. Because despite losing my home, my job, my income, my belongings, my clean record, my dignity, my anonymity and the love of my life, I'm still here. I'm sat on a blind date, because I believe that there is someone out there that will love me and treat me right like I will them, and you turning up tonight is the revelation I needed. You've made me feel like I'm a weak person for having loved you. But the truth is, when someone puts all of their heart into loving someone, that

313

doesn't make them weak or stupid. It's a privilege to be loved by someone, because not everyone experiences this in life and someone like you certainly doesn't deserve this, because you need to appreciate what love is first. You're not a good person, Reed. You need help, because to treat people the way you do and to destroy people's lives in the way you have is not okay. I do need to say thank you to you, though."

Reed looks puzzled.

"Thank you for what?"

"For letting me go. A wise woman once told me I was a caged bird, and I needed setting free. I couldn't see it when she said it, because the broken version of myself wasn't ready to hear something so profound. But it turns out she was right. For the first time in a long time, I feel like I'm ready to meet even more versions of myself, I'm excited to meet all the versions of myself that are undiscovered and the best part is I've learned so much about myself from the version of me that loved you."

I look up. "Oh, here comes the grand finale."

Walking towards the table is Beatrix. I texted her when Reed arrived because I wanted her to know that the man she's dating is currently on a blind date.

Reed looks up at her, and his eyes are full of fear.

"Bea," he fumbles.

"You're dumped, Reed, and find yourself a new job because I've spoken to my father about you, and you're not right for our brand and business."

"Bea, wait…I"

Beatrix puts her hand in front of his face to usher him to stop."Don't be pathetic, Reed. Now one last thing." She turns around and grabs a plate of food from another diner's table and it just so happens to be a plate of spaghetti bolognese. The shock on their face as this fierce and confident blonde beauty swipes their food from right under their nose.

Beatrix turns around and drops all the plate contents over Reed's head.

He sits covered in bright red sauce with spaghetti hanging down his shoulders.

"Charity, I think Reed said he'd like some sauce with that."

She ushers her fingers to the pot of condiments on the table.

"Oh, of course." I grab a bottle of HP brown sauce, give it a shake and aim it directly above Reed, squirting sauce all over his head.

Everyone in the restaurant has stopped eating and is interested in watching the final act at our table play out; 3/4 of the people are filming it, and I marvel at the possibility that Reed may get his fifteen minutes of fame after all.

Beatrix turns around to the people in the restaurant and declares, "This man here is a cheating, lying, two-faced, nasty piece of work; please don't any of you feel sorry for him; he's getting what he deserves."

With that, an older lady stands up from her table and walks over to Beatrix, where she hands her a bowl of ice cream.

"Please, it would be my pleasure, dear."

And with that, Reed gets his freezing cold just dessert, as they say.

It's at this moment where it's confirmed to me that revenge really is best served freezing, because this moment couldn't have played out any better if I've tried to imagine it.

The whole restaurant claps and cheers.

I look around, and everyone is laughing, including the waiter.

This is one of those moments I will never forget; Reed losing his fake public persona in front of everyone in the restaurant.

It was more than I ever needed to know that I'm going to be okay and that there's good people in the world. Good people who know the difference between right and wrong. All this time I thought I was alone inside this never ending twister, and yet tonight, I feel the opposite of alone, with a united front in the restaurant.

This feeling is one I will never forget.

I have nothing more to say while Reed sits covered in the mess he created.

The waiter comes over, and Beatrix tells him that Reed will pay the bill for my drinks and the food from the other customers' tables.

I look at Beatrix in her element, taking control and I admire how strong this woman is; she's a force to be reckoned with.

"Girl code." Beatrix winks at me.

"Girl code."

All I wanted was revenge on Reed. I wanted him to feel unwanted, jealous, humiliated, and I wanted him to beg for me to take him back. I guess 3 out of 4 isn't bad, and I can live with that.

"Fancy a Starbucks?"

"Absolutely." I smile at her.

Who knew that a blind date could end up this good?

With that, Beatrix and I leave the restaurant to the roaring sound of people clapping, both on the road to a Reed free life.

Chapter Forty-Seven
Facing The Music

Today It's highly likely that I'll be going to prison.

While serving my sentence, I know I will lose my soul; it will be sucked away from not being able to get my frappuccino caramel cream from Starbucks and not being able to snuggle up with my favourite throw and watch the next crime documentary that drops on Netflix and from not having access to whatever junk food I want.

I accept I deserve the sentence because my behaviour has been unacceptable. I didn't mean it; I got caught up on a rollercoaster I did not willingly ride.

I look back at where I was six months ago, and I was different. A person who thought she had it all: the perfect home, the perfect man, the perfect life. I was so wrong; I was living in a bubble of lies. I got comfortable, and I never imagined my life would be pulled from underneath me, knocking me into tomorrow. I lived in denial, thinking I had it all, but when I look back, I realise I had nothing but a fake version of the life I thought I wanted.

I didn't even know who I was until this mess started. It's taken a broken heart for me to realise who I am.

I've seen sides of myself during this time that I don't like and never want to see again in the future.

I've also seen a desperate side to myself. One I didn't know was hidden inside of me.

I'm embarrassed when I think of how I begged for something that wasn't real. I hurt other people whilst I was hurting, and that wasn't fair to them. I was just so desperate to get Reed back, to get him to see me and look at what he lost.

But the truth is, he lost nothing; he never wanted me; he wanted whatever he wanted, regardless of other people's feelings. I've realised through this madness that he isn't all that. He's selfish, vain, deceitful, cruel, a womaniser, petty, and he comes across as more desperate than me when I add all his bad traits up.

I no longer feel the same love for him as before; I simply feel pity for him. I don't know how I didn't see it before; I don't know; maybe I was too close, and my eyes and brain were washed out to what was in front of me; one thing I learnt during this is that I am worth more than how I was treated. I deserve someone who will love me for me, by someone who won't try to change me to suit their needs and tastes, but can look at my bad traits and appreciate that we all have them, and hopefully see that mine aren't that bad.

I never asked for a man full of muscles, who's airbrushed from head to toe, who spends all his hard-earned money on me and puts me on a throne as his queen, worshipping the ground I walk on. All I ever wanted was companionship, a friendship that's built on trust and love; I don't need materialistic objects; I don't need to be pampered, I just need a best friend, someone to snuggle with and watch Netflix with, someone to watch the sunset with, someone I can talk too without judgement, someone who is always there for me and I'm there for them. A best friend that wipes away my tears and makes my face glow again on the gloomiest of days.

As I reel off in my head the events that have happened, I realise I can't take anything back now; I have to face up to what damage has been done; I have to accept it, deal with it, and probably go to prison, because it's the least I deserve after my behaviour and once I've completed my sentence, then I can rebuild my life after, closing all the chapters of this heartbreak and start actually living my life again, maybe even living my life how I want to for the first time in my entire life.

Della's always there for me, and I don't deserve her; I'd be lost without her always bringing me back to reality, and if I'd listened to her more, I wouldn't have so many charges in court today. She's packed me a bright yellow suitcase, which she's filled it with clothes, makeup, books, sweets, and sexy underwear. You may wonder what I'll do with sexy underwear in prison.

Well, Della being a glass half full type of woman, has a theory so she's packed me a suitcase for two reasons, the first one is, if I don't get sent to prison then I'll be able to get on the flight later today to New York alone. Della thinks I need to spend some more time with myself and really get to know who Charity is; she had a plan where if I got sent to prison, she would cause a massive scene in the courtroom, allowing me time to escape and get on the flight. Where I could be in New York within 8 hours and free to start my life under a new alias. I admire she thinks something like this could work, but remind her she's seen far too many movies and it's highly unlikely we could pull this off this in real life.

Which leads me to the alternative option Della has come up with. If this fails, and I have to go to prison. I will at least have sweets, books, and clothes to swap for essentials with the other inmates, and the makeup and sexy underwear will come in handy if I end up with a new girlfriend. However lighthearted we are about this situation, I think we're trying to play down how devastated both of us will be if I get sentenced.

Della creeps into the bedroom.

"Are you ready?" she speaks with such a soft, concerned tone, like a mother taking her child to the doctor, but neither wants to go for fear of bad news.

"Yeah, I'm all ready to go."

I look at Della and see how beautiful she is, not just on the outside but also on the inside.

I reach over and hug her; and as we hold each other tight, we are both trying hard not to get emotional and all worked up.

"Right, you smooth criminal, let's get this show on the road. Your banana case is in the car full of supplies; remember, as soon as I scream, you run to the door, head to the car park, the keys will be under the front wheel, get in the bloody car and get to the airport."

We both laugh, but I worry as I don't think she has any intention of letting me just walk into prison; knowing Della, it has to at least be on the front of every newspaper if that's happening.

After all, I am the famous Charity Fletcher, so why on earth would I go quietly?

Chapter Forty-Eight
Surprises In Court

As we arrive in the courtroom, my first thoughts are, who are these people?

I don't know this many people, but the court is packed. People are waiting outside, hoping to get in. This looks like the trial of the century, but it isn't. It's a trial about a petty criminal, that criminal being me.

Having all of my charges read out in front of so many strangers is intimidating. I look behind me and notice there are reporters here, which makes sense, as the outcome of my trial will be plastered all across the newspapers first thing in the morning.

I look over my shoulder, and I see Reed is here. Why on earth would he even make the effort to come here today? No doubt to get some more details of what I've been up to so he can sell another story. I can see the headline - **My life with Charity Fletcher. She was always destined for prison.** However, he spins it. I'm sure he will look like the victim, and he'll somehow make himself look good, as always.

I also spot that Beatrix is here; she isn't sitting with Reed, though; she winks at me, gives me a reassuring smile, and then mouths to me, "Starbucks is on me." This makes me smile. Who knew Beatrix and I could be on civil terms? I realise I like her, and after all of this is wrapped up, I plan to continue meeting up with her; who else will teach me about coffee and men as she can? I would instead like some fashion advice from her. I still don't know who Kurt Geiger is, but I'm sure I'd like him.

I quickly observed that the judge didn't seem to like me; I was getting vibes from her that suggested she wasn't impressed with my recent activity. While the charges and details are being read out, I look to my right and see Rupinder staring at me. Derek is seated next to her. I smile at her, but she looks back at me as though she couldn't even force a smile at me if she tried. Instead, she rolls her eyes at me and then continues looking forward.

I look at the jury and wonder what they think of me. After all, they are hearing about me assaulting a Police Officer, and I wonder if any of them have ever been in my position before and accidentally got themselves caught up in a mess like mine. I hope they have humility and some sympathy for my situation.

I think the nail in my coffin today will be because of people like Rupinder, because once she takes the stand and assassinates my character, I'm done for.

As the proceedings continue, my mind zones out as I think about what Dalton will feel when he reads the news and gets the finer details of what I'm charged with. I would love to hear what he says about it because something inside of me tells me he would somehow make me laugh about it all and not take it as seriously as I should. The judge is talking about a witness, and I try to focus back on what's happening in the courtroom. But it isn't easy to relive the past few months again. Even if someone else is telling the story about it, it still happened to me, and the sooner I can forget about it all, the better.

But my focus is quickly regained when I hear the words:

"We'd like to call Dalton Rivers to the stand."

Chapter Forty-Nine
An Unexpected Statement

Your honour, members of the jury and people in the courtroom. My name is Dalton Rivers, and I'm an actor.

I've come here today to give a character reference for the accused, Charity Fletcher.

I met Charity a few months ago when she accidentally exposed herself to me at a Comic Convention, where people come along to meet and greets with celebrities like myself.

Her exposure was an accident; I must clear this up; the velcro on her skirt got caught on my belt, and it became an embarrassing situation for her.

Pictures soon went viral, and Charity faced public scrutiny over the incident, which made me feel terrible for her.

In my profession, I'm faced with this most days, and it can be pretty unpleasant for strangers to make derogatory remarks about you, especially commenting on your visual looks. People can tear you apart when it comes to what you look like, like you somehow had a choice of the nose you were born with or the size of your teeth. Social media seems to have an abundance of negative and hateful opinions and comments, which is challenging to see, especially when it's targeted directly at you.

Charity met me, not because she was a fan of my work.

But she was seeking revenge on her ex-partner, who had recently broken up with her in an unforgivable way. She knew how much of a fan he was of me. Being borderline obsessed would be a correct statement (he's a bit of an idiot, I've heard from a few excellent sources). She wanted to make him jealous by meeting me, because she had purchased tickets to meet me as a gift for him, but he broke up with her before she could surprise him.

My first impression of Charity was that she was pretty cold towards me. It was almost as though I wasn't there, and this struck me as odd because it's not the usual way fans greet me. But she intrigued me because I had forgotten what it felt like to be treated as though I was no one, a complete stranger.

I wanted to get to know her, and most importantly, after seeing all the comments on social media, I wanted to check on her to make sure she was okay. People were being very cruel towards her.

We went for a picnic, and once again, she seemed somewhat distant and distracted. It was like I was someone sitting in a waiting room with her, and we were complete strangers, just making small talk.

We followed this up with dinner because I'm a believer in third time lucky, and once again, she appeared somewhat of a loose cannon; I believe one of the charges she has today in this hearing comes from that night, where she smoked an illegal substance in the toilets at the restaurant we met at. Charity does not appear to be a recreational drug user; the man who drove her to the restaurant, gave her the marijuana and in her naivety, she took it and lit it and also smoked it. Do I think that's the first time she's tried it? Yes, do I think she would try it again? Probably not.

I sensed something more to her because she was acting erratically. After texting each other frequently and meeting again for a sightseeing night, she opened up to me. She told me about her broken heart and that her ex-partner, who she loved more than anything in the world, had broken up with her on their ninth anniversary. On the same night, she discovered he had been cheating on her for months with someone from work. On this night, she had got it into her head he was going to propose to her, and when he didn't, and she discovered the betrayal, her entire world came crashing down. She drank wine and ended up with another charge that she is up for today, which was drunk and disorderly and also assaulting a police officer, which she has said was a complete accident.

That night, her whole world changed...

She lost the love of her life

She lost her confidence

She lost the ability to trust someone

She lost her home

She gained a criminal record

And a few days later, she lost her job

Nobody has ever said that dealing with heartache is easy; we all know it isn't. It changes us, and we lose ourselves momentarily because everything we know is now no longer. It can make even the most stable person unstable.

Grieving for someone alive can be just as hard as grieving for someone who has now passed away.

All the decisions she made following this breakup were during a time when she was crying out for help, when she needed more support than ever, at a time when she didn't even recognise herself. I'm not saying she should be let off the charges because the decisions made, sadly, she made herself.

But would she have made them if she wasn't suffering from a broken heart?

That is what we have to consider.

So, who is Charity Fletcher?

This question has been asked a lot recently, and everyone seems to have an opinion on it. I myself can only speak for the Charity that I've come to know.

She's beautiful, funny, caring, and somewhat brilliant; she's also intelligent, creative, and insecure.

I didn't think meeting anyone more insecure than me would be possible until I met my match in her.

She's a good person who has made disastrous decisions, but she isn't bad. She lost her way, but is now back on the right path.

She's…everything yellow. Even if she can't see it in herself, I can see it and so can others around her. When she's happy, rays of sunshine are beaming off of her, and standing next to her is a great place to be, because you get to experience feeling the warmth of her rays first hand.

I'm asking you, your honour and the jury, to recall when you had your heart broken and how it made you feel. Can you remember what you went through? Please ask yourself if you behaved in a way that wasn't how you usually behaved.

Please don't send Charity to prison because she doesn't belong there. She's learning from her mistakes, and she's spent a lot of time recently focusing on herself and bettering herself, and that came from a trusted source (her best friend who lives with her). She's got future aspirations, and she's a really good person, and sending her to prison would just be further punishment for her. We can see she's been through enough recently after losing everything.

So, as a good and honest character witness who has got to know her well, I'm asking you to please give her a chance.

I can guarantee you that you won't see her in this courtroom anytime soon, if ever at all.

Thank you.

Chapter Fifty
Leaving On A Jet Plane

So, not getting sent to prison is one of my achievements this year.

Apparently, the judge is also somewhat obsessed with Dalton. As soon as he started talking, she just started seeing stars, and how could she possibly send me to prison after he asked her not to? The Dalton effect has really helped me on this one.

Would I have been imprisoned if he hadn't come and saved me like a knight in shining armour? That's a high possibility. But people love and respect him, and thanks to him, I will not be getting a prison girlfriend anytime soon.

I was shocked that he came to my rescue.

I don't deserve it, but I'm really grateful that he did. He looked as beautiful as ever. This is as close to him as I will ever get now.

But I'm glad to know he doesn't hate me for what I did, and I really hope he can forgive me one day.

Della explained he had been messaging her to check on me and wanted to ensure I was okay.

I was shocked that she had kept this from me. I thought we shared everything, but I can see why she didn't distract my focus when I was slowly getting my life back together again. So, I appreciate the fact she kept it from me; I understand it was the right thing to do.

We discussed the emergency flight we'd booked in case I needed to escape and go on the run, and after leaving the court, we both decided it would be really good for me to take the flight still, continue with some soul searching, and spend time focused on me.

It would be a waste of money not to take the flight, and my suitcase was already packed in the car's boot, so Della dropped me off at the airport, and I was going away for a week.

I called the court just before we got to the airport because the last thing I wanted to do was get into any further trouble. I asked if it was a problem for me to go, and the judge was fine with it.

The punishment I was given was community service and a small fine. Surprisingly, the community service is working at a local library, where I'll be helping them for 40 hours. This. This will start next month and be spread over one week because it won't interfere if I secure employment. I wonder if Dalton also played a part in that decision when specifically it was referred to that I would assist with the children's books.

Another surprise, before I left the court, was Rupinder came over and asked to speak to me.

She told me the love of her life had recently dumped her and she wished I'd told her what I was going through; she said it would've helped to understand why I was behaving the way I was, but that it wouldn't have made a difference, she would've still charged me.

And now I'm off to a different country. It's quite nerve-racking and scary, flying to a different country all on my own. I've never done it before.

I've always travelled with family, friends, and Reed, but I've always dreamed of going back to New York again.

I haven't been since I was younger, and there are a few tourist places I missed the first time because there's just so much to see there.

I wish Della had come with me, but it was impossible because she has an exhibition of her flower paintings she has to finish. I was so excited when she got the call to say an art gallery wanted to add them to a collection they were exhibiting. I promised her I would be back before it opened so I could be there with her on opening night.

I'm so proud of her; she's always stuck with me through thick and thin, and something I've learnt through all of this is to not take her for granted because if I thought I was losing my mind before, I'm not sure how I would've coped not having her on my side and talking sense into me, even if I didn't listen at times, but what I've learnt is she's only ever looking out for me. She only wants the best for me in life, so I will listen to her advice in the future, and hopefully, I'll never make the same mistakes I've just made.

She's begged me to bring her back anything that says 'I Love New York' on it and a miniature yellow taxi, which I've promised her I will. I'm confident these items won't be hard to find.

When she dropped me off at the terminal, it felt as though she couldn't wait to get rid of me, and I wondered if there was an ulterior motive for her wanting me out of the picture. She seemed very pushy about me taking this trip, and I suspect she has plans while I'm away. Maybe she's met someone? I haven't asked her lately if any dates are on the go. Still, whatever it is, her excuse about not getting charged for being in the drop-off lane didn't really wash with me, especially as she practically asked me to get out of the car while it was still moving.

While waiting to board, I sit in a coffee shop, watching the world go by. I love people-watching; I play that game in my head, creating stories for the people I'm looking at. There's Niall and Flora eloping to get married. Flora's family is wealthy, and Niall's isn't, so Flora's family won't give their blessings. I imagine they're boarding the flight to Las Vegas, a lovely, cheap, quick wedding with minimal planning and Elvis as the registrar.

There's Violet. She's awaiting the arrival of a man she's been dating virtually for five years. This will be the first time they actually met in real life. Violet looks so pretty and very excited; she's somewhat walking on clouds. I hope he turns up.

I realise that despite the heartache I've gone through this year, love is still within me. I can still see it out there, and I know there will come a time when my heart will open up to someone new again. I hoped it would be with Dalton because he's very special to me, but it wasn't meant to be.

I open my phone and pull up a note I've created.
It's a list of all the places in New York that Dalton told
me he's never visited but wants to go to, and despite
living there, his comeback was more substantial than
mine for not seeing the local sights, he told me there
was so much to see, which was his excuse for not
ticking off some places he desperately wanted to go to.

I think back to our night of sightseeing in London and
how much fun it was to finally see all the iconic
landmarks and how it took him kicking my ass and
arranging it all for me to actually get around to seeing
them.

I look at his list:

Strawberry Fields in Central Park

Ice skating on the Woolman Rink

Breakfast at Ellen's Stardust Diner

The Crown inside of the Statue of Liberty

Washington Square Park

Beetle House for a themed cocktail

Grand Central Terminal

Lunch from Black Seed Bagels (he specified it had to
be a peanut butter and jelly seeded bagel, toasted)

To see a show on Broadway (he specified he doesn't
mind which show)

Tick Tock Diner for apple pie and coffee

The Ghostbusters station

I have mapped out my week and included every one of these places in my itinerary; I wish I could have taken Dalton along and repaid the favour of the fantastic night of sightseeing he gave me. Still, the least I can do is visit these places for us both. I plan to get a selfie for my little NY scrapbook at each location.

If there's one thing Dalton gave me, it was inspiration.

He helped me remember there's so much out there in the world and to grab it all whenever I can. I envy his drive; I look at his story, where he came from, and the hardships he faced to get to where he is now.

He helped me find my imagination again, and he's helped me get on the right path with my writing; for that, I thank him.

I check the time, and my flight is now boarding, so I close my notes, grab my bag, and head off to the gate.

Airports are always difficult to navigate quickly because of the lack of a structured flow of where people should walk.

You always find yourself weaving in and out of people, and it's hell when you're running late. Luckily, I'm close to my gate. I arrive at the gate and realise I'm a bit later than I should've been, as everyone has nearly boarded, that was the people watching distracting me.

I show my ticket and passport to the man in the security booth, and he ushers me through. It feels like miles walking through the tunnel to get onboard the plane, which is weird, as it's not long.

The hostesses all look very smiley. Standing to attention in their pristine uniforms, they welcome everyone onboard. One woman checks my ticket and ushers me to the back of the plane.

Luckily, most people had sat down, so maybe it was a good thing I was a little later boarding as there's nothing worse than that lengthy half a centimetre at a time shuffling to walk through the plane to your seat because everyone in front of you is taking their time to put their belongings in the overhead lockers and get out everything from their bags, including the kitchen sink just for an eight-hour flight.

I temporarily regret my choice for the last seat at the back of the plane, but I like the back seats because no one can sit kicking my chair from behind; I also don't get to see someone's creepy long feet saying hello from underneath my chair. I don't get the shock when I'm sipping my wine of someone pulling my chair back to pull themselves up every time they get up to go to the toilet; oh, the joys of economy flying.

I put my bag under my chair, as the rest of my stuff has gone into the hold. I remove my jacket and squeeze it into the last tiny space in the overhead locker. This is the downside of getting on late: Everyone takes up all the room in the lockers. I bet the person who put all of their stuff into my overhead locker is sitting 30 rows down the plane because it's always the way in economy. It's a dog-eat-dog world we live in.

I take a seat and click my seatbelt together. I get my earphones out because economy earphones are close to putting tiny sharp knives inside of your ears for eight straight hours. It always baffles me they can't create softer earphones for more comfort on a flight, but we can put people in space.

I look up, and the air hostess who checked my ticket at the door stands over me.

"Hello. Is it Charity?"

"Erm, yes."

Marvellous, what have I done now?

Don't tell me my criminal record has been flagged on the system. The last thing I want is to walk out of this plane in shame, especially given that I'm in the last seat and everyone owns smartphones.

"Could you come with me and bring your belongings," she's smiling at me in a way that smiling assassins do.

For the love of…. seriously, couldn't this have flagged at the gate instead of putting me through this shame and embarrassment. "Have I done something wrong?" I ask, and all heads turn around. Everyone close by knows something is going on. Oh, quick, get that smartphone at the ready. I'm sure I will be shared across the internet if I make a scene, and I'm not going to do that ever again, so I'm going to stay as calm as possible.

"No, please don't worry. You haven't done anything wrong; we're upgrading you."

Upgrading me?

I didn't pay for an upgrade.

Ugh, am I going to end up in Premium Economy, where it then becomes my responsibility to sit next to the exit and assist if there's an emergency?

I really don't want that job on this flight, and for what?

The reward of a few extra inches of space.

"Oh, thank you for the offer, but I like this seat more than the ones in Premium."

Everyone is now looking at me, trying to figure out what got me a free upgrade.

They're taking tips for their return journey, no doubt.

"Oh no, we're not upgrading you to Premium; we're upgrading you to First Class. Can you gather your things and come with me."

The air hostess seems a little impatient, but I get that, considering we are flying shortly, and she's got a job of getting everyone where they need to be.

Hang on, did she just say FIRST CLASS?

Without even thinking about it, my seat belt is unclipped as quickly as a wax strip is torn off. I'm up with my belongings, and I'm following the air hostess back down through the plane.

There is a slight smugness in me, as people are watching me and wanting to know how it was possible I got such a luxurious upgrade free. These situations are what dreams are made of. We walk through what I thought was First Class and go through another curtain into what looks even more exclusive. The hostess holds her hand out, shows me my seat, and smiles. As if by magic, a glass of champagne appears in her other hand. I take my seat, quickly followed by the glass of champagne.

"If there's anything you need, please let me know. I'm here to make sure you have the best flight. Your menu card is there, and after take-off, I will come back and show you all of your accessories."

"Erm, thank you." I'm stunned…

How did I just get upgraded?

I quickly pull out my phone and take a selfie with my champagne, which I send to Della:

No idea how this happened, but I've been upgraded to FIRST CLASS WTF OMG!!!!!

I put on my new seatbelt, and despite having massive imposter syndrome in this class, I'm excited about my trip, especially with a start like this.

And then something I thought I would never see…

I look to my right.

Dalton is in the chair next to me, smiling at me.

That thing where my words get stuck in my throat is happening again, and I feel like I'm being strangled.

We stare at each other profoundly, and there are no hostilities between us. He looks just as beautiful as he did in the courtroom.

"Hey Charity, fancy seeing you here." He smirks..

"Did you….just….get me upgraded?"

He nods yes to me, with an expression of the same smugness I just had walking through the peasant class of the plane into the exclusive club area.

"How, why?" I'm so confused. How did he even know I would be on this flight?

"Well, I had help from a little birdie and look around you; it wasn't hard; I bought the whole cabin." I hutch myself up, with my seatbelt digging into me, and see there is no one else in the cabin but us; all the seats are empty; oh, how sad; all of those missed opportunities for some people in the economy to experience this class; it seems a waste.

I grab my phone and quickly text Della:

You arranged this. You told Dalton I was on this flight??!?!?!?!

I see the bubbles typing, and she replies with:

You're welcome ;) Now please don't mess it up this time; love ya xxx

I'm speechless. She's hoodwinked me again. She not only liaised with him about how I was doing, but she also helped set me up on my solo trip.

I look over at Dalton. "I'm really sorry for everything. I really am. I didn't mean to do what I did." It feels such a relief to finally get these words off my chest.

"I know." He has that sincere look, and I sense he believes me.

He holds his champagne glass out to me, and we chink glasses.

"To fresh starts."

This flight really couldn't get any better.

"To fresh starts."

"Dalton, can I ask you a question"

He nods yes and smiles at me.

"We're not really going to have this whole cabin to ourselves, are we? Couldn't we upgrade some more people"

He seems really happy with my question.

"How shall we do this? Seat lottery numbers; we'll pick random numbers together."

"Oh yes, that would be great fun."

Dalton ushers the air hostess over and explains what we'd like to do with the cabin seats. She agrees that once we're in the air, we can give her the numbers, and she will bring in the lucky people who are getting upgraded

"So, do you have any plans for when you're in New York?" he asks.

"Well, I do, actually, I have this list someone special shared with me of all the places they wanted to go to, from the Ghostbusters station to ice skating on the Woolman Rink, and so I'm going to go to them and get selfies."

"Oh, how interesting. I've always wanted to see the Ghostbusters station and go ice skating on the Woolman Rink…Would you like some company? After all, I live in New York, so I'm a great tour guide; I could also show you my apartment, it's quite the thing, you know, and I have three new paintings to hang up when I get home, so maybe you could advise me on the best places to hang them, after all, they'll be familiar to you."

I'm shocked; Dalton bought the paintings; no wonder we got so much for them, I think. "You were the anonymous buyer?"

He flashes me that devilish grin of his. "Anyway, on the tick list for New York, I will only agree to be your tour guide for this on one condition."

"One condition?" I raise my eyebrow.

"I'll only agree to it, if we can fit in going to Central Park Zoo as well, followed by a picnic in the park." He gives me that sultry look, and I feel flustered because I know exactly what he's insinuating.

The woodpecker is back inside of my heart.

I look Dalton in the eyes and say, "I thought you'd never ask."

343

Epilogue

I don't know if it was the flowing champagne or the deliciously sexy man I sat drinking it with.

Still, either way, the combination of these two elements was always destined to lead to me joining the Mile High Club, a club I never once thought I would become a member of.

There was no plan for this to happen, I just looked over at Dalton, and it was almost as though we were both in sync with our urges towards each other and before any words could be spoken, he was leading me to the toilet, and I certainly didn't put up any objections on this. I let him willingly take me in there; we couldn't have got in there any quicker.

And what happened in that toilet was most definitely sex and not making love because the passion was through the roof. There was very little time to get our clothing off, and it had an animalistic drive to it; I did not expect an upgrade and an orgasm on this flight. But, this moment will go in my memory bank to remember for all of time.

And even though getting passionate in a toilet cubicle thousands of feet in the air is a complex operation, it's exciting.

If we'd had been in economy class on this flight, then this type of behaviour would've been stopped in its tracks the minute an air hostess saw us both going into the toilet together because, let's face it, what other reason would two people be going into a small bathroom for on a plane, everybody knows why people go in twos in this situation.

But one, Dalton is, after all, Dalton Rivers, and two, he's bought out the entire first-class cabin, and I doubt any air hostess would ever feel brave enough to challenge him. It's probably not worth losing their job over when the airline boss reminds them of how much the man paid for the flight and that they don't care what he's doing thousands of miles in the air because he is, after all, paying their wages.

As I take my luxury seat back in the cabin, I smile, thinking as if that just happened. An air hostess comes over and offers me some sparkling water. We both look at each other, knowing full well what's just happened, but neither of us is going to say anything about it.

She smiles at me in a way that says, y*ou go, girl, I'd have done it.*

I feel like another new version of myself, one that is brave and now sexy, one that has the admiration of the air hostesses onboard this flight.

I blush when I think about what I've just done with Dalton because who knew that version of me was even inside? I certainly didn't, but this man makes me feel brave.

He makes me feel like there's no one else around us in the world; it's just me and him.

And I feel exhilarated that I've just committed another crime.

One Rupinder and Derek will never find out about ;)

About the Author

Penelope Bond (known as Penny) studied a BA in American Studies, followed by an MA in Journalism, along with several other courses including Fiction Writing, Criminology and Private Investigator.

Her writing style is conversationalist and is usually personal to her in some way. Her book *Letting go of the rain* is an honest account of her story of dealing with grief and trauma from childhood. She uses writing as her therapy and escapism and her thoughts and emotions are often captured in her books, including *Tired Bones* and *Shattered Bones*, which are a collection of prose and poetry books.

She's a huge fan of film, dogs, travel and breakfast food. She is not a fan of tin foil or early morning alarm calls. One of her biggest achievements was receiving a British Empire Medal for her volunteer work during the pandemic in 2020. One of her not so biggest achievements is despite her age, she still hasn't mastered how to cook a proper meal.

Her aspirations in life are to have a log cabin in the middle of nowhere surrounded by snow, dogs and a good internet connection.

Books by the Author

Tired Bones

A collection of prose and poetry pieces about love, life, laughter and loss. A tattered teddy, the moon, the lovers and the candle of life are among the things that have been twisted into some short thought provoking pieces to inhale....... If the wind could talk what would it say…?

Shattered Bones

This is the second book in the Tired Bones series. It is a new collection of poetry and thoughts shared on life, love and loss.

From thoughts on broken relationships, to a mothers love for her daughter, from real life friendships to dream friends and from daisy chains to walking in a snow globe.

The short book aims to be relatable, with key themes around grief and life and encourages those reading it, that we all feel similar emotions, we may just experience them in different ways.

Letting go of the rain

From childhood to adulthood, one girl learns about understanding Complex-Post-Traumatic-Stress disorder, and finally it all makes sense to her. Her imposter syndrome, her triggers, her emotional flashbacks, the way her emotions are. She always thought it was just her, that she hadn't grieved properly and that she herself had somehow ignited her own self-destructive behaviour, always thinking she deserves nothing good in life. She shares her experiences in the form of letters she writes to her dad over the years, whose death was the biggest trauma of all for her.

"I feel sad when it rains, it controls my emotions and my mood. Sometimes I sit by my bedroom window on those rainy days, when the sky is grey and that rumbling sound echoes above from the sky, and I run my finger down the window pane trying to touch the glass, telling myself I have nothing to fear, but still that haunting feeling is there."

The book shares an honest account of a child's journey experiencing grief, trauma and guilt, into adulthood.

Printed in Great Britain
by Amazon